VALLEY 6/1
5069001080   W9-AYX-291
Hitchcock, Mark.
The Mayan apocalypse

VALLEY COMMUNITY LIBRARY
739 RIVER STREET
PECKVILLE, PA 18452
(570) 489-1765
www.lclshome.org

june 22, 2011

The Mayan Apocalypse

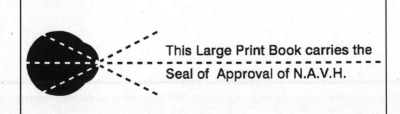

This Large Print Book carries the
Seal of Approval of N.A.V.H.

THE MAYAN APOCALYPSE

MARK HITCHCOCK AND ALTON GANSKY

THORNDIKE PRESS

A part of Gale, Cengage Learning

VALLEY COMMUNITY LIBRARY
739 RIVER STREET
PECKVILLE, PA 18452-2313

GALE
CENGAGE Learning

Detroit • New York • San Francisco • New Haven, Conn • Waterville, Maine • London

GALE
CENGAGE Learning

Copyright © 2010 by Mark Hitchcock and Alton Gansky.
Unless otherwise noted, Scripture quotations are from the New
American Standard Bible®, © 1960, 1962, 1963, 1968, 1971, 1972, 1973,
1975, 1977, 1995 by The Lockman Foundation. Used by
permission.(www.Lockman.org)
The quote from Psalm 23 on page 80 is from the King James Version of
the Bible.
Thorndike Press, a part of Gale, Cengage Learning.

ALL RIGHTS RESERVED
This is a work of fiction. Names, characters, places, and incidents are
product of the author's imagination or are used fictitiously. Any
resemblance to actual persons, living or dead, or to events or locales is
entirely coincidental.
Thorndike Press® Large Print Christian Fiction.
The text of this Large Print edition is unabridged.
Other aspects of the book may vary from the original edition.
Set in 16 pt. Plantin.

LIBRARY OF CONGRESS CATALOGING-IN-PUBLICATION DATA

Hitchcock, Mark.
    The Mayan apocalypse / by Mark Hitchcock and Alton
Gansky.
        p. cm. — (Thorndike Press large print Christian fiction)
    ISBN-13: 978-1-4104-3695-5 (hardcover)
    ISBN-10: 1-4104-3695-0 (hardcover)
    1. Geologists—Fiction. 2. Maya astrology—Fiction.
3. Prophecies—Fiction. 4. Two thousand twelve, A.D.—Fiction.
5. End of the world—Fiction. I. Gansky, Alton. II. Title.
PS3608.I84M39 2011
813'.6—dc22   2011005216

Published in 2011 by arrangement with Harvest House Publishers.

Printed in Mexico
1 2 3 4 5 6 7 15 14 13 12 11

THE MAYAN
APOCALYPSE

PROLOGUE

December 26, 2010

Andrew Morgan was aware of only four things: the slight hint of cedar that hung in the air, the darkness that surrounded him, the rows of hanging clothes that lined his self-created sepulcher, and the effort it took to draw a breath.

He should have been aware of the time, but he wasn't. He should have been conscious of his position, but he wasn't. He should have realized the position he was in, but he didn't care.

Numbness continued to eat away at his brain like insects boring through his gray matter. Most mornings, that thought would have made him shiver with revulsion. Now, at whatever time it was, he found it strangely comforting. If he was lucky and he wasn't imagining creepy crawlers were devouring his brain, then the little buggers would do him a huge favor once they reached the part of his mind that controlled the beating of his heart.

But there were no insects in his brain. If he wanted to die, then he'd either have to do something about it or stay here until he perished from thirst or hunger — or sorrow.

He would stay here. In the large walk-in closet his wife loved so much. On the floor. Pressed into the darkest corner.

"You know," she had said when the mansion was finished and he showed her the large space with more room for shoes, clothes, and coats than she could use, "I'm going to make it my mission to fill every square foot of this."

She followed that with a laugh.

Oh my, she could laugh. When she did, birds stopped singing just to listen.

Morgan had laughed too. He laughed less when the credit card bills began to come in. Not that it mattered. He had money. Lots and lots of it. *Forbes* magazine listed him in the top twenty-five wealthiest men in the country.

He'd give it all away now. Every dollar, every dime, every cursed penny of it.

He raised the strapless black dress to his nose. He could smell her on it. She had last worn the slinky dress at a fund-raiser for their alma mater, Oklahoma State. That was two weeks ago. She had never looked lovelier. At forty, she had only become more stunning. More than once he had accused her of defying normal aging.

"How come you get better looking, and I only get older?" He said that two weeks before as they dressed for the event.

"I know how to use chemicals." She smiled, and the lightbulbs in the master bedroom dimmed. "It's all about the right alchemy. And makeup. The right makeup makes a big difference."

"So if I use your makeup —"

"You will creep out everyone, especially me."

Morgan slipped on his tuxedo coat. "Hunter would think I was cool."

"Are you kidding? Your son would run screaming from the house."

"He'd come back."

She raised an eyebrow, leaned closer to the mirror of her vanity, and pressed the tip of her Plum Fizz lipstick to her mouth. "I wouldn't be so sure."

"I am. His video games are here."

"Okay, you got me there."

Two weeks ago. Two weeks that seemed locked in eternity past.

Tears ran from his cheeks to the black dress. His body convulsed.

9

Marybeth — blond, tall, lanky, smart, and soft to the touch — was gone. Marybeth, wife of eighteen years . . . forever gone. Marybeth, the smartest, funniest woman he had ever met . . .

His shoulders rose and fell with each sob. When he threw his head back, it struck the wall. He took little notice of it. What was physical pain compared to the grief shredding his organs like a meat grinder?

Remembering the conversation seared his heart again with the rest of the truth he struggled so hard not to believe. Hunter — fifteen, tall like his mother, honors student, dark hair like Morgan's, same hazel eyes — was also gone. No more playing basketball on the half-court on the back acreage. No more tennis. No more fishing. No more . . . no more . . . *oh, dear God* . . . no more.

"Mr. Morgan?" The man in the deputy sheriff's uniform seemed to shrink when Morgan answered the doorbell that morning.

"Yes?"

"I'm Deputy Morris." Somehow that didn't seem important. He could see through the man's tough exterior. He was melting inside that uniform like a candle in an oven as he gestured to a round man with gray eyebrows who was standing next to him. "This is Reverend Bill Lacy, the chaplain for our department."

The bones, ligaments, and muscles in Morgan's legs began to dissolve.

"What? What's happened? Something at one of our plants?" *Please, God, let it be that. Let it be a fire. Let one of the board members be a crook.*

"No sir. I'm sorry to be the one to tell you this, but there's been an accident. A plane crash. Your jet."

"No . . ." He could think of no words to follow that.

The chaplain spoke. "May we come in?"

By Morgan's estimation, it took less than ninety seconds to crush his life.

PART 1

CHAPTER 1

July 8, 2011

Andrew Morgan was pretty sure he was still on Earth, although the number of extra-terrestrials surrounding him made him wonder. To his left was a six-foot-tall gray alien with bulbous black eyes that reflected the glare of streetlights overhead. As an alien, he would have been more believable if he weren't handing out fliers for a bar-beque joint two blocks down the main drag. And the woman with green skin, an extra eye glued to her forehead, and a pair of wire antennae sprouting from her coal-black hair would have been more convincing if she weren't wearing a worn pair of New Balance sports shoes.

Morgan had expected to see people dressed in homemade costumes wandering the streets of Roswell, New Mexico. He had done his homework, and like everyone in the United States, he knew about the 1947 alleged UFO crash in the nearby desert and the ensuing cover-up.

Entertaining as the tourists were, and fascinating as Roswell's history was, Andrew didn't care. He wasn't there for aliens or crashed UFOs. He cared nothing for such nonsense. His mission was serious. He had come because the end of the world was less than a year and a half away. Then the world would change for him and a few billion others.

December 21, 2012, or 12-21-12, would arrive, and everything would be different — assuming anyone survived.

Sixty-three years earlier, a flying saucer supposedly crashed seventy-five miles outside of town — all UFO aficionados knew the crash was closer to Corona, New Mexico. Roswell, however, got all the credit. Over the last two decades, the city of less than 50,000 had become Mecca to every kind of oddness, cult group, and paranormal adherent.

Morgan had been to the town before, but never during the annual UFO festival. Watching the costumed tourists crowding normally quiet streets made Morgan shake his head. Roswell could well be remembered for many things. Rocket pioneers did much of their work here. Former Dallas Cowboys

16

quarterback Roger Staubach played football at New Mexico Military Institute. Demi Moore, John Denver, and other famous people were born in Roswell. *Does anyone remember that? Nope.*

Morgan was a man of science as well as business. Being CEO and president of Morgan Natural Energy made him wealthy and able to pursue his passions, a passion that narrowed from a spotlight to a laser beam. He enjoyed mysteries, and he had done his share of investigation in UFOs, cryptozoology, and other fringe subjects. He didn't believe the stories, but he did find them entertaining. That was before he learned the world was coming to an end. Such truth tended to push other thoughts from the mind. He had many thoughts he *wanted* pushed away.

Struggling to move through the crowds, Morgan pressed forward like a salmon swimming upstream. He reminded himself to be patient and enjoy the ambience. He was a man on a mission.

Five blocks from the parking lot where he left his Beemer, Morgan arrived at a movie theater built in the early sixties. This week, Morgan imagined, the owners were making far more money renting the facility to groups bringing in experts from the far regions of the world (and of reason). One, however, was different.

Morgan was here to see Robert Quetzal, the last Mayan priest.

Marcus McCue was a drunk, but he was a dedicated drunk. He took to drinking like Mozart took to music — like Michelangelo took to canvas and marble. Rare was the man who understood his skills and his limitations like Marcus understood his. Marcus had many limitations but only one skill: He could hold his liquor, at least most nights.

It was still early in the evening when Marcus pushed open the marred blue door leading from the Tavern on the Green bar and into the Arizona evening. The door was the only thing in Tacna, Arizona, that bore more scars than he.

Marcus glanced at the bar's sign: TAVERN ON THE GREEN. The name always amused him. There was nothing green around the bar, and aside from the occasional lawn in front of some home, there was no green in Tacna: just sandy dirt, pitiful-looking desert plants, dust roads, sidewalks, and tumbleweeds.

Overhead, a bejeweled, cloudless sky returned his gaze. This part of town had few streetlights, allowing the stars to shine without interference. The only art Marcus could appreciate was that created by the constellations.

As a boy, he spent many of his evenings staring through a telescope at the twinkles in the sky. The small refractor lacked enough power to render the rings of Saturn, but that didn't matter. Marcus's imagination filled in what was missing. The warmth of memory rose in him, and he smiled at the moon. *Good times. Good times until the old man got home.*

Marcus's father had also been a dedicated drunk. Marcus came by it honestly. He started drinking when he was thirteen, following an especially severe beating from his dad. At first, he would sneak sips from his old man's stock, but Marcus Sr. would catch him, and he would communicate his displeasure with his fists.

His mother, a saint with graying red hair, begged him to stay away from booze. He promised to do so. That was when he became a dedicated liar. She left six months later, and he never heard from her again. His father said she died in Phoenix. He had no idea if that was true. Forty years later, he wasn't sure he cared.

His gaze drifted across the street to the

auto repair shop he inherited from his father. He hated that shop. He hated its origins. It smelled of his father. Still, it provided enough income to pay for his mobile home, frozen dinners, and Jim Beam. He worked during the day, just as his father had, in a slight fog and with a persistent buzz. He had been staining his hands with grease since he was sixteen.

"Too many years," he told the night.

He felt depression coming on. He scolded himself for the thought. Of course he was depressed. He'd been depressed since his eighth birthday when he realized his family was nothing but trash. Drinking a depressant didn't help.

"You ain't so bad." This time he mumbled to himself. "You kicked drugs, and you didn't bring any kids into the world that might turn out like you. Nope, you ain't so bad. Just two more battles to win."

The first battle was his chain smoking. Marcus had quit smoking many times. He was quitting again, just as soon as he finished this last pack of Marlboros. Maybe after he finished the carton. The last battle would be the booze, but there was no sense taking on too much at one time. He had time. He had nothing but time.

He pulled a cigarette from the pack he

kept in the front pocket of his stained overalls and placed the filtered end in his mouth, and then he drew a lighter from another pocket and flicked on the flame.

The glow seemed brighter in the dim light. He squinted, blocking out the glare and the twisting smoke of tobacco.

He released the lighter's starter, but the glare remained. *Odd.*

A distant glow in the sky captured his attention. A falling star? No. He took a drag on the cigarette then pulled it away from his lips, his eyes frozen on the greenish light hanging in the sky.

"Nova. That's gotta be it."

Marcus thought he heard a distant roar. That's when he realized the spot of light was moving — and growing.

"It can't be."

Over the years, Marcus had seen meteors streak the sky. It was one of the few benefits of living in a town that was little more than a wide spot on the road. The kind of place people passed but never visited.

He had only been drinking for a few hours, so most of his brain cells had yet to be pickled for the night. *There should be a tail. Where's the tail?*

As if on cue, a short green and white tail appeared. So did fiery globs that dropped from the moving object and trailed behind it, creating their own tails.

Should be longer. Tail's too short.

A boom rolled along the desert as the object broke the sound barrier.

Yup. Tail should . . . be . . . longer.

A frightening realization wormed through the alcohol-induced haze: The tail wasn't too short — Marcus couldn't see it because the object was coming right at him.

Nah. Can't be.

A second later, he changed his mind.

"Boys. Boys! You gotta see this." A voice in the back of his mind tried to remind him that no one in the bar could hear him over the raging country music and loud conversation.

Another boom. This one rattled the bar's blackened windows and the blue door. The light had grown from distant star to plummeting fireball. Smaller pieces rained from the main body.

"Hey, Marc, what'd ya do? Bump into the building?" It was Gary's voice, a trucker who broke up his routine drive with two beers every night. Not even Marcus was that stupid. "If you can't stand on your own two feet . . . What is that?"

"Meteor." His voice was so low he could barely hear himself.

"It's a UFO, ain't it?" Gary stepped to Marcus's side.

"Don't be a fool, Gary. It's a meteor."

The light doubled in size. "It looks like it's headed right for . . ." Gary was gone. Marcus heard the blue door open and shut. A muted shout that sounded a lot like Gary pressed through the walls and windows.

The object was close enough that its light blocked out the stars.

What remained of Marcus's instinct for survival screamed in his head. "Uh-oh." Marcus threw himself to the ground, pressing himself against the wall. If he could, he would have started digging through the concrete walkway.

He could hear it approaching. He thought of a train. The ground shook. Or maybe it was Marcus who shook.

He felt it. The concrete seemed to lift a foot off the ground. The sound — a bomb-sized explosion — stabbed his ears and vibrated through his body.

There was light.

There was heat.

There was ear-pummeling noise.

So this is it. This is how I die. Drunk. On the ground. Crushed by a big rock from the sky. At least it has class.

Marcus didn't die. He lay curled like a

fetus, his hands covering his head, arms protecting as much face as possible.

Glass broke. A thousand bits of space shrapnel pounded the parking lot and pummeled the wall next to him. It sounded like someone had pulled the trigger on an automatic rifle and refused to let go.

"Marcus! You okay, dude?" Big Bennie the bartender stood over him. "Talk to me, man."

Slowly, Marcus opened his eyes and then sat up. Behind Bennie stood the rest of the pub's patrons.

"You hurt, pal?" Gary's voice. It sounded distant. Marcus's ears rang and felt as if someone had packed a pound of cotton in each ear.

Without speaking, Marcus stood, wobbled, and looked at his auto shop across the street. Its roof and two walls had collapsed. The sheet-metal wall facing the street that separated the bar and shop bowed out.

Turning, Marcus saw dozens of holes in the wall of the bar and several broken windows. Fragments had hit the wall like pellets from a shotgun blast. That raised a concern with Marcus. He looked at his arms, legs, and body. No blood. No pain.

"It missed me. Not a scratch."

"You're one lucky drunk," Bennie said. "You fared better than my bar."

"Not so lucky, guys." Gary pointed at the shop. "You won't be salvaging much from that mess, Marc. That big rock ruined you. What are the odds?"

Marcus felt something well up inside of him. It took a moment to realize what it was. He bent and placed his hands on his knees. His shoulders began to shake. His head bobbed.

"It's all right, dude." Gary put a hand on Marcus's shoulder. "Let it out. Ain't no one here gonna blame you for crying."

Marcus straightened, unable to hold back the emotion. A loud guffaw erupted from deep inside him.

"What're you laughin' at?" The bartender seemed offended. "Maybe you're drunker than I realized."

Another roaring laugh filled the night. Marcus wiped a tear from his eyes. "Don't you bums get it?" He pointed at the burning remains of his shop. "I'm rich, boys. I am rich."

CHAPTER 2

Andrew Morgan never rushed anywhere. Not anymore. In high school and college, he had been so impatient that he jogged across campus to whatever place he needed to be at next. When he drove, he drove fast, as if he didn't want to waste one moment of his life.

He read fast, he spoke fast, and once he became an executive in his father's oil business, he conducted meetings fast. He was a race car with only one pedal-to-the-metal speed.

The day he learned of the plane crash that took his wife and son, Morgan slowed. At first, he dawdled because he didn't want to face life. Why get out of bed? What reason was there to answer the phone? Morgan Natural Energy had the best executive team in the business, men and women smarter than he and more conscientious. If he never stepped foot in his CEO's office again, the firm would continue to grow and pay hefty dividends to investors and stockholders.

It took less than a day for him to realize he was unneeded: no wife to love and support and no son to guide. The rushing whitewater river that had been his life had declined to a slow-moving, muddy, polluted creek.

Morgan hadn't decided to slow his pace. His grief and confusion had shackled his legs and thickened the air around him so much that it pressed him down.

The Tinsel Town Theater displayed art deco on the outside, as was popular for theaters of this age.

Just as Morgan laid a hand on the angular door pulls, a woman stepped to his side. Without thinking, he opened the glass doors and moved aside to let the woman in. She was rushing. Like Morgan, she was five minutes late.

"Thank you." The words came without a smile.

"My pleasure." He followed her through the doors.

The woman was, he judged, five-foot-six, slim, and well-dressed in a tan pantsuit with a bright, decorative scarf. She had shoulder-length auburn hair that bounced as she walked. She wore bone-colored flats. The shoes indicated she was a sensible woman who cared more about the condition of her feet than how shoes made her legs look.

The lobby was empty except for two beefy men with arms the size of redwoods who paced the worn carpet. Morgan recognized security when he saw it.

Pale colors accented the geometric shapes on the walls and ceiling. The carpet, which had to be decades old, proudly displayed its faded designs. At one time, the colors must have been bright. Now, they were difficult to distinguish from the beige background. Although the snack bar was closed, the place smelled like popcorn.

The woman fast-stepped to the doors. Morgan followed a few feet behind. Soft New Age music wafted from the theater.

Just over the threshold stood a teenage blonde holding a thin stack of folded paper. He saw her hand one to the impatient woman. Then, spying him, she held one out for Morgan to take. He took the program.

"You're just in time." The blonde sounded as if she'd been taking in helium. "These are the last two seats." She motioned to movie-style chairs in the last row and next to the aisle. "No one is allowed in once the program starts."

The woman slipped into the first chair,

saw Morgan sanding there, and moved over one spot. He smiled and lowered himself into a seat a thousand other fannies had used over the years. The cushion had lost the ability to cushion long ago. A chunk of plywood would have been more comfortable.

He glanced at the woman and saw a lovely face with bright, blue eyes and a serious expression. He knew better than to ask, so he guessed: mid-thirties. Her face, her body, and her confidence were everything necessary to attract a man. The ring finger of her left hand was naked. So why didn't that matter to him? His marriage had been a happy one, and he had been a faithful husband: no dalliances, no flirtations, no liaisons, no affairs. Other women didn't tempt him. In those moments, when he was especially honest with himself, he'd admit to allowing his gaze to linger on the form and faces of other women, but he likened it to admiring art.

That was then. He was a widower now. He had the right to pursue romantic interest. And yet he never did. He felt no inclination to start.

He watched as the woman rifled through her purse until she found what she had been searching for: an identification badge hanging on the end of a neck strap. She slipped it over her head. First, Morgan noticed PRESS/MEDIA emblazoned in large red letters across the top of the plastic card. Just below that, he saw a photo of the woman and the name LISA CAMPBELL.

"It looks like we just made it, Lisa." Morgan paused a half second. "May I call you Lisa?"

"How do you know my . . ." She pursed her lips. "My press pass. Of course."

"I'm Andrew Morgan." He held out his hand, which she shook.

"As you've already surmised, I'm Lisa Campbell. I'm with —"

"The media." The words came out harsher than Morgan intended.

"I take it you don't like the press." She turned her eyes forward.

"Sorry. I didn't mean to . . ." He sighed, then smiled. "I've had a couple of bad experiences."

"With reporters? So you've been in the news." She returned her gaze to study his face. "Your name is familiar. Why?"

It was his turn to look away. "So you're covering the UFO festival?"

"An evasive change of subject. You *have* dealt with reporters before. To answer your question, yes and no."

Morgan chuckled. "Now who's being evasive?"

"I'm not trying to be. I'm not covering
the UFO junk. I'm here to cover this meeting." A second later, she added, "I'm sorry,
I shouldn't have called it UFO junk."

"Doesn't bother me. It is junk. At least
most of it. Like you, I'm here to hear what
Robert Quetzal has to say."

She nodded and started to speak, but then
the lights lowered. Morgan looked over the
heads of several hundred people to the front
of the theater. The movie screen had been
raised so the area behind it could be used
as a stage. Another screen — the rear
projection, Morgan assumed — hung at the
back of the platform. A pair of high-backed,
red-leather chairs faced each other and had
been angled so people in the theater would
be able to see the faces of those who sat in
the chairs. Next to the chairs were end
tables, each with a glass and a pitcher of
water.

The audience applauded as the lights grew
low. Their wait was just about over.

The stage lights grew brighter, and a man
in a three-piece suit stepped on the platform. Morgan had seen pictures of Robert
Quetzal, and this man wasn't him. The man
on the stage was painfully thin, his cheeks

31

drawn. His suit hung on him as it would on a closet hanger.

"Good evening, ladies and gentlemen. My name is Charles Balfour, executive assistant to Robert Quetzal, prophet and priest." He paused to allow applause. "It is my daily pleasure to travel with Mr. Quetzal and help him share the ancient and contemporary message. It is a message at which many scoff, but we know the truth. The world as we know it is coming to an end."

Morgan glanced at Lisa in time to see her shake her head in disgust. He concluded she wasn't a believer.

Balfour continued. "*You* know the world will end in 2012, and *I* know it. Because of that we know, we'll survive while others . . . don't. But enough of me. You came to hear wisdom from the one who carries the knowledge of ancient times." Again he paused, this time raising his left hand and pointing to the right side of the stage. "Ladies and gentlemen, Robert Quetzal, final and exalted Mayan priest."

The crowd shot to its feet. The applause was nearly deafening. Music poured from the wall-mounted speakers. It reminded Morgan of Native American songs. The drumbeat vibrated his bones.

Standing, Morgan looked over the heads of the others and watched as a man in a charcoal gray suit walked onstage. His hair was long, raven-black, and hung down his back in a ponytail. He had shoulders as wide as a linebacker's and stood six-foot-six. His skin was the color of pale leather. The references to Quetzal being the last Mayan priest made Morgan expect a serpent headdress. Instead, he was looking at a man who could have sat in one of the seats of his boardroom.

A video camera zoomed in on the man, and his image was projected on the screen behind him. Morgan saw a pin on the man's lapel: the snake god Quetzalcoatl and two feathers.

Quetzal placed an open hand over his chest and bowed deeply, an action he repeated several times. He did nothing to stop the applause. Morgan imagined the man enjoyed the adulation, and why not? If he was right, he deserved it.

"Welcome, my friends. Welcome." Quetzal's rich baritone thundered from the speakers. "Welcome to the end of the world . . . Welcome to the *beginning* of the world."

"Oh, brother," Lisa said. Morgan looked at her. Lisa didn't look back.

COMMUNITY LIBRARY
739 RIVER STREET
PECKVILLE, PA 18452 - 2313

33

Morgan had insisted. It went against every desire, severed every fiber of logic and reason. Still, he went.

The southern part of Utah was barren, desolate, devoid of important life. Just like Morgan. The Jeep pulled to a stop fifty yards from the charred remains of what had once been a 2009 Falcon 200EX corporate jet. The once sleek-white aircraft rested in a crater of its own making. Jet fuel had fed the fire that turned the aircraft from a flying object of art to a scorched hulk of twisted, blackened metal. It had also reduced the bodies of his wife, son, and the plane's crew to burned bone. Authorities had removed the bodies the day before and sent them to the nearest coroner to determine the official cause of death. Not much work involved there.

Morgan had already made arrangements to have the remains moved to the cemetery where his mother and father were buried. Marybeth and Hunter would be entombed in the family mausoleum. When news of the death reached Morgan's town news service, friends and acquaintances began to call. Pastor Johansson of Berkley Street Baptist Church had been one of the callers. Berkley Baptist was the church Hunter had taken

34

an interest in. For the last six months, he had been attending services and activities for youth.

"Are you sure about this?" Ranger Reid Tasker sat in the driver's seat of the Jeep. "I don't see how this can help you."

"You say that as if it matters." Morgan released his safety belt and popped open the passenger door. Tasker sighed and followed suit. Together, the men traversed the red soil and rocks of the desert area, Morgan's boots pressing rocks into the sandy soil. He kept his head down. As they neared the wreckage, Morgan could see signs of previous activities. The parched ground had held the images of boot prints and tire tracks in place as if waiting for his arrival.

He and Tasker walked over a circular area blown free of loose dirt and sand. *Helicopter landing area.*

Morgan continued forward, ignoring the nagging plea deep in his gut to turn around. He had already seen too much to be able to forget.

A yellow caution ribbon attached to wood stakes surrounded the aircraft carcass and the crater. Morgan stepped beneath it.

"Hey, Mr. Morgan, this is a crime scene. I can't let you walk around —"

"Try to stop me."

Tasker didn't. He slipped beneath the legal barrier and joined Morgan as he stood by the airplane. The craft had hit with such force that the tail section had compressed in on the cabin area like an accordion. The sides of the cabin had split apart like the husk on an overripe watermelon.

Morgan had always been good at math. He wished that wasn't true. An image — garish, brutal, and impossible to scrub from his brain — rose to the surface of his consciousness: the faces of his wife and son as they watched the ground five miles below racing toward them. Dying was unfair; to know you're about to die and have time to think about it was soul-scorchingly cruel.

He closed his eyes. The tears burned.

His ears filled with the whine and roar of seizing engines — the banshee scream of wind rushing past metal hull.

Morgan tasted copper. He was biting the inside of his cheek.

A hand rested on his shoulder. "Has the NSTB and FAA come to any conclusions?" Tasker's words were solid and encased in kindness, the way one man comforts another.

Morgan shook his head. "Too early. They tell me it might take months before we know anything conclusive." He paused and let his eyes scan the debris. "The pilot reported complete engine failure in his Mayday."

"Complete? Both engines?"

"Yes."

Tasker lowered his hand. "That's odd. Bird strike?"

Morgan shook his head. "They were flying at thirty thousand feet. Not many birds fly that high."

Tasker started to speak and then stopped. Morgan knew the man was doing him a favor by not asking for full recounting of the events.

They stood in a silence broken only by the wind and the cry of an eagle circling overhead.

"I lost my wife a little over two years ago."

Morgan looked at him. His brown eyes seemed to melt in their sockets. "You're not going to tell me that it will get easier, are you? I don't think I could stand to hear that again."

"Easier? There's nothing easy about it. Time makes it manageable — most days." He gazed into the distance, seeing only what he could see. Morgan could almost smell the sorrow on the man. "Every time I look at her side of the bed, someone stabs me in the gut."

"I'm sorry for your loss." Morgan wished

he sounded more sincere.

"She lost control of her car on a snowy day. It rolled. They say she died quickly." Tasker took in a noisy breath. "Sorry, I should be trying to encourage you, not drag you down. I just wanted you to know you're not alone. It won't change anything, and it won't make you feel any better."

Morgan was surprised to feel a smile cross his face. It didn't rise from amusement, just the knowledge that the man standing next to him had endured the good intentions of others who offered a balm of kind words.

"I can walk away for a while. You know, answer nature's call if you want to . . ." He motioned to the crumpled hulk.

"No need. I've seen everything I need to." Morgan walked back to the Jeep.

"I welcome each of you to our humble gathering." Quetzal's voice filled the theater. Lisa thought the man could be an actor on a Broadway stage. He stood near the edge the platform and slowly paced like a man considering a leap into a bottomless abyss.

He held no notes but spoke like a man who was well prepared.

"I am the last descendant in a line of Mayan priests. Does that sound odd to you? Perhaps you assumed we Mayans dropped off the face of the earth centuries ago." He paused, and nervous titters rolled through the room. "Well, I have something to tell you: *Weee're baaaack.*"

By Lisa's estimation, it took a full second for the crowd to get the joke. She glanced at the man sitting next to her to see if he appreciated the humor. His face bore a grin. It took only a moment to see that, but she let her eyes linger and then snapped them away when he returned her gaze.

"The truth is, congregation, we never left."

Interesting. He addressed us as "congregation." He's working this priest thing.

"Let me be honest: We have been a small religious group, but it may surprise you to know that we have over fifty thousand adherents now. I know, I know, that's not much when you compare it to the many millions claimed by the Roman Catholic Church worldwide or even the millions of Baptists. But that doesn't matter. We are not for everyone. We are for those who appreciate the past and want to change the future."

He paused. The audience applauded.

"We are here for people like you — people who know that everything will change on December 21, 2012. I am here to guide you."

Quetzal continued with his opening remarks as Lisa jotted down notes in a small, spiral-bound notebook. She also held a digital recorder with one hand, hoping it was picking up the audio from the speakers.

As Quetzal spoke, Charles Balfour, the man's rail-thin assistant, received a note from a worker who stepped forward from backstage. He read it quickly and approached Quetzal, who paused mid-sentence. If the interruption irritated him, he didn't show it.

He read the note, exchanged glances with Balfour, and then turned back to the audience. "If you've followed my writing, read my book, listened to my interviews, or kept track of my e-newsletter, then you know that I have spoken of signs in the sky indicating the beginning of the end — the end only our followers will survive." He held up the piece of paper. "I've just been handed a note that informs me of a meteor which struck a small town in Arizona."

Gasps and excited chatter swept through the theater. Quetzal held up his hands. "Quiet. Please, quiet, everyone. The damage is minimal and there has been no loss of life." He straightened and stared at the crowd. "Yet."

Lisa set her pad and recorder on her lap

and retrieved her BlackBerry. In a moment she was online, searching the web. She found confirmation on a news site.

"It's true." Lisa spoke to herself but the man next to her overheard.

"You had doubts?"

CHAPTER 3

Albuquerque International Sunport Airport
was crowded and noisy. Morgan had cleared
security and was making his way through
the mired mass of humanity clogging the
walkways. He'd flown into this airport on
several occasions to conduct business for
his firm, but this was the first time he had
found it so crowded.

The crowd didn't bother him. He would
have preferred more elbow room, but at
least he wasn't in a rush to catch a plane.
He hadn't had to do that for years.

He moved slowly through the terminal,
too slowly for those behind him who
grumbled and elbowed their way past him.
He didn't care. What other people thought
of him had ceased to matter. Behind him he
towed a small, rolling suitcase.

Unrecognizable music mixed with the
sound of footsteps, crying children, and
people on cell phones. Some of the faces

looked familiar, fellow travelers to Roswell now returning home in droves.

One woman looked especially familiar. Same auburn hair, same height, same outfit from the night before when he sat next to her in a theater and listened to a man talk about the coming end of the world. He had hung on every word, and she had grumbled through the entire presentation.

Lisa Campbell. The name floated forward in his mind. She was studying the screen of her cell phone. He was still twenty feet away when he saw her lean her head back and stare at the ceiling. Whatever was on the screen had upset her.

"Bad news?" He stepped close. A large overnight bag rested near her feet. Next to it sat a computer bag.

"My plane —" She looked at him, wrinkled her brow, then offered a polite smile that he read as, "Oh, it's you."

"What about your plane? Run out of pretzels?"

"That I could live with." Lisa peered at the small screen of her BlackBerry. "My flight has been canceled. Mechanical trouble of some sort. I guess I'm going to have to spend the night in the terminal."

"What about a hotel?"

"Everything around the airport is full."

Morgan slipped his hands into his pockets. "Where are you headed?"

"San Antonio by way of Denver."

"That's on my way. I can take you home if you want."

She examined him as if trying to read his mind. It amused Morgan. "What makes you think your flight has an extra seat?" she said.

"I didn't say I could get you on a flight. I said I can take you to San Antonio."

"Why should I get in a car with a total stranger?" Her eyes narrowed.

"Did I mention a car?" He pointed to a window at the end of the terminal. "Follow me."

She hesitated.

"Got something else to do? Come on. I'm harmless." Morgan took the extended handle of his case and pulled it behind him. A glance over his shoulder showed Lisa was also in tow, her bag hung over her shoulder. She followed in his wake as he pressed through the milling crowd like the bow of a ship through the ocean.

He edged close to the large window. Lisa moved to his side but kept an arm's distance between them.

"That's mine. The one with the blue stripe along the fuselage." At one time, he would have said those words with pride and a

44

smile. Seeing the Cessna Citation Sovereign resting in the business area of the tarmac reminded him of another jet — the one that preceded this one.

"That's yours?" Lisa eyes widened.

"Yes. Well, it belongs to my company; not to me personally. How about it? Can a guy offer you a lift?"

"What did you say your name was again?"

"How soon they forget."

She shrugged. "I was preoccupied with my work."

"Andrew Morgan from Oklahoma City."

Lisa chewed her lip for a moment. "That name still rings a bell with me."

"I probably owe you money. Come on — let me take you away from all this. You can keep me company. It's lonely being the only passenger."

Lisa let out a melodic laugh. "That sounds like heaven to me."

"I'll take that as a yes."

"You know, San Antonio isn't on the way to Oklahoma City."

"It is the way I travel."

She straightened. "Wait, are you saying you're the pilot?"

"No. You wouldn't want that. The plane comes with a two-man crew. You'll have to fetch your own snacks."

Lisa grinned. "I can do that. I've never been in a private jet before."

"Well, let's fix that." He took her computer bag. "We go through that door. We have a little time, but the pilot will need to file a new flight plan."

An airport employee checked their identification and matched it against the manifest of private flights. He then escorted them through a security door and onto the tarmac. Minutes later, Morgan led Lisa into the luxurious interior of the finest business jet made.

San Pedro Yancuitlalpan, Mexico

It was just 10:00 a.m., and the heat was already oppressive. The sun, which still had two more hours before it would reach its zenith, shone like a huge gold coin in the deep blue sky. Bob Newton stepped from the adobe-lined community building and onto the dusty street. Profirio Galicia followed him. Both men glanced around the impoverished community. A man rode a burro down the street; a teenage boy peddled his bicycle in the other direction. Newton sensed tenseness in the air.

"El Popo was upset last night," Profirio said, nodding to the mountain just outside of town. "Soon villagers will be taking offerings again."

"I'm afraid that won't do them much good, Profirio," Newton said as he studied the 17,887-foot tall, snowcapped volcano. "Cooked chickens and fruit might make *me* feel better, but it won't do anything for El Popo."

"It couldn't hurt," Profirio countered.

"Couldn't it?" Newton turned his eyes from the volcano to his interpreter. "I don't think you want to be on the mountain if she goes. That would hurt."

"You think her time is soon?"

"Popocatépetl has been acting up for years now and may continue to do so with very little danger, or it could go at any time."

"You think she will erupt, don't you?"

Newton turned and faced the man. He was tall, thin, and quick with a smile. Although only thirty-eight, he looked much older. In addition to serving as interpreter to Dr. Newton, Profirio was also the town clerk. "I can't be sure, but the latest readings indicate that something is up. I think it may be time to call for an evacuation."

Profirio shook his head. "We have had too many evacuations over the years. The people lose wages when they leave. It will be hard to get them to abandon their homes again."

"They'll have to, Profirio. San Pedro is in

the worst possible situation here." Newton removed the New York Mets baseball cap he was wearing and wiped his bald head. Newton was forty-two years old and a senior project manager for the US Geological Survey in Menlo Park, California. He had spent the last three months in San Pedro monitoring Popocatépetl, the volcano that residents called El Popo. He returned his attention to the road that led from the town.

"You seem worried, *amigo,*" Profirio said. "Your friends will be back from the mountain soon."

"I can't help but worry. In April of 1996, five hikers died up there. That's five too many deaths. My group should have been back by now."

"Maybe it took longer to fix the radio monitor."

"Perhaps, but that . . ."

They felt it before they heard it. A rumble — borne along by the hot wind of the day — echoed from the side of the mountain. A moment later the ground shook, vibrating everything within fifty miles. Fifteen seconds later, it was over.

"Another earthquake, *amigo.* A big one too."

Newton ignored Profirio. His mind was

on the mountain. "Where are they?" he asked aloud. "What could be keeping them?"

Once again the earth shook. Once again Newton's heart skipped a beat.

"Wow."

Morgan smiled at Lisa's expression as they walked around inside the jet. "First time in one of these babies is always memorable."

"I imagine it's old hat to you."

"Not really. I still have to pinch myself."

The passenger compartment sported leather seats that faced each other. On the right side was a table crafted from teakwood, situated between a pair of seats. A cobalt blue carpet covered the deck.

"The restroom is in the back. There's a tiny galley behind the front bulkhead. And opposite that, there's a business center with fax, notepads, pens, and that kind of stuff. We have a wet bar if you're interested."

Lisa grimaced. "I don't drink, but thanks. Tried it once in college. That was enough for me."

"I don't drink either."

"Then why the wet bar?" Lisa took a seat at the fuselage-mounted table.

"I'm not the only one who uses the aircraft. It's not my jet. My company owns it, and some of our clients and vendors like a beverage now and then."

"But not you. It was the taste that put me off."

"I like the taste of booze. I like what it does to me more."

Lisa raised an eyebrow. "What it does to you?"

"Numbs the mind. I got too close to it for a while. I'm a bit of a health fanatic these days. I'd rather work out than drink."

Lisa sputtered.

"Too honest? Life has taught me to be honest with myself about myself." He waited for a response that didn't come. "I need to talk to the pilots about our little detour. Can I bring you a soda or coffee?"

"I'm fine."

"Let me know if you change your mind." Morgan exited the aircraft.

Lisa felt fortunate; she also felt uneasy. Here she sat in a custom leather airplane seat on a business jet simply because a good-looking CEO had offered her a lift. She felt like a hitchhiker. Of course, this kind of hitchhiking she could learn to love.

She took in her surroundings again, impressed by the kind of wealth necessary to create an interior like this. Outside, the sound of the jet aircraft leaving solid ground to take to the air filtered in through the open door.

Drumming her fingers on the table, she resisted the urge to look in the drawers and galley. Instead, she retrieved her BlackBerry and checked the signal strength. Three bars were good enough. She activated the Internet browser and did a search for "Andrew Morgan."

"Nuts." The name was so common that Google returned over fifteen million hits. Most of those would only be vaguely related to the name. On the bulkhead that separated the cabin from the cockpit, there was a logo woven into the cloth covering: *Morgan Natural Energy.* She entered, "Andrew Morgan Morgan Natural Energy." A few seconds later, she had several good hits.

Using journalistic skills honed since her college days, she scanned the sites. She learned he wasn't yet forty and had been CEO for the last seven years following the death of his father. A business evaluation site gave the company five stars for leadership, innovation, and service.

On a whim, Lisa clicked on "Images." Scores of photos appeared, too many to scan on her phone's small screen. She did see photos of him in a tuxedo at a fund-raiser for some charity. She also saw images of him in what appeared to be foreign locations.

She reached for her computer, hoping her wireless service would be fast enough for another quick Internet search. Before she could unzip the bag her host reappeared.

"Look out the window." He stepped in the craft.

"What?"

"The window. Look out it."

"At what?"

"Oh, for the love of . . . Just look." Morgan pointed at the window by her head.

Lisa turned and scanned as much of the airport as the window allowed.

Morgan sat in the seat at the opposite side of the table and stared out the window.

"What am I supposed to be seeing?"

"The airplane."

Lisa snapped her head around. "You don't mean it! There's an aircraft at the airport? How could that happen?" She followed the words with a chuckle.

"Cute. I thought reporters were supposed be observant. The Bombardier."

"The more you talk, the more confused I become."

He chortled. "The other business jet. The

one taxiing on the tarmac. Look at the tail section. That's the tall metal thing sticking out of the back of the plane."

"That much I know." She studied the sleek craft. "What about it?"

"The logo. It doesn't look familiar to you?"

"Should it?"

Morgan sighed for effect. "The snake. The feathers."

Lisa didn't know what to say.

"Robert Quetzal was wearing a lapel pin just like that."

Lisa furrowed her brow. "How could you see something as small as a lapel pin? Oh, the projection screen." Her attention had been divided by Quetzal's speech, the crowd, her notepad, and her recorder. She hadn't looked at anything beyond the man's appearance. "That's his jet?"

"That'd be my guess."

"I suppose if I said, 'Follow that plane,' you'd get right on it."

"Sure. As long as he's going to San Antonio."

"Mr. Morgan?"

Lisa looked forward to the open door. A man in dark pants and a white shirt with a captain's chevrons on the shoulders' epaulets stepped into the cabin. A younger man

53

with only three gold stripes on his shoulders followed and then slipped into the cockpit.

"Yes, Steve."

"We're ready, sir. With your permission, we'll see if we can get this thing to fly."

Morgan rose and walked forward.

Lisa sneaked a look at her cell phone, toggled over to the search results, and was about to sign off when she saw a link that caught her eye. It was listed under "News." She followed the link, which took her to an archived article for an Oklahoma newspaper: OILMAN'S FAMILY DIES IN PLANE CRASH.

Fifteen minutes later, the jet took to the air.

CHAPTER 4

As the jet flew east, Morgan moved across the cabin and took a seat next to one of the port windows. Below, the desert was painted in ever-changing hues of brown. He knew he couldn't see the area where it happened. It was too many miles away and behind them. Colorado was to their north, the red-painted Utah.

"Is that where it happened?" Lisa's voice was soft and measured, just loud enough to be heard over the engine noise.

Morgan tore his eyes away and looked at his guest. "Where what happened?"

She didn't answer his question. "Do you know who Horatio G. Spafford was?"

"No. Should I?"

She shrugged. "He was a successful lawyer in the late 1800s. He lived what some considered a charmed life. He had fame and more money than he knew what to do with. He was also a man of faith and very involved in the evangelistic movement led by Dwight Moody and others."

"Why are you telling me this?"

She shifted in her chair. "They lost a son to scarlet fever. The boy was only four. Not long after that, the family lost much of its wealth in the great Chicago fire. Still, they remained faithful, and Spafford continued helping in evangelistic work. His wife, Anna, however, still struggled with their losses. They decided to take a cruise to Europe, but a business emergency kept Spafford home. He sent his wife and other children on ahead."

"There's a point to this." Morgan didn't like where this was headed.

"The ship his family was on was rammed and sunk in three miles of water in less than twelve minutes. Out of three hundred and seven passengers, only eighty-one survived. Anna Spafford was one of them. They found her floating unconscious in the water. Later she would describe being towed under by the sinking ship. The current, filled with debris, pulled one of her children from her arms. A young man had rescued two of the girls, but they were too weak to hold on to the planks he used as a life preserver. They slipped beneath the surface. When she reached shore, she sent a telegram to her

56

husband telling him she was the lone survivor."

"Lisa —"

She held up a hand. He could see tears in her eyes. "Survivors watched Anna closely. They thought she might take her own life. Who could blame her? Lost one child to disease and three more by drowning."

"You think I'm suicidal? You don't know me well enough to —"

"She heard a soft voice: 'You were saved for a purpose.' That voice got her through." She inhaled deeply before continuing. "Horatio Spafford sailed for Europe to be with his wife. The captain of his ship called him to the bridge and told him that they were passing over the spot where his wife's ship went down. That night, he wrote the words that became one of the best-known hymns in Christendom: 'It Is Well with My Soul.' Have you ever heard it?"

"I grew up in the Bible Belt. Of course I've heard it." He looked away. "I take it you're one of the faithful."

"I'm a Christian, yes. I write for an online Christian newspaper."

"I should have known."

"Shall I step out of the plane?"

That made Morgan smile. "That might tarnish my image as a gentleman. How do you know so much about Spafford?"

"I wrote a feature article about him while working for my college paper."

He pinched the bridge of his nose. "So how did you find out?"

She held up her cell phone.

"You're not supposed to have that on."

"I turned it off before we got to the runway."

He reclined his seat and stared at the ceiling. "So you told me that story so I can feel better about my dead family?"

"Feel better? Is that possible? I've never lost someone that close."

"Yet you're going to tell me that you understand and that life will get better."

"Not at all." Her words carried a touch of heat.

"Then why the story?"

"Never mind. Sorry I brought it up."

Morgan glanced at her. She had turned her face back to the window but not before he saw it redden.

"My son was one of you."

"A woman?"

"Again, cute. No, he was a Christian. Got involved in a local Baptist church. I think it was all the youth activities that drew him in. You know, people his age. Girls his age."

"It couldn't be that he was searching for

the truth?"

Morgan's temper rose. "I guess I'll never know."

"It's time." Bob Newton wished he had more data, but the radio relay between the monitors on the volcano and his equipment in San Pedro was still incapacitated. "We can't wait any longer."

"Are you sure?" Profirio Galicia asked.

As if answering his question, a deep rumble rocked the community building. "As sure as I can be without hard information."

"What about the others?" Profirio referred to the team that had gone up El Popo three hours before.

"They radioed that they were on their way back down. They couldn't fix the relay board. They said the mountain is becoming more active. CO_2 and SO_2 levels are lower, which means El Popo is not degassing properly, and the number of tremors has increased substantially. The time has come. We can't take any chances."

"But last time —"

"But last time the volcano didn't erupt. I know, Profirio, but what if it had? I'd rather go down in history for being too early than being too late."

"I'll inform the mayor."

"Don't inform him. You tell him in no uncertain terms to clear this town out and to do it now. He needs to deliver the same message to the other communities. I'll notify the Mexican Civil Protection Agency, although they've been monitoring things from Cuernavaca. They probably already know."

Profirio nodded. "I understand." He ran from the room.

Newton wondered if Profirio really understood. Popocatépetl had been active over the last few years and there was clear evidence about two previous major eruptions in 400 B.C. and A.D. 822. Entire towns had disappeared. Over the last few years, the volcano had made a lot of noise but had done very little damage. It would vent from time to time, throwing gray ash and fiery projectiles high into the air, which would later rain down on the earth. Quarter-inch bits of debris called *clasts* had fallen as far as seven miles away. Ash had been propelled 27,000 feet in the air. And those events were mere belches compared to what a volcano like El Popo could do.

Bob Newton stepped from the building and into the street, leaving the door behind him open so that he could hear the radio. He turned to face the mountain. A thick column of smoky ash rose into the sky. But it wasn't the sight of a pillar of smoke that made Newton uneasy — it was what he couldn't see.

El Popo wasn't the biggest volcano in the world, nor was it the most dangerous, but it was dangerous enough. Thirty million people lived within fifty miles of the peak, including those who resided in Mexico City. A significant eruption would impact them all. The worst hit would be the smaller towns near the foot of the mountain. These would be choked with ash and bombarded by burning projectiles. There would be mudslides, avalanches, and — depending on how El Popo blew — possible lava flows.

It would be the realization of Dante's Hell.

Newton stared at the mountain. Where were his people?

"Tell me you think I'm brilliant." Robert Sanchez, known to his followers as Robert Quetzal, sat in one of the white leather seats in the Bombardier's passenger compartment. The seat was reclined, and its padded leg support extended in front of him. In the seat next to him rested his expensive suit coat, neatly folded. The sound of the aircraft filled his ears with white noise and was close to lulling him to sleep.

"I always think you're brilliant." Charles Balfour sounded slightly miffed. Quetzal heard the man tapping the keyboard of a laptop computer.

"You don't say it enough. We creative types are an insecure bunch."

"So I've noticed." More keyboarding.

"Must you always work? Or are you playing a video game?"

"Yes. No. I wouldn't know how to play a video game."

Quetzal imagined the man's matchstick fingers doing their disco dance on plastic keys.

"Maybe you should learn. It would give you a relaxing diversion."

"First-person shooter games are relaxing?"

"You could start off with solitaire or checkers."

Balfour snickered. "I have an IQ over a hundred and eighty, and I'm an expert in several fields. I don't think checkers would do anything for me. I enjoy what I do. I don't need diversion, especially now. The 2012 clock is ticking. I'm not going to spend those seconds pushing digital cards around on a computer screen."

"Then what are you pushing around?" Quetzal turned his head and expended the energy to open his eyes. The thin man sat hunched over a table, face close to the screen, sharp shoulders threatening to pierce the thin shoulder pads of his coat. "You could at least take your coat off and act like you're comfortable. This is the most luxurious jet you'll ever be in."

"You sure about that? If I have my way, we both will have a fleet of these."

"Dream big, friend. Dream big." He waited a moment. "You never answered my question."

"I'm digging up more research on the meteorite strike in Arizona. I can't believe our luck to have that hit while we were in Roswell. I've already sent a directive to the PR firm. We need to make hay off this."

Quetzal snickered. "Make hay. I haven't heard that for a long time."

Balfour sighed. "Reports from the general media state the thing destroyed a mechanic's shop." He turned the screen of the tablet PC so Quetzal could see.

"Guy won't be using that building anytime soon."

"He won't need to. Recovered meteorites are as valuable as gold. The Peekskill meteor of 1992 hit a parked car. That car has traveled the world raking in big bucks. The H6 meteor was about the size of a bowling ball."

"I bet it did a job on the car."

Balfour grunted. "You could say that. Blew through the trunk. Other large meteors have brought in hundreds of thousands of dollars. The owner of the car shop won't need to get his hands dirty for a long time."

"Too bad it was so small." Quetzal brought his seat upright.

"What do you mean by that?"

"Look, I haven't studied like you have, but judging by those pictures, the crater it left must be pretty small."

Balfour nodded. "The early reports say the rock ripped through the roof and knocked down a couple of walls. It also fractured the foundation."

"See what I mean? Interesting as that is, it's not a life-ending event. It will be forgotten in a few days."

"Let's let PR find the right way to spin this. We pay them barrels of money to do that."

"You can only spin things so far, Chuck. People, especially Americans, have very short attention spans. If something new isn't shoved in their face from time to time, they go on to other things."

"What do you suggest?"

"I agree we should see what the PR people come up with, but I'm planning on referring to it as the 'first strike.' "

"First strike." Balfour licked his lips as if tasting the idea. "First . . . strike. Hmm." He leaned back. "So something like this? Media girl asks, 'Mr. Quetzal, do you and your followers see significance in the meteor strike?' You look concerned, even worried — but not surprised. 'Yes, my many researchers and I think it is a very significant event.' Media girl: 'But it damaged only one building.' You: 'Which is what we expect from a first strike.' You —"

"Me: 'I can't say any more. I refuse to be responsible for a panic.' Then I shake my head sadly and refuse to answer any more questions."

A grin spread across Balfour's narrow face that made Quetzal think of a smiling skeleton. "What do you know? You *are* brilliant."

CHAPTER 5

Bob Newton watched as trucks and cars loaded with people slowly drove by. A large construction truck filled with people instead of building materials lumbered along the street, its tires spewing dust into the air. Some of San Pedro's inhabitants rode on motor scooters or bicycles, and some walked to waiting, aged buses.

Another tremor rolled through the ground. They were becoming more frequent and therefore more frightening. Newton was beginning to second-guess himself. Maybe he should have called for the evacuation sooner. Volcanoes were fairly predictable and normally gave sufficient time for evacuation. Ground tremors were one of the key indicators. What couldn't be predicted was the level of activity a volcano might take. Violent eruptions could happen quickly. It had with Mt. Pinatubo in the Philippines, but there had been enough time to evacuate the area as well as the local air force base. He was hoping for the same luxury.

Newton wished for two things now: more time, and the return of his team from the mountain. They were overdue. They had radioed a report earlier, but that was now two hours past. There had been no contact since, which was unusual. Something was wrong, and Newton didn't know what.

Perhaps he should go look for them. As he weighed the idea, another tremor shook the ground. *Too many tremors,* he thought. They were experienced field scientists, they knew how to take care of themselves, he reassured himself. But the reassurance rang hollow. Mt. Pinatubo took the lives of two experienced scientists, as it had other scientists before them.

He saw it before he heard it. Facing the northwest side of the mountain, Newton raised his binoculars to his eyes and saw a cloud of dust, followed by sudden jet of ash and steam rocketing skyward. "It's beginning," he said to himself. The face of the mountain collapsed on itself as the magma chamber below gave way. As a child, Newton imagined an eruption as fire and lava squirting out the peak of the volcano and running down its side. While such things did happen, many volcanoes erupted explosively through their weakened sides. The ash continued to rise like a mushroom cloud after a nuclear explosion. Then came the billows of pyroclastic flow. Heavy billows of black smoke, laced with rock and debris, began to cascade down the mountainside.

Newton felt his heart stop — the deadly cloud was heading straight for San Pedro. It was also traveling down the dirt road used by the scientific team, if they were still on the mountain.

Turning, he saw the citizens of San Pedro staring in disbelief at El Popo. "Run," Newton screamed. "Run!"

There was pandemonium. People scattered in different directions. The few who had cars sped down the dirt road that ran through town, barely missing their pedestrian neighbors.

The deadly, toxic cloud approached.

Thud.

Newton turned to see what had made the sound behind him. It was a rock, red with heat and the size of a grapefruit. The object didn't surprise him; he had been expecting such flying burning materials — known to volcanologists as *pyroclastic ejecta.* They were common in major eruptions. Another dropped, then another, burning missiles fired from deep within the mountain. Soon there would be mudflows like the one that killed 23,000 people in the Nevado del Ruiz eruption in 1985. One of the things that had captured Newton's scientific curiosity was the numerous ways in which a volcano could kill.

Directing his attention to the ash cloud above the mountain, Newton saw that it was *also* headed northwest. Ash would begin to fall from the mountain to well past Mexico City forty-five miles away.

Sadness filled him. He was sure his team was dead, and even if they had survived by some miracle, the town of San Pedro wouldn't. He had shouted a warning to the stunned inhabitants who had stood dumbstruck by the sight of the cataclysm they were witnessing, but he knew that many would still die. He felt responsible. If only the monitoring devices on El Popo hadn't failed, perhaps then they would have had more warning. Still, there had been enough indications, and he had hesitated. After all, El Popo was supposed to be relatively safe, some even defining its destructive capabilities as mild. They were wrong. He was wrong. And now many would die. Perhaps the other towns would fare better.

Another falling rock jarred him from his thoughts. The mountain was now surrounded by a massive ash cloud. Already lightning was beginning to flash from the cloud as it created its own thunderstorm. The rumbling of the mountain was set counterpoint to the newly added claps of thunder.

"Fire and water. How ironic."

He turned to face the community building that had been serving as his field office. A woman, not much more than a girl, huddled in fear by the doorway. She was clutching an infant in her arms. Stepping to his Toyota Land Cruiser, he opened the passenger door and quickly motioned for her to come. She hesitated but then complied. Then he loaded the car with as many as would fit, jumped in the driver's seat, and started down the street.

The afternoon sky darkened as the ash cloud obliterated the sun. Gray ash began to fall. Soon the ground, the buildings, and the bodies of those who died would be covered in a gray funeral shroud that had been created in the depths of the earth.

"I haven't been a very good guest," Lisa said. She had been watching Morgan out of the corner of her eye. For a while she assumed he was sleeping, but every once in a while, he would open his eyes and stare at the jet's ceiling. He hadn't spoken for the last hour, and every minute of that hour cut her soul like tiny knives of guilt. She had come on too strong. She was always doing that — pressing the subject of a story for a more quotable line, nagging her editor for better assignments, and even engaging in arguments with herself.

Why was she so polemical? What did she have to prove? She didn't know, but she felt she had to prove something. Maybe it was her upbringing. As a child, she had learned to hold her own at the supper table, which was more of a debate forum than a place to eat the evening meal. Her father taught philosophy at a Christian college, and her mother taught English literature. As a family, they never had much money, but they did abound in passion.

Her one brother was too smart for his own good. Smarter than the other kids in school, the best he could do was circle the outer orbit of social interaction. Until he got to college. Through college and med school, he had all the friends he could want, including pretty coeds. How he resisted their tempting smiles, sweet laughter, and youthful bodies was beyond her, but she knew he had. He married two years out of med school. Three years later, he took his wife to

East Africa to work as a medical missionary.

It was the way of her family: Everything centered on Christ. What Lisa lacked — and she told herself this repeatedly — was restraint. Perhaps she was trying to live up to her brother's level of commitment. Perhaps she was just argumentative.

"I'm sorry," Morgan said. "Did you say something?"

"I was apologizing for being rude."

He sat up. "Rude? Did I miss something?"

"You've gone out of your way to help me, and I repay that kindness by offending you."

"Really? Am I offended? I hadn't noticed."

She smiled at him. "I think you're just being gentlemanly."

"Ah. It's a fault among men of the South."

Lisa chuckled. "I know lots of Southern men, and they know nothing of being gentlemen. I'm afraid that art died a long time ago." She shifted in her seat so she could see him better. "Anyway, I tend to be a little —"

"Aggressive?"

"I was going to say *assertive*."

He tipped his head to the side. "That's a much more positive term. *Assertive*. I like it."

"I'm trying to apologize here. I can be a little pushy."

Morgan grinned. "A pushy reporter. Who could imagine such a thing?"

Lisa began to speak, but Morgan cut her off with a raised finger. "You did your research. You know I've suffered the worst loss a man can experience, but that doesn't mean I'm fragile. I'm not. You don't need to apologize."

"But you haven't said a word in over an hour."

"So? I've been thinking. I do that a lot. Trust me, my board of directors puts me through more than you can ever dream up."

She leaned back and wondered why his refusal to let her apologize bothered her so much. "Do you really believe all this Mayan calendar . . ."

"Mumbo jumbo? Nonsense? Garbage? Superstition? Which term do you prefer?" He leaned his head back against the seat rest. "Yes, I believe it."

"But you seem . . . I mean . . . I'm doing it again."

He didn't move. "Seem what? Intelligent? I am. I have an MS degree in geology from Reynolds University. Had my father not died, I might have pursued a PhD. As it was, I inherited a business. The boardroom is a very different place than a barren field."

"You prefer the outdoors, don't you?"

"More of your research?"

"I saw the online photos of you in far-off places." She reached for her phone. "Want to see?"

"No thanks. I was there."

"So why believe this stuff about the Mayans and 2012?"

He waited a few moments before answering. "Because, Lisa, it's the only thing that makes sense."

"Okay, I'm working hard to not cross the line again, Mr. Morgan —"

"Just Andrew is fine. I'm a casual man. Most people just call me Morgan."

"Okay, Andrew, how is it that the Mayan prophecies make so much sense to you?"

He turned his head to face her. A smirk rose on his lips. "Call it faith."

CHAPTER 6

December 30, 2010

The pastor was a chunk of a man, pear-shaped, who waddled more than walked. Morgan didn't trust men who refused to take care of themselves. He spent a significant portion of his day working out and taking enough vitamins and health enhancements to constitute a small meal. Why every man didn't do the same puzzled Morgan. Although the reverend wore an expensive suit, Morgan could tell that there was more fat than muscle beneath the finely stitched black material.

Pastor Johansson sat in a red oak chair behind and to the side of the mortuary pulpit. Quincy Doolittle, the portly pastor who stood behind the lectern, was Berkley Street Baptist Church's minister in charge of pastoral care. It had been explained to Morgan that Berkley Street Baptist was a megachurch and therefore need many staff members. It wasn't news. The South was filled with such churches. He had assumed that the senior pastor would be the one doing the funeral and felt cheated because the duty had been passed off to another man.

As the CEO of a major corporation, Morgan knew the importance of delegation. Still, it didn't seem right. His wife and son deserved the best in life and even more in death.

In his heart, he knew it didn't matter. Dead was dead, and even if he buried his family in caskets of gold and hired the world's most famous preachers to conduct the service, he would still go home alone to an empty house.

Quincy Doolittle took care of the weddings, hospital visits, and funerals. Johansson was there for support. Johansson had been the first to visit Morgan after the crash. He deserved credit for that. After that one visit, Doolittle made all future contact. Why that bothered him, Morgan didn't know. Of course, everything bothered him. Stop lights were too long, birds sang off key, grass was too green, and sugar too sweet. It didn't matter what it was — it was wrong.

Morgan took a deep breath and noticed it came in a shuddering flow. He promised himself he would not cry. He had done little else since the cops showed up at his door with the small words that ground his world to dust.

A few moments ago, the room was filled with subdued action. Soft conversation bounced off the walls of the Benjamin Atwood Memorial Chapel in Oklahoma City's most prestigious mortuary and cemetery: Eternal Trails. Morgan had been here twice before: once to bury his mother; once to bury his father. Now . . .

He had no brothers or sisters, so an elderly uncle and even older aunt sat with him on the family pew. Marybeth had also been an only child. The pew seemed under-filled and for reasons he couldn't explain, it bothered him.

Behind him sat the twelve members of his board of directors. Each had shaken his hand as professional men do, said how sorry they were, and offered to help in any way they could. Morgan shook each hand and said thank you.

Young people — people Hunter's age — filled up half the seating on the right side of the large chapel. The girls wept; the boys tried not to. Behind them were teachers who had Hunter in their classes. Morgan had seen the principal of the private school enter. They exchanged nods — nothing more.

When Morgan arrived, soft music, mostly hymns Morgan remembered hearing as a child in church, wafted from concealed speakers overhead like mist before a rain. They were smooth, soft, gentle, and meant to comfort the grieving. They irritated Morgan. The moment Doolittle stepped behind the pulpit, the music ceased. The operator failed to trail the music off; it sounded as if he just hit the off button. Jarring.

"Good afternoon." Doolittle talked through his nose. "My name is Reverend Quincy Doolittle of Berkley Street Baptist Church, where I serve as minister of pastoral care. It is my honor to officiate at this difficult time. On behalf of Mr. Morgan and extended family, I thank you all for being here. As we begin, I would like to introduce Senior Pastor Bryan Johansson, who will lead us in prayer and offer our first Scripture reading."

Johansson was unlike his fellow pastor: six-foot and stout. Morgan took him to be one of those guys who ran five miles a day — ten if he wanted to work up a sweat. He spoke with the kind of voice that made radio personalities envious. Although he needed no microphone, one had been provided, most likely for Pastor Wimpy.

"At times like these, there is no better place to turn for comfort and strength than to our Lord and Savior, Jesus, and to God's Word. Stand with me as I read the twenty-third Psalm." The sound of two hundred people standing — most of whom Morgan couldn't name — echoed through the chapel.

"The LORD is my shepherd . . ."

Morgan stopped listening. His ears no longer wished to function, and he was grateful. His eyes, however, were a different story: They drifted to the pair of shiny black coffins at the front of the chapel. Unlike the memorial services for his parents, these caskets were closed and locked. No amount of wax and makeup could make what remained of his wife and son presentable. What lay in those boxes were the charred remains of what had once been the heartbeat of his life.

He had not seen their bodies. The mortuary people had warned against it. "This is not what you want to remember." He agreed. He didn't need to see their broken and burned bodies. He saw that every time he closed his eyes. Instead of open caskets, large photos in gold-painted frames stared back at him: Hunter in his school's basketball uniform; Marybeth in her Sunday best.

Movement around him brought Morgan back to the moment. Lost in his thoughts, he was the last to sit. Doolittle was up front again, his mouth moving but Morgan heard only snippets, none sharp enough to bore through his grief.

Johansson's reading of David's psalm swirled in his head.

"The LORD is my shepherd." *Not my shepherd. Apparently not my wife's or son's shepherd either.* "I shall not want." *I will forever want.* "He maketh me to lie down in green pastures." *Or plunge my family to their deaths in a desolate desert after a thirty-thousand-foot fall.* "He leadeth me beside the still waters." *He drowns me in sorrow.* "He restoreth my soul; he leadeth me in the paths of righteousness for his name's sake." *He driveth my soul away.*

It was at that moment that Morgan began his war with God.

Morgan's corporate jet set down at the San Antonio International Airport and taxied to an area reserved for private jets. The copilot exited the cockpit and opened the air-stairs, descended, and waited for Morgan and Lisa to exit. As she reached the last step, the young airman held out a hand, and she took it.

"It was a pleasure having you onboard, ma'am."

She detected a New England accent. It sounded strange to her Southern ears. She smiled at the courtesy. "It was a greater pleasure being aboard."

The steps bounced slightly, causing Lisa to turn. Morgan was descending; the pilot stood in the doorway. He caught her eye. "A gentleman always walks a lady to the door."

"This is an airport, not my home."

Morgan smiled. It seemed genuine. "You don't live at the airport?"

"Not anymore."

"Touché. Hungry?"

"I've already put you out of your way."

Morgan placed a hand on her elbow and directed her to a stairway that led to the terminal wing. "I'm hungry. The crew is hungry. Besides, security has to go over the plane again. Did you know that we can't carry golf clubs onboard?"

"Why is that?"

Morgan shrugged. "Beats me. Maybe terrorists like to play a few holes before destroying something. I'm sure security has their reasons."

"Seems strange to me."

He chuckled. "I didn't say they were good reasons. Are you in a hurry to get somewhere?"

"No, I can spare some time for the guy who gave me a lift on his private jet."

"In that case, let's chow down."

The terminal looked similar to every terminal Lisa had been in. It sounded the same. Although not a world traveler, she had been in most major airports in the United States. Each one proved form followed function.

Finding a spot to sit proved more challenging than Lisa expected. Wading through the crowd reminded her of experiences as a child playing in the surf on family vacations to the Gulf Coast of Texas. The waves would rush her and then attempt to draw her deeper into the sea. Here, however, ocean waves had been replaced by swells of people, each lost in their own thoughts. Airports were great places to be ignored.

"How about here?" Morgan gestured to a sports bar. A crowd stood around the perimeter, but she could see two or three empty tables. "It's a bar."

"I can see that."

Morgan blinked a few times. "What I mean is —"

"You're wondering if I as a Christian can eat a sandwich in an airport sports bar."

"I just don't want you writing an article about how I, a fallen man, tried to lead you to the road of destruction."

Lisa couldn't tell if he was serious. "I don't think I'll melt. Let's go."

Morgan led the way, politely elbowing his way to the entrance. Lisa followed in his wake. She noticed very few people bothered to look at them. Their eyes were glued to the flat-screen televisions mounted to the walls.

They sat at a sticky, round table barely big enough for two plates of food. Snatching up a menu, her eyes traced the soup and sandwich offerings.

A teenage-thin waiter dressed all in black approached and stood in silence by the table.

"Do you have a soup of the day?" Lisa barely glanced up from the menu. When he didn't respond, she raised her gaze and looked at his youthful face. His forehead looked like a freshly plowed field; his eyes were fixed on one of the televisions. She pursed her lips in frustration and turned to Morgan. He too was fixated on the screen. She started to make a snide remark about men and sports when she noticed everyone

— men, women, and children — were hypnotized by the image on the screens. She turned. A moment later, she raised a hand to her mouth.

Images from what Lisa assumed was a helicopter filled the televisions. Dark, billowing smoke rose from a mountain. The gasses and ash were so thick they seemed more liquid than anything else. There was a caption at the bottom of the screen: VOLCANO ERUPTS NEAR MEXICO CITY. One of the bartenders behind the bar picked up a remote and cranked the volume. A man with a two-hundred-dollar haircut was speaking.

"It's too early for definitive reports, but estimates of dead run in the thousands. Popocatépetl has been rumbling for years. Scientists had earlier dismissed the idea of such a violent explosion. Villages in the San Pedro Mountains are the most severely hit."

"Oh my . . ." Lisa had joined the ranks of frozen viewers.

The news anchor continued: "A team of scientists from MIT had been studying the volcano for the last few months. Nothing has been heard from them, and the worst is feared. Video from cell phones are being sent worldwide. We have one here." He touched his ear and tilted his head. "I'm

84

being told to warn you that this is rather graphic."

The newsman disappeared, replaced by a grainy, bouncy image. At first, Lisa could only see a dirt path and the feet of frightened people. Suddenly, the individual with the camera fell. The lens of the device pointed up, revealing a funeral shroud of black smoke hovering overhead. A face appeared. Lisa assumed it was the phone's owner. Dirt covered his skin, streaked clean by flowing tears.

He picked up the phone and turned it back to the wrathful mountain, just in time to see a blazing red explosion. Moments later, fiery pieces of molten rock began falling like blazing basketballs.

The device recorded the screams of men, women, children, and even animals.

The image changed from a boiling mountain to fleeing villagers to the face of the man who the owned phone. He spoke. Lisa knew enough Spanish to translate the man's words: "I love you forever . . . forever . . ."

The video stopped.

"Oh, my soul," Lisa said. "Oh, my dear Jesus."

"Quetzal was right." Morgan spoke softly and respectfully. "It's begun."

CHAPTER 7

December 30, 2010

The funeral and reception lasted less than three hours, which seemed slightly less than a week to Morgan. After the funeral, scores of people came by and patted or shook him on the shoulder, each expressing the deep sorrow they felt for him at his loss.

He nodded.

He said thank you.

And when they commented about how wonderful his wife was, how talented his son had been, he agreed and tried not to let on that each word sliced off a piece of his heart.

They held the reception in a large fellowship hall at Johansson's church. Volunteers had brought every imaginable form of casserole, fried chicken, potato salad, and Jell-O concoction. They had laid the food on a series of long tables that reminded Morgan of a buffet line.

When he first arrived, a dour seriousness hung in the air. People spoke in low tones and ladies with decorative aprons ricocheted from the kitchen to the hall and back to the kitchen. None looked up from their work. One gray-haired woman moved a serving tray of spaghetti and meatballs to the end of one of the tables and then disappeared from view. A moment later, another woman with grayer hair moved it back. Morgan wondered if spaghetti protocol had been broken.

A few days ago, the thought would have been funny.

In the center of the room sat the largest table in the room. In the center of the table sat a placard with his name on it. A flash of memory burned his brain. The last time he saw his name on a table placard was at the fund-raiser he attended with his wife shortly before . . . well, before. The placard had more than his name on it: ANDREW MORGAN AND FAMILY.

Was this the way it was going to be? Reminders in every room, at every corner, in every sentence? Whoever made the little sign couldn't have known it would evoke such a scorching memory. Not even he could have predicted it.

Morgan took his place at the table and someone offered to fix a plate for him. He looked in the sad eyes of a woman who teetered on the threshold between middle age and matronhood.

"I'm not hungry, but thank you."

"I'll just bring a little bit of everything."

Morgan doubted she was strong enough or had a plate large enough to bring a sample of everything. "No, really —"

Apparently the woman had never encountered a "no" she couldn't ignore.

People took turns sitting at Morgan's table. Some made small talk as if his life hadn't been snuffed out; others just sat and looked at him with pity.

A half-dozen pastors and an equal number of deacons flew in, expressed their sadness, then flitted away like hummingbirds.

He stayed for nearly an hour before excusing himself. He felt as if he were being rude, but it was either leave or explode. What did it matter if they thought he was rude? He would never see these people again.

The drive home took four times longer than necessary. He needed time. Like a diver who has been too deep for too long, Morgan needed to decompress, if such a thing were possible. So he drove with no destination in mind. He cruised residential streets and plied the freeways. Tears blurred the traffic, and sadness rolled over him. He tightened his grip on the steering wheel until his knuckles threatened to break through his skin.

As the fuel gauge tipped toward the large E on his dashboard, Morgan headed for home.

Raw emotions wore him down. He had no energy and longed for the blissful nothingness of sleep. But he had one more difficult task to do. He disrobed, slipped into a pair of pajamas, and did something he hadn't done since the accident: He crawled into the bed he shared with his wife. Surely he was weary enough to defeat whatever memories sought to keep him from a restful night.

At 1:15, he thought he heard Marybeth breathing beside him. He reached for her but his hand found only cool sheets, unwarmed by a body.

At 2:10, he caught a whiff of her deodorant.

At 3:10, he was certain he heard her soft snore.

At 4:30, he heard her talk in her sleep.

At 4:35, Morgan went downstairs and curled up on the sofa. In the darkness, he did something he hadn't done since he was a kid. He prayed.

"God, You killed my family. How about

You kill me?"

The last few days had left Lisa worn and frayed. Her dad would say she felt like a dog bone chewed to the marrow. Her apartment was large, and if she stood in just the right place and looked over the balcony at just the right angle, she could see a portion of the horseshoe section of the San Antonio River. It was one of the two hallmarks of the city — the other being the Alamo. Lights from the River Walk glowed warmly. Lisa had lived alone for many years, which left her subject to mild depression and loneliness. When the dark emotions clouded her heart, she would go to the shops and restaurants along the famous river and watch the stream of tourists meander the walkway, or dine on barges that plied the waters.

A good meal, a fine coffee, or a clear night was usually enough to scatter the emotional gloom. A part of her — a large part — wanted to do that very thing. The last few days had been tense and a sense of foreboding rose in her. She took a moment to wonder about it, but could pinpoint nothing to explain the emotional haunting.

"Too much travel; too much uncertainty." There was no one on the balcony to argue with her.

Her body longed for bed, but her mind wouldn't settle.

Still, there were some good things to ponder. She had been rescued by a handsome man who carried her off in a multimillion-dollar aircraft. That was a first.

Could it be? No. She dismissed the idea. Her wakefulness and overactive mind had nothing to do with Andrew Morgan. She knew plenty of women who would salivate at the opportunity to fly in a corporate jet with a billionaire hunk. But she was different. Money, fame, and good looks had no effect on her. Or so she told herself.

Moving back into the apartment, she strolled over the worn brown carpet, past the secondhand sofa and coffee table, beyond the small television, and into the kitchen. If she worked for a larger news organization, a secular news organization, she could afford a better place. But she didn't, nor did she want to. Working for the *Christian Herald* was her mission. And since it was online, they could provide news in a more immediate fashion.

After fixing a cup of Earl Gray decaf tea, she went to the second bedroom of the apartment — the room she called her office. With just the light of her computer screen to illuminate the small room, Lisa sipped tea and answered e-mail.

Then she paused.

No, she had gone too far already. "Leave the poor man alone." The computer didn't answer.

Once again, Lisa started an Internet search for Andrew Morgan of Morgan Natural Energy.

The rental limo dropped Morgan off at his home. Although the exterior lights painted the stone walls with yellow splashes, the interior looked as dark as a tomb. It seemed fitting.

Everything looked the same as he had left it: same emptiness. The blankets he had left in a pile on the sofa in the great room were undisturbed, but the sight of them was disturbing. His home was huge, seven bedrooms in all, and he couldn't sleep in one of them. The only place his brain would shut down long enough for him to sleep was the family room couch. The sofa was comfortable to sit on, beautiful to look at, but made a lousy bed.

He dropped his bag and garment bag on the mahogany flooring, slipped from his shoes, flicked on the flat-screen television, and plopped into the leather easy chair his wife had given him for his birthday two years prior. The light from the television struggled to press back the blackness of the room. Morgan had no idea what program played on the screen.

Morgan closed his eyes and tried to lower the revolutions per minute in his mind. Thoughts tumbled in his head. He thought of Roswell. Then he thought of Lisa. He forced his thinking to the words of Robert Quetzal. A moment later, the image of the last Mayan priest was replaced with that of Lisa.

"This is stupid."

He sat up and glanced at the television. Someone was selling something in an info-mercial. He rose, moved to the kitchen, poured a glass of two-percent milk, downed it in several gulps, and then poured another and moved back to the family room.

No matter how he positioned himself, the normally comfortable overstuffed chair felt like it had been filled with chunks of con-crete.

The clock showed eleven minutes past ten. Unless travel made it impossible, Morgan liked to be in bed by ten. He had become a man of routine: in bed by ten, up at six, exercise, in the office by nine, home by seven in the evening.

Not tonight.

"Do you know who Horatio G. Spafford was?" He could hear the words as if Lisa were in the room with him. He hadn't let on, but the question and the conversation that followed stung him.

"So what?" He spoke to the dimness. "I don't care who has lost whom. Just because someone else lost a family doesn't mean . . ."

He rose and began to pace. He took another long draw on the milk, and, for a moment, he wished it was something stronger. He didn't keep booze in the house anymore. He told himself it was because he had become consumed with health and fitness, but the hidden, brutally honest part of the brain reminded him that he was too weak to limit his intake. Drinking only deepened his ever-present depression.

The room closed in on him. The darkness grew thick. Disciplined in every area of life, Morgan grew more frustrated that he could not evict Lisa from his thoughts. She was annoying, nosey, preachy, and someone who walked around in a fog of irrational faith.

So why was he missing her?

Morgan opened the sliding glass door and crossed the threshold into the cool, moist night. The smell of mowed grass mingled with the aroma of chlorine wafting on the large pool a short distance away.

The night painted dew on every surface. Bracing himself against the doorjamb, Morgan removed his socks then walked barefooted across the concrete patio. Still compelled to pace, he walked around the pool to the half-court basketball area he shared with his son so many times before. A basketball covered in condensation rested in a nearby patio chair. He retrieved it, stepped to the free throw line, and shot for the basket. The ball hit the rim, the backboard, then bounced away, landing in the pool with a soft splash. It floated to the center of the pool, well out of reach.

Morgan looked at the safety pole hanging on a post a short distance away. Its length and the gentle curve of the end meant to help a struggling swimmer to the side would be perfect for retrieving the wayward ball.

Instead, Morgan sat in one of the damp chairs and wondered how difficult it would be to drown himself.

CHAPTER 8

The offices of the *Christian Herald* were small and cramped. Several desks, each with a computer and monitor on the surface, populated the central area of the space. The news outlet occupied one-half of the first floor of an old building in downtown San Antonio. It wasn't the best location, but it was what the small organization could afford. Started ten years prior by a former journalist-turned-pastor, the *Christian Herald* was one of the few purely Christian news organizations in the world, and it was one of the few that survived the recession of 2009 and 2010. Lisa was among the scarce field reporters left.

She entered the office, walked to the battered desk purchased from a used office furniture store, set her purse in the large bottom drawer, smoothed her pantsuit jacket, and retrieved a notepad, pencil, and her BlackBerry.

The conference room was at the front of the building, just a few feet from the entryway and reception area. A glass wall separated it from the "bullpen," where the half-dozen reporters, researchers, and web gurus worked more hours than they were paid for to put out a daily online newspaper that offered a Christian worldview on current events.

Lisa was the last to enter the room. At the head of the table sat the editor in chief, Rodney Truffaut, an artificially dark-haired sixty-year-old man with a well-lined face. Several others, mostly women, lined the perimeter of the table. Coffee cups and diet soda cans rested on the marred surface. Some of the employees held iPhones and BlackBerrys, poised and ready for note taking. Two had laptop computers. As much of a technophile as Lisa was, she preferred taking meeting notes with pencil and paper.

"You made it." Lisa couldn't tell if Truffaut was smiling or grimacing. Like a bear, he was large and looked cuddly, but he could take an arm off with one swipe of his meaty hand. She had never heard him raise his voice, but his glare was deafening.

"Sorry, chief, late night. I overslept." She walked to him and laid the unused ticket on the conference table. "I did manage to save the company a few bucks."

"Your airline ticket? What'd you do? Walk?"

Lisa grinned. "Hitchhiked." She moved to the other end of the table. "My flight was canceled."

"How'd you get home?"

"A man I met —"

"Ooooooh." The others mocked her in unison.

"All right, knock it off." Lisa couldn't hold down her smile, and it bothered her. "My flight was canceled, and he took pity on me and flew me home."

"How did he do . . . You don't mean —"

"Yes, he had a business jet." Lisa's face felt warm.

"Is he good-looking?" Marge Lyman, a dark-haired woman living on the other side of forty-five, leaned over the table.

"Who cares? He has his own jet." Jennifer Garcia was all smiles. She was the political reporter and one of the best writers Lisa knew. Which was remarkable because English was her second language.

"All right, guys," Truffaut said. "Let's get back to work. Lisa, I was just introducing Garrett Vickers to everyone. He's our newest hire."

Lisa studied the young man for a moment.

He looked too young to go to college, let alone be a graduate. His skin bore a slight tint, causing Lisa to assume that he had Mediterranean roots in his past.

"Hi." Lisa followed the word with a nod.

"Back at ya." Youthfulness and confidence flavored his voice. When Lisa got her first "real job" out of college, she had been a bundle of apprehension and fear, worried that people would learn before lunch just how ignorant and naive she was. Garrett acted as if he were the chief's nephew.

"Garrett graduated at the top of his class." Truffaut beamed. "Journalism, of course."

Lisa couldn't resist. "Nephew? Grandson? Great grandson?"

"I resent that, young lady. I'll have you know that Garrett's distant relation to me had nothing to do with my hiring him. And what do you mean by *great* grandson?"

"Did I say that?" Lisa smiled. The others chuckled. "Okay, I'm going to go with nephew."

Garrett turned to the editor in chief. "You're right, Uncle. She is the sharpest scalpel on the tray."

"At work, you may call me boss, sir, or chief. Save the uncle stuff for family dinners."

"Yes, Uncle — boss."

He sighed loud and for effect. "If it's all right with the rest of you jokers, maybe we can return to being a news agency."

The chuckles evaporated.

"Since the rest of us were slaving away in the office while you were vacationing in Roswell and flying around the country on some rich guy's air yacht, we'll start with you."

Lisa straightened in her chair. "As everyone knows — well, everyone but newbie here — I was in Roswell, New Mexico, to research Robert Quetza—"

"The Mayan priest guy?" Garrett's eyes widened.

"Yes, newbie, but don't bet your paycheck that he's a real Mayan priest. Anyway, I sat through his spiel, which was held in a small movie theater. The place was packed. I got one of the last seats."

"What's he like?" Marge asked.

"Tall, built like a lineman, articulate, well dressed, and rich."

Truffaut cocked his head. "How do you know he's rich?"

"While I waited for my plane to taxi to the runway, Morgan noticed a business jet with a Quetzal logo on the tail."

Jennifer leaned Lisa's direction. "You mean while *you* sat in a corporate jet, you saw another corporate jet with Quetzal's logo?"

"Let it go, girl." Lisa raised a hand. "I can't help it if God likes me better than you."

"Who is Morgan?" Truffaut was trying to keep things on track, something he often likened to herding cats.

"Andrew Morgan. He's the CEO of Morgan Natural Energy and the guy who came to my rescue at the airport. I told you I got one of the last seats in the theater; he got the other. Anyway, he pointed out another private jet and identified it as belonging to Quetzal. Quetzal wears a gold pin in the image of a snake and two feathers."

"Makes sense," Garrett said. "Ancient Mayans were polytheistic. One of their gods was Quetzalcoatl, a snake."

"Right," Lisa said.

"That seems rather coincidental," Jennifer said.

Lisa shook her head. "Not really. Albuquerque International Sunport is one of the places people use to reach Roswell. You fly in there and drive the rest of the way. Roswell is not a big city. It makes sense that Quetzal and Morgan parked their aircraft there."

"Did you get an interview?" Truffaut

pressed.

"I tried. The man didn't stay around long. By the time I got to the stage, he was gone. His security people made it clear that he seldom gives interviews after a presentation." Lisa inhaled deeply. "He offered nothing new. Same nonsense as is on his web page: world coming to an end, 2012 comes and the lights go out, only a few will survive. The gods of the universe have chosen him to lead the select few to safety. The rest of us are toast."

"A lot of people don't think it's nonsense."

All eyes turned to Garrett.

"Hey, I didn't say I was one of them. You said the theater was packed, right?"

"I did. And recent events are going to make more people turn to him."

"The volcano? Popokrakatoa." Jennifer stumbled over the Indian name.

Lisa corrected her. "Popocatépetl. I'm sure you've been following the broadcast media. Before the mountain blew its top, something else happened. In fact, it happened in the middle of Quetzal's presentation. A meteorite smashed a mechanic's shop in Arizona. Quetzal didn't miss a beat. He told the audience it was one more sign of the coming end."

"You say Andrew Morgan was in the audience?" Marge's eyes narrowed. She had more experience in journalism than Lisa and the others combined — not counting the chief.

"Yes. He sat next to me."

Her head bobbed slightly. "How did he react to Quetzal?"

"My focus was elsewhere, but I couldn't help noticing that he did a lot of nodding, and . . ."

"And what?" Truffaut leaned over the conference table.

"He's a believer. He told me as much on the flight."

"How can a successful man like him be taken in by a charlatan like Quetzal?" Jennifer never held a conviction she didn't share with others.

"He's . . . I can't be sure. I think much of it has to do with the tragedy he experienced."

"Tragedy?" One of Truffaut's eyebrows rose.

"His wife and son died in an aircraft mishap."

Truffaut scratched his forehead. Lisa had seen this response many times before. He was searching the file cabinets of his memory. "That was what? A year ago?"

"December 26, 2010."

"The day after Christmas." Jennifer shook her head. "Doesn't seem right."

"Would it feel any more right if it happened on any other day?" Marge looked at Lisa. "There's your hook."

"I agree," Truffaut said. "If I know you, you've already started doing research."

"Maybe."

"Lisa?"

"All right, chief, I may have done a little Internet snooping, but that doesn't mean I found a story —"

"Here's your story, Lisa. Andrew is a rich and powerful man. He has influence, and I assume a pretty good education."

"He has a degree in petroleum geology. In fact, he told me if he had his way, he'd —"

"There's the angle. Right there, staring you in the face."

"I know what you're getting at, boss, but —"

"Wait," Garrett said. "Someone fill me in. I'm new, remember?"

"Your uncle thinks there's a story about a wealthy, successful, educated man following Quetzal."

"I don't *think.* I *know.*" Truffaut squirmed in his seat. A good story still stoked his fires. "We know people will follow almost anything, but guys like Morgan are different.

104

Why would this guy buy into this nonsense? That's what I want to know. And if he's taking the bait, there might be others. That's what I want you to work on. I'm telling you, it's got Pulitzer written all over it."

Lisa turned to Garrett. "That's known as *hyperbole,* newbie. Christian news organizations don't get nominated for the Pulitzer Prize."

Truffaut pointed at his nephew. "Garrett will help. It'll do him good to see how real world journalism works. He needs something more than a college newspaper to cut his teeth on."

"Chief, you know I work alone."

"I know you *used* to work alone."

CHAPTER 9

"Okay, since we're going to be working together, fill me in on this whole Mayan apocalypse thing."

Lisa glanced over her shoulder at the trailing Garrett. "From your comment about Mayan gods, I assumed you were up to speed on all this." She worked the bullpen area, sidestepping desks. There was work room for twice the reporters and web-ninjas than actually worked for the *Christian Herald,* but the economy being what it was and no real way to charge for subscriptions, the small nonprofit had to work on a shoestring.

"Well, I know a few things that I picked up in world history classes, but I don't know much about the end-of-the-world stuff — well, except what I see on television. There's a lot of that, but it all seems contradictory."

"That's because it is." Lisa stopped at her desk, set down her writing pad, and grabbed her laptop. "Since we have to work together,

I guess I should fill your newbie brain with facts."

Garrett's shoulders dipped an inch. It was enough for Lisa to notice.

"Sorry, kid, that came out harsher than I meant." She gave him a long look and then forced a smile. "You know how the movies show star reporters as aloof, antisocial, and loners?"

"Yeah."

"Well, that's me — except the antisocial part. I'm usually easy to get along with."

"Unless someone gets in your way."

Her smile dipped. "Your uncle tell you that?"

"Yes . . . I mean, he said something similar. I wasn't trying to be rude. I tend to repeat what I hear."

"You need to break that habit, right now. Clear?"

"Yes, ma'am."

"And if you call me 'ma'am' again, I'm going to have to hurt you."

"Okay, but what should I call you?"

"I'm fine with *amazing,* but if that's too much of a stretch, you can call me *Lisa,* like everyone else."

"You mean not everyone calls you *amazing?*"

"Now you see how quickly we've come

107

back to my need to hurt you?" She smiled. "You'll get used to my sense of humor. Probably. Follow me."

"Where?"

"The library."

Lisa moved to the back of the office space and opened the door to a long, narrow room with a narrow conference table that had so many scars it looked as if it had served as an aircraft runway. Scars and stains gave it character.

Along the walls were rows of out-of-date encyclopedias, stacks of magazines, and the latest editions of major newspapers. The library was the most useless room in the office complex. Almost everything a reporter needed could be and was found on the Internet. The room existed only because of Truffaut's allegiance to the old way of doing business. To Lisa, her boss was a paradox. He led an organization that distributed news digitally, but his heart still pumped ink. These days, the library served as a place to heat a sack lunch or to slip away from the rattle of computer keyboards, phone conversations, and chit-chat.

"Take a seat." Lisa pointed at a rickety, dining-room-style chair near the head of the table. She pulled back a chair, sat, and set her laptop on the table. A few moments later, the laptop was humming. "Okay, I'm going to do a brain dump, so listen fast."

"I'm all ears."

Lisa resisted the urge to make a joke. "Talk of end times is not new. It's part of the Christian doctrine. There is an entire branch of theology devoted to eschatology — the study of Christ's return and end times. As you probably know, there's a fair amount to debate about the details, but most Bible-based churches agree that Jesus will bodily return."

"I'm familiar with the concept." Garrett leaned back.

"I assumed you were. Christians are not the only ones to believe the world will someday end. People share a collective sense that the world is getting near closing time. Apocalyptic thinking is everywhere. Especially now. According to the Pew Research Foundation, about one in five Americans believe that Christ will return in the current generation. A *US News & World Report* poll revealed sixty percent of all Americans — from all faith backgrounds — believe the world will end eventually."

"Sixty percent?"

"Yup. About twenty percent say Earth's life expectancy is just a couple of decades, and people are getting pretty nervous about it. December 21, 2012 is less than a year and a half away."

"And the closer we get to that date —"

"The flakier things are going to get. Already we've seen the rise of cult groups and crazies. More and more people are predicting that December 21, 2012, is the apocalypse deadline — history's final day. The stroke of midnight. The galactic tipping point. The astronomical grand finale."

"Okay, okay, I got it." Garrett leaned forward and tried to peer at Lisa's computer screen. "What makes that date so special? I know that December 21, 2012, can be written 12-21-12. Is it some kinda code?"

"Several people have made a big deal of that, but it's silly. We work on the Gregorian calendar, a system developed by Pope Gregory XIII. That's a long time after the ancient Mayans."

"So that part is just an interesting coincidence?"

Lisa nodded. "December 21, 2012, marks the end of the five-thousand-year cycle by the Mayan Long Count calendar. According to meticulous Mayan calculations, the world as we know it will reach its expiration date. They're not the only ones to say this. The ancient Aztec calendar corroborates the Mayan date." She paused. "Shouldn't you be taking notes?"

Garrett grinned and tapped his forehead. "Eidetic memory."

"You have a photographic memory?"

His grin spread. "That I do. Want me to prove it?"

"No."

He seemed disappointed. "Okay."

"Let's get through this first." Lisa took a breath. "The origins of the Mayans is a mystery. Some believe the Mayan lineage stretches back two thousand years. No one can be sure about much of anything, but there are some things we do know. The Mayans were not alone in ancient Meso-america. The Toltecs, who lived about five hundred miles to the west of central Mexico, spoke a different language but shared many of the Mayan beliefs about time, nature, and cosmology. The Toltecs arrived late on the scene, emerging to power in about A.D. 900. There were also the Olmecs, who were the first in the region to establish a major civilization. Their cultural influences peaked between 1500 and 600 B.C. Other Mayan neighbors were the Zapotecs and Aztecs.

"Mayan civilization grew until the population numbered five to fourteen million. That was around A.D. 800, but then the real mystery begins. One hundred years later,

111

the population had diminished by eighty to ninety percent. No one knows why, but there is no shortage of theories: social or political upheaval, environmental breakdown leading to famine, or even sudden climate change. Others suggest a deadly plague."

"Sounds logical. The plague, I mean."

Lisa nodded slowly. "It seems so, but no vast gravesites indicating the sudden death of large numbers of people have been found. Perhaps several catastrophes took them out." Lisa let her mind drift for a moment as she thought of the strange disappearance of millions of people.

"You okay?" Garrett looked puzzled.

"Sorry. Just thinking. Are you sure you shouldn't be taking notes?"

Garrett straightened and closed his eyes. "Mayan civilization grew until the population numbered five to fourteen million. That was around A.D. 800, but then the real mystery begins —"

"Okay, okay, you win. No need to repeat everything I said."

"Sorry. I like to show off."

Lisa pursed her lips. "I see that." She cleared her throat and glanced at the notes she had been accumulating over the last few weeks. "We may never know why they disappeared so quickly, but here's one thing we do know: They left behind a remarkable legacy — and a bloody one."

"I think I know the bloody part: They performed human sacrifice and would cut the hearts out of their victims."

"Correct. There's evidence that they would drop the bodies in a reservoir they used for their drinking water, thereby contaminating it. It's been suggested that macabre indiscretion may have been the cause of the Mayan demise."

Garrett squirmed. "Sick."

"Human sacrifice, an annual ballgame in which the losing team was killed, and other practices can make a person think the Mayans were crude and barbaric. But they weren't. Well, not completely. They proved themselves to be master builders and keen observers of the sky and time. They were sky-watching timekeepers."

Lisa tapped a key on her computer and read her notes. "The Mayans weren't just interested in time, they were *obsessed* with it. The Mayan calendar keepers charted the cycle of the moon with painstaking accuracy. They did the same for the sun and Venus. Their uncanny accuracy could not be duplicated until modern times."

"How accurate is accurate?" Garrett was

showing real interest.

"Without using telescopes, Mayan astronomers determined the length of a lunar month to be 29.53020 days, within thirty-four seconds of the current value. That was two thousand years ago."

Garrett looked stunned. "They got it down to within thirty-four seconds? That seems impossible."

"You're right. It does seem impossible, but it is still true. They did the same with the solar year. By their calculation, a year was 365.2450 days. Modern science sets the length of a year at 365.2425. And the Mayan astronomers did all of this without the help of telescopes, computers, or calculators. And if you think that's impressive, listen to this: They didn't just keep track of time for a few years, or even a few decades. They kept track of time for millennia."

"How many millennia?"

"Just twenty-six thousand years."

"Oh, is that all?"

"Here's the key: for the Mayans, time was holy. Time was reflected in events. To them, time formed history; not the other way around. We think of time as a string of hours or days. The Mayans saw it as part of a cosmic plan. A calendar was not something to jot down a business meeting on; it was the schematic of the past and the future. That's why they spent so much time and precision in making their calendars. The Mayan time codes are very elaborate and precise."

Garrett rose and paced the room for a few moments. "So where we see time as a series of events on a time line, they saw it as something bigger. Is that right?"

"Yes. They saw time, not as a line, but as series of repeating cycles. We measure the passing of days; they measured cycles."

"And they did this on one calendar?" He returned to his seat, his brow knitted in thought.

"No, newbie, the Mayans had more than one calendar. They had about twenty different calendars, but they relied upon three main time-tracking calendars. These three calendars are most relevant to the 2012 date. The solar calendar, known as the *Haab'* — sometimes called the 'Vague Year' — was based on the celestial cycle. It contains 365 days split into eighteen months of twenty days, each with a five-day period or 'month' left over. They considered that time as very unlucky."

Garrett asked, "Why a twenty-day month? That seems odd."

"To the Mayans, the number twenty was

sacred because humans have twenty digits."

"Oh. I guess that makes sense."

"They'll be happy that you approve." Lisa softened the words with a slight smile. "The second calendar is called the *Tzolk'in.*" She spelled it aloud. "It was a ceremonial and sacred calendar related to Venus. It contained 260 days known as the 'sacred cycle.' It's believed to be based on the nine-month period of human gestation. It was the oldest and most widely used calendar in Mesoamerica."

Lisa didn't wait for Garrett to comment. She plowed forward. "The third Mayan measure of time is known as the Long Count calendar. This is the biggie. It was used to document the ever-repeating age cycles of the world. They divided this calendar into five units that extended forward and backward from the mythical creation of the Mayans, which they believed was August 11, 3114 B.C. That day is represented on the Mayan Long Count calendar as 0.0.0.0.1 — Day One. The fifth cycle is supposed to end on December 21, 2012, or 13.0.0.0.0 — Day Last. The day after will be 0.0.0.0.1. It all starts over, but many believe that day will never come — at least not for humans. According to the Mayans, all five great cycles end in destruction. The year 2012 is the year the fifth great cycle is supposed to end."

"And that's where the end of the world comes in?" Garrett asked.

"That's it. I hope you don't have plans for that day."

"Funny. How did they come up with their dates? It can't be arbitrary."

"It wasn't arbitrary. The Long Count calendar is based on the procession of the equinox."

"That sounds scientific. I avoided science classes."

"I'm no scientist either," Lisa said, "so I have to break it down into simple terms. A processional cycle is the amount of time it takes for the earth to complete one full 'wobble.' You know the earth turns on its axis, but what some don't know is that as the earth rotates, it wobbles very slightly. If you imagine a pole extending through Earth's axis, then the end of pole would inscribe a small circle in the sky called the 'procession.' Earth wobbles one degree every seventy-two years. It takes about 25,800 years to make a full circle. This is very close to the Mayan grand cycle."

"So the 2012 date marks the end of the . . ."

"Fifth cycle. Five cycles of 5160 years.

And to make matters even more interesting, the end of the fifth cycle coincides with the great 'galactic alignment,' in which the sun and the earth align with the galactic equator that bisects the black hole at the center of the Milky Way — something that occurs once every twenty-six thousand years. Around December 21, 2012, the earth will make this alignment just as it finishes one complete wobble."

"And that's supposed to bring about the end of the world? A wobble?" Garrett frowned. "What's supposed to happen?"

Lisa shrugged. "Recorded history goes back only about six thousand years, so there are no records of what happened the last time the earth completed a wobble."

"And you believe this, um, stuff?"

"Did I say that, newbie? Since you've been assigned to me, you need this info. Since I have to work with someone, then I might as well work with someone who is up to speed."

"I'm always up to speed."

"Sure you are. Let's just test that, shall we? What is the significant fault in the wobble argument?"

"That it's untrue?"

"No sir, not even close. The fact that the earth wobbles and the length of time it takes

118

to do so are both scientifically established."

"Okay, I give up."

"It's arbitrary. True, the length of time to complete a wobble matches the Mayan long cycle, but that doesn't mean the two are related."

"So that could be a coincidence."

Lisa nodded. "Yes."

"Unless the Mayans knew things we don't." He sat back in his chair.

"Do you think they did?"

He shrugged. "What do I know? I'm just trying to drink all this in."

"Okay, drink this in: At the winter solstice for the Northern Hemisphere, the sun and the earth will line up with the galactic center of the Milky Way. We will cross the threshold of the Milky Way's equator in 2012. When that happens, we will begin a new 5125-year world age and also a new 26,000-year processional cycle." She tapped a few more keys. "Mayan cosmology predicts five cycles, each lasting 5125 years. According to the contemporary mythology, each previous cycle allegedly ended in destruction. Of course——"

"We have only six thousand years of history, so we don't know if that's true."

Lisa grinned. "You have been listening. The fifth cycle is set to end on December

119

21, 2012 — and not just the end of the one cycle but two. Two interlinked cycles of time: the 5125-year great world cycle ends, as does the greater 26,000-year processional cycle."

"A double whammy."

Lisa paused. "Um, sure, a double whammy. An alignment like this won't occur again for another 26,000 years. The big question is this: What does it mean?"

"If the Mayans were so advanced, then why didn't they just write all this down instead of leaving future generations to guess about their calendars?"

"They did have a highly developed writing system and kept detailed records of religious and historical events, but very little of it remains. Almost all of their writing is lost to history. Spanish conquistadors invaded Mesoamerica in the 1500s. Their — behavior — led to documents being lost or destroyed. Only three books and a fragment of a fourth remain. They are known as the Dresden, Madrid, Paris, and Grolier Codices. The best of these is the Dresden Codex. It's an eleventh-century mind picture book, seventy-four pages long, and was made of a material from fig tree bark. It is nearly twenty feet long, covered with paintings of the Mayan gods. The book was written in Mayan hieroglyphics. It provides invaluable information about Mayan culture. The book is shrouded in mystery."

"I like mystery."

"Then you'll like this. A common theory about the Dresden Codex is that it was taken from the Mayan temple and observatory at Chichen Itza by the Spanish conqueror Hernando Cortes and delivered to Emperor Charles V sometime around 1520. It's called the Dresden Codex — officially *Codex Dresdensis* — and it gets its name from the place where it resides today: the Royal Library in Dresden, Germany. The director of the Royal Library of Dresden purchased the codex in 1739 from a collection in Vienna and donated it to the library in 1744. How the codex made its way to Austria is anyone's guess. Most likely the King of Spain sent it there. At that time, he was also the king of Austria."

"So what is the book about? I'm assuming it's something more than a cookbook."

Lisa sighed and closed her eyes. She opened them again, choosing to ignore Garrett's flippant remark. "The Dresden Codex is an astronomy book. It contains numerous astronomical calculations and eclipse-prediction tables. It focuses specifically on Venus."

"Venus?"

"Venus represented their god of war, and they believed its cycles could be used to predict the outcome of war. Due to its predictive nature, some consult the codex to discover important clues about the end of the world and any relation it has to the 2012 end date.

"The last page of the codex shows a great flood. Some assume it predicts a worldwide flood, but that's far from certain."

"A flood like Noah's?"

"Perhaps. Others believe the Mayans taught the world will be destroyed by fire."

"Fire? Flood? Which is it?"

"I don't think it's any of those things. I just want you to see that there is a lot of disagreement among the doomsayers."

"Go back to the Milky Way thing again. Why is that so important to the Mayans?"

"They believed the center of the galaxy was the womb of the world — the place where stars are born. What's amazing is that modern science has discovered that there is a black hole at the center of the galaxy where all the stars in the Milky Way were born. An ancient Mayan symbol portrays the center of the Milky Way as a turning disc. It's eerily accurate. They came to these astronomical conclusions without the help of high-speed computers and complex software.

"On December 21, 2012, according to disaster theorists, the sun will eclipse the center of the galaxy, interrupting energy flow from the galactic center to our planet. Many think that will hasten the end of the world."

"And I just thought these guys built some interesting buildings and performed human sacrifices."

Lisa agreed. "I'm still stunned by their astronomical sophistication and their obsession with time. The buildings you admire were positioned to align with the heavens. That includes all major buildings and even their houses, which they carefully positioned so the corners of the structure aligned with cardinal compass directions. Windows were situated to allow the sun to shine on specific objects at certain times."

Lisa brought up a photo on her laptop. "Did you know the Mayan pyramids are older than those in Egypt?"

"No way."

"Yes way. To put it in historical perspective, the Mayans constructed the pyramid at Cuicuilco, Mexico, in 2750 B.C. That's about the same time as the building of Stonehenge in England. Egyptians erected the Great Pyramid about two hundred years later — in 2560 B.C. It's fascinating that all these mysterious stone structures came to be around the same time and in such diverse places."

"And all this has led to the doom boom." Garrett smiled.

"Doom boom?"

"Yeah. Movies, books, articles, conferences, everyone is talking about this. It seems like the world loves the idea of its own demise."

"Doom boom." Lisa chuckled. "I like that. You're right. People can't seem to get enough of this. I can understand why Christians look forward to the return of Christ. That makes sense. Who wouldn't want that to happen soon, but the end of life on the planet?"

"Maybe people are tired of life."

Lisa frowned. "I'm not. I've compiled the various end-of-the-world scenarios."

"I figured you had."

"You want to hear this, or do you want to take over the obit desk?"

"I'm all ears." Garrett folded his hands in front of him like a grade school student.

"Okay. While there are those who think December 21, 2012, will usher in rainbows and happiness, the majority of 2012ers see apocalypse."

"Like Earth has an expiration date."

"Exactly. Some think a huge cloud of electromagnetic particles will be released into space, taking out all our satellites. Whammo, end of communication. Others predict massive earthquakes and volcanic eruptions."

"Volcanoes like the one that just blew its top in Mexico."

"Yes, but bigger. Are you familiar with the Yellowstone caldera?"

"A little."

Lisa studied Garrett for a moment.

"Okay, I heard something about it but wasn't really listening."

"Beneath Yellowstone National Park is a volcanic caldera some think is nearing eruption. Many call it a supervolcano because of its potential to cause more damage than a regular volcano. I've read studies that say an eruption could be devastating and impact most of the United States. Scientists, however, have been monitoring things there for a long time. It's unlikely that it will blow any time soon."

"Didn't they say that about the Mexico volcano?"

"Yes, they did."

Garrett seemed pleased. "Well, there you go."

"No, there *you* go. I'm moving on. Others have predicted drastic weather changes that will leave much of the United States and Europe in a new Ice Age. Add to that tsunamis that destroy and contaminate food and water supplies — not to mention the devastation of harbors and ships. That would affect food imports and exports, especially in many foreign countries.

"Imagine the devastation should an earthquake destroy a nuclear plant," Lisa continued. "Can you fathom the consequences if solar activity takes down our power grid? Magnetic storms would make air travel impossible and hamper or destroy communications. Some areas might lose access to health services. Some predict the arrival of the new Dark Ages."

"But these are all ideas of crazy people — right?"

"Not all of it." Lisa stood and stretched her back. "Here are some sobering thoughts. The year 2012 will be a peak year for sun cycles. That means more solar flares. NASA predicts the most intense sunspot activity since 1958. They also predict that the planetary tidal force — that is, the impact of our planet on the sun — is also expected to peak in 2012."

She sat again and leaned back in the chair. "The National Academy of Sciences — NAS for short — issued a study about the possible impact of a solar storm."

"Do I want to know?"

"If you're going to be a reporter, then you must know. Facing the unpleasant is something every reporter does on a regular basis. If you want to avoid the ugly, then go start a blog."

"I can take it. Give it to me."

"The sun goes through an eleven-year cycle. Nothing new there, but it reaches its peak activity in 2012. The NAS created a worst-case scenario that goes like this: The active phase of the sun's cycle can emit powerful solar magnetic storms that are capable of frying electric transformers. Many experts are expecting a sunspot megacycle in 2012 that could produce a 'Katrina from outer space.' If a sun storm cooks the US electric grid and satellites, then the resulting devastation would be Katrina times ten. Everything from sewage systems to Wall Street banks would be affected, paralyzing the United States and other highly developed nations for months and maybe even years."

Lisa took a deep breath and let it out

slowly. Then she continued. "Experts say that such a solar storm could cause serious electrical damage. Power failure would be massive in the United States — let alone the world. Such a catastrophe would devastate our natural resources, seriously affecting worldwide communication, medical care, and transportation. The economy would suffer dramatically, and we would need a long time — maybe months — to recover."

"But how likely is that?"

"A colossal solar storm struck the United States in 1859 long before satellites and in-home electricity were developed. It shorted out telegraph wires in the United States and Europe."

"But 1859 was a long time ago."

"Not that it matters, but some storms have affected North America more recently. In 1989, the sun unleashed a tempest that knocked out power to all of Québec, Canada. A remarkable 2003 solar rampage, which included ten major solar flares over a two-week period, knocked out Earth-orbiting satellites and crippled an instrument aboard the Mars orbiter."

"It all seems a tad wacky to me." Garrett drummed his fingers on the table.

"Bored?" Lisa motioned to Garrett's restless fingers.

"Me?" He looked down. "No. Sorry. I do that when I think."

"Check this out: A man named Percival Lowell thought for a long time that a ninth planet beyond Neptune was part of our solar system — this was known as the Planet X hypothesis. But after discovering Pluto, astronomers soon discovered a *tenth* planet. There are those who say this is the planet Nibiru, spoken of by ancient Sumerian astronomers five thousand years ago. The official name of the planet is 2003 UB313 — you might have heard that it was recently called Eris."

"That's fascinating, but what does that have to do with 2012?"

"Here's where another 2012 doomsday theory comes in. In this scenario, the earth is on a collision course — or at least a near-collision course — with 2003 UB313. Technically, it should be called a dwarf planet even though it is larger than the dwarf planet Pluto. It has a long elliptical orbit, which doomsayers say will intersect with our inner solar system and create havoc on the earth as it sails by."

"You know, you sound like you believe this stuff." Garrett leaned back a few inches as if he expected Lisa to slap him.

"I don't believe in the 2012 prophecies. I don't believe that December of that year will be any worse than any month in any other year."

"So everyone is wrong?"

"Only those who think the Mayan calendar predicts all this."

Garrett drummed the tabletop again then caught himself. "Still, there's been the volcano in Mexico and the meteorite in Arizona."

Lisa rubbed her eyes. "First, the volcano in Mexico — it's a tragedy. Hundreds died, including some of the scientists studying the mountain, but eruptions are not as rare as most people think. From my research, I've learned that over a hundred and fifty volcanic eruptions occur in a decade. Italy's Stromboli volcano has been erupting for more than a thousand years."

"No."

"Yes. There are years with as many as sixty eruptions. Some we hear about; some we don't. Some are small; others are very large. And as far as meteorite strikes go, approximately forty thousand tons of material fall to Earth from space. Most of it is the size of a dust particle. Of course, there are some that are as large as a Volkswagen, but that's rare."

"So what now, boss?"

"I'm not your boss, Garrett. I'm just another reporter, albeit more experienced."

"Isn't *more experienced* an euphemism for —"

"Watch it." Lisa stood, closed her laptop, and lifted it from the table. "I'll forward the background research to you. Study it."

"What are you going to do?"

"I have to figure out a way to get Andrew Morgan to meet with me again."

CHAPTER 10

Andrew Morgan grunted. He grunted again, then again. Fire blazed in his arms and down his back, threatening to scorch him from the inside out.

The pain grew, expanding into the small of his back and around his ribs. Dots of perspiration spread to form rivulets of sweat coursing from his forehead and cheeks. He closed his eyes to block out the room and — it seemed to him — to keep his eyes from popping out of their sockets. His vision had turned blurry anyway.

He struggled to suck in a lungful of air. He needed oxygen, and he needed it badly.

"Easy, pal. You're gonna bust a gut."

Morgan ignored him and mustered enough strength to push against the bar, moving it inch by inch to the stops, exhaling noisily as he did.

"I'm serious, man. What are you trying to prove?"

Morgan wanted to do another rep to prove the man with him wrong. He could take it. No matter how much his muscle complained, he could do another set.

The muscles in his shoulders and arms quit. The chrome bar with knurled handles snapped back to its resting position.

Morgan rubbed his arms to prevent knots from forming in the muscles. Lactic acid burned the fibers of his triceps, biceps, and everything connected to them. Morgan leaned forward and groaned.

"Need a nurse. Maybe a pretty nurse."

"I'm fine, McNair. Stop fretting over me."

McNair Adams sat on the bench of the adjoining bench press machine, a towel dampened by his own sweat in his hand. Even while seated, he was tall. On his feet, he stood six-four and carried two hundred and forty-five pounds of muscle. His black skin glistened under the overhead lights of the Rockpoint Fitness Gym.

"You may be my boss, but you don't get to tell me who to be concerned about. I am a free moral agent."

Morgan sat up and smiled. "I've seen your paycheck. There's nothing free about you, and as far as being moral —"

"Hey — I'm a good boy, and you know it.

I'm also a pretty good chief financial officer."

"That's because everyone is afraid of you."

McNair chuckled. "As they should be. As they should be."

"Most high-level execs lead by example, not intimidation." Morgan buried his face in a white terry-cloth towel.

"Lesser men, my friend. Lesser men. Besides, you know that's not true. Most guys in our business lead whatever way we can."

"I know. I agree with you. Not because you're right, but because I'm afraid of you."

A laugh exploded from McNair. "I've known you since you were a teenager, Morgan. You're not afraid of anything."

Just the dark and loneliness. "It's all part of the act."

"So what's eating you?"

"Who says anything is eating me?"

McNair leaned forward. "Like I said, I've known you for a long time. We've been working out together for the last five years. Aside from your little foray into alcoholism, we've been coming here three times a week to keep old age at bay. I know your routine better than you do. You're overworking everything today. Why?"

"I was out of town for a few days and

wasn't able to work out. I need to work out the kinks."

"You're doing a lot more than working out kinks, pal. You're being self-destructive. What's got you going?"

"Nothing. I just need to expend some energy, that's all. Now leave it alone."

"Nope. You may be my boss, but you're also my friend."

Morgan tossed the towel aside. "And that gives you the right to poke your nose in my business?"

"As a matter of fact, it does."

"I can replace you, you know."

McNair shook his head. "I'm the best-looking chief financial officer in the business. The board loves me."

That made Morgan laugh. "We need to work on your self-esteem problem."

"Hey, truth is truth. Now spill the beans. Are the nightmares back?"

"No."

"When was the last time you had one?"

Morgan stood and stretched his back. The blazing pain had subsided, replaced with a growing stiffness. "I had one the other day."

"The other day?"

Morgan shrugged. "I may have had another one last night."

"*May have had?* You don't have the kind

of nightmares people forget about. Did you have one last night, or not?"

"Yeah." Morgan looked away. He always had nightmares. Talking about them didn't help. They came. They went. They left him gutted and curled up like a fetus on the sofa.

"You never went to the shrink like you said you would, did you."

"He can't help." Morgan picked up the towel.

McNair rose and wiped his face again. "First, he is a she; second, I'm sure she could help you."

"I'm not going to do it. I've got to learn to live with it. No psychiatrist is going to make it go away."

McNair put a hand on Morgan's shoulder. "Come on, chief, let's go to the bar, and I'll buy you a fruit smoothie. Something with bananas. You're going to need the potassium."

"You don't care about my potassium level, do you? You just want to poke around in my private life some more."

"Why, yes, I do. Thank you for the invitation."

"That wasn't . . . Oh, never mind."

The Rockpoint Fitness Gym refreshment bar was a health nut's dream. Patrons could order everything from oatmeal to whole-wheat bagel sandwiches. McNair ordered two large fruit smoothies and then moved to a small, metal table in the corner of the room. The table was next to a window overlooking the parking lot, one floor down.

"Something in New Mexico get your goat?"

Morgan gazed out the window. McNair was impossible to stonewall. "Not really. Sometimes things just pile up."

"Things?" the CFO asked. "Emotional things? After what you've been through, you've got every right to have some issues and nightmares."

"It's not that." Morgan looked at his friend and saw the concern on his face. Most people offered their regrets, looked sad, and then did their best to avoid the topic of his family's death. Not McNair. Of all the senior execs, McNair treated Morgan honestly, never shying away from the darkness Morgan sometimes brought to the office. "I've almost gotten used to the dreams. I imagine they'll be part of my life forever."

"Maybe."

A gym employee brought the smoothies to the table. Rockpoint catered to the wealthy and offered services not normal to lesser gyms.

"Anyway, I'm just off a little — that's all."

"You have no idea how much restraint I'm showing by resisting that setup line."

Morgan smiled. "I'm testing your mettle."

"I was born with lots of mettle." He paused. "If this is none of my business, just say so. Why did you go to New Mexico?"

"You mean, if I told you to butt out, you would?"

"Of course not. Now answer the question."

"First, is it you who's asking, or someone else?" Morgan kept his eyes on McNair as he took a sip of thick drink.

"I'm the one doing the asking, but I won't lie to you. A few members of the board have stopped by to ask me questions."

"About me?"

"Yep. There is growing doubt about your fitness to run the company."

"They know my family started the corporation."

McNair nodded. "Yes, they do, and you should know that when your father took it public, he surrendered certain rights to the board of directors."

Morgan did know that. The fact that he could be replaced was never far from his mind. The problem was, it didn't bother him.

"What did you tell them?"

"It wasn't an official inquiry, just a couple of the members asking casual questions."

Morgan clinched his jaw. "Doesn't sound casual."

"My bad. I should have said informal. That's a better word."

"Okay, what was your informal answer?"

The corners of McNair's mouth rose. "Let's just say they won't be asking me again. Know this, Andrew: I am now and always will be on your side."

"I know." Morgan directed his eyes out the window and watched a UPS driver pull packages from his large brown van. "If I told you why I was in New Mexico, you might change your mind."

"I doubt it. I like my mind. Why would I change it?"

"You know what I mean." Morgan inhaled deeply and turned his gaze back to McNair. "Do you know who Robert Quetzal is?"

"The 2012 nutcase? I've heard of him. Saw him on some interview show. Why? Oh, don't tell me . . ."

"Too late. Remember, you insisted."

"So . . . this Quartzman guy was there?" The CFO leaned over the table.

"Quetzal. Robert Quetzal. The name is linked to a Mayan god. It's probably an assumed name. Yes, he was there. He's the reason I went."

"You don't believe that manure he's slinging, do you?"

"I do."

McNair ran his hand over his face as if doing so would change what he heard. "How can you trust a man who uses a fictitious name? If he lies about his name, doesn't it follow that he might be lying about all this end-of-the-world garbage?"

"You're right. I should toss his ideas aside because he has a pseudonym. While I'm at it, I think I'll start a movement to have Mark Twain books banned from school libraries. After all, his real name was Samuel Clemens. We might as well pass a law preventing the showing of John Wayne movies. His real name was Marion Morrison —"

McNair raised a hand. "Okay, okay. No need to get worked up. I concede the point. Still . . ."

"Still what?"

"If I were you, I'd keep that to myself. You know the board. They're composed of facts-figures people: engineers and Harvard business MBA types. If they hear that you're . . . interested in this doom-and-gloom guy, then they'll have more reason to question your loyalty and business acumen."

"I didn't want to tell you, McNair. What makes you think I'd tell anyone else?"

"True. So what attracts you to this guy?"

"I'm not attracted to him. I'm concerned that he might be right."

McNair leaned back as if the statement pinned him to the chair's backrest. "Right? About the world ending next year?"

"About the Mayan prophecies; about the things we're seeing. Do you believe the world will go on forever? Don't all things come to an end sometime?"

"Sure they do, but no one can put a date on it. Not even this Quetzal guy."

"Are you sure?"

McNair frowned. "Yes, I'm sure. You are too smart for this, Andrew. Much too smart. When you walk into the room, the corporate IQ goes up twenty points. I'm . . . I'm stunned."

"Let me see if I have this right: You praise my intelligence as a way of saying I'm being stupid?"

"That's not what I'm saying — okay, it is what I said, but it isn't what I meant. Ever since that day —"

"My family's death. You can say it."

"Okay, ever since your family died in that

141

plane crash you've been . . . How do I put this?"

"Crazy as a loon?"

"You are many things, but crazy isn't one of them. You've been . . . without an anchor. You've been drifting like a boat looking for a harbor. You went through the deepest grief and turned to alcohol to get through it. You kicked the juice through hard work and medical help. Now look at you — still young, fit, and determined. Nonetheless, you're drifting from place to place."

"This isn't an infatuation with an idea. I've done my homework on the subject. I know as much as man can know about the topic."

"And you believe it?"

He nodded slowly. "Yes, I believe it."

"Well, this will teach me to poke my nose in where it doesn't belong."

Morgan rose and tried to force his anger back into its cage. "I'm going to take a shower."

Thirty minutes later, he had changed into a dark gray suit and retrieved his wallet and cell phone. He had missed a call. The caller ID read LISA CAMPBELL.

Morgan deleted the voicemail.

CHAPTER 11

Morgan's office was on the top floor of the twenty-six-story Morgan Natural Energy building in downtown Oklahoma City. The building reflected his father's love for the new and the old. Unlike the tall glass rectangles that loomed over many cities, the Morgan Natural Energy building sported smaller windows and an earth-toned facade. Under his father's leadership, the architect managed to create something that honored the past while embracing the modern. Shortly after construction ended, one architectural reviewer described it as a "building without identity, which neither detracts nor enhances the Oklahoma City skyline." To Morgan's surprise, his father had taken that as a compliment.

The limo driver pulled into the subterranean parking garage through an entrance reserved for upper-level execs. To outsiders, a limo, a private entrance, and private elevator might seem the affectation of the wealthy. At one time, that would have been true, but the twenty-first century had evolved into a dangerous place where executives like him could be kidnapped and held for ransom, or simply be killed by a zealot from any number of causes.

The driver, one of several used by the company, each trained in evasive driving and personal protection, opened Morgan's door and escorted Morgan to the basement's private elevator. Morgan ran a microchip cardkey through the slot of a security lock, placed his thumb on a black piece of glass, and waited until he saw the green indicator light flash and heard three soft beeps. The elevator was a "capture container." If someone tried to defeat the security system, the elevator would open, allowing entrance and then initiating a lockdown until the police arrived. Twice a year, the head of security held a meeting with all key personnel in order to remind them of procedures and the growing threat from foreign and homegrown terrorists. It still surprised Morgan how many people hated oil companies.

Once inside the lift, Morgan looked up and to the left. A small, dark glass plate filled the corner. Behind it was a security camera. There was also a microcamera hidden in the display that flashed floor numbers as the cab moved up and down the shaft.

"Alpha floor," Morgan said. The voice recognition software responded with the same words, and the elevator began to rise.

What a world we live in. Morgan hated living in a security cocoon. For a short time there was concern in the company that the plane crash that took his wife and son had been the result of foul play. Police, FAA, NTSB, and the company's private security investigators found nothing to prove the point. It was just an accident.

Just an accident. When the two people you love most die, it's not "just an accident."

Twenty-six floors later the elevator doors parted, and Morgan exited into a plush, contemporary chrome-and-glass lobby.

A receptionist desk sat empty fifteen feet away from the elevator. It was a throwback to the original design, a time when security was less demanding. Because no one came to this floor without an invitation, no receptionist was necessary.

Five offices and one massive conference room filled the floor space. Morgan's office was twice as large as the others, and the conference room was filled with high-tech toys.

Large double doors made from walnut stretched to the ceiling. There were no signs or plaques to identify this as the entrance to the CEO's office. Morgan twisted the polished brass doorknob and crossed the threshold into his cavernous office. No man needed an office this large. It was a showpiece for visiting foreign executives, major stockholders, and state and national politicians. Beyond that, Morgan often thought, it was wasted space.

As the door automatically closed behind him, Morgan crossed the room, treading on royal blue carpet. The room was decked out in warm wood tones of walnut with ebony trim. His desk, which had belonged to his father, was a gift from a grateful senator and large enough to sleep on. The kneehole could house a small family.

A trim woman in a close-fitting brown pantsuit stood behind his desk, silhouetted by the bright morning light pouring through floor-to-ceiling windows. She straightened as Morgan drew close. "You're here early."

"Working out seemed more like work today." He rounded the desk as she stepped away.

"Isn't that why they call it working out?"

Janie Horner stood tall and straight as if someone had surgically implanted a steel

146

rod in her back. She not only *stood* that way, but Morgan had seen her *sit* for hours without her shoulders ever touching the back of her chair. He guessed he wouldn't last ten minutes sitting like that, and he was as fit as a man could be.

"I suppose so." He plopped down in his brown-leather executive chair, also a hold-over from his father's day, and tapped a key on the computer keyboard set to one side of his desk. The thirty-inch monitor came to life, revealing several windows. His computer was networked with Janie's. A glance told him his calendar was still free, something he had requested Janie to arrange, but there were several phone messages.

Most of the messages looked routine, the kind of matters he dealt with daily, but there were several from Lisa Campbell.

Janie rested a hand on the desk. "Is there anything I can do for you this morning?"

"No. I'm going to spend some time planning and thinking."

"Shouldn't that be the other way around?" She smiled, flashing expensively maintained teeth. Morgan paid her more than most execs received in other firms. Janie was intelligent, intuitive, and knew as much about Morgan Natural Energy as Morgan did. He considered her indispensible.

"So that's what I've been doing wrong."
He paused and looked at the messages. "Let
me ask you something."

"Anything, boss."

"This Lisa Campbell." He pointed at the
displayed message. "She called me on my
cell phone this morning. Did you give her
my number?"

"Of course not. I never give out personal
information about you or anyone in the
firm. What did she want?"

"I missed the call and haven't called
back."

"So you don't know her? She's a stranger,
and she's calling you?"

"She's not really a stranger, Janie. I've met
her. In fact, I gave her a lift to San Antonio
from New Mexico."

"I don't understand. If you know her —"

"I told her where I work, and she knows
who I am, but I didn't give her a business
card and certainly didn't give her my cell
phone number."

"Who is she?"

Janie sounded defensive, jealous, and
protective. "A reporter. She's an all right
person, but . . ."

"But what?"

"She put me off. Came across a little too pushy."

Janie nodded. "Saying a reporter is pushy is just being redundant. You flew her from New Mexico to San Antonio?"

"It seemed like a good idea at the time. I was going to give her my card, but . . . it doesn't matter."

"Do you want me to call her and tell her you're unavailable?" Janie stiffened.

"No. You're my administrative assistant, not my protector."

"Okay, boss, but I'm here if you need me. I know how to handle the media. Is she from a big paper? Network?"

"No, she works for a small Christian outlet. I think they're only online."

She put a hand to her hip. "Really? A Christian newspaper?"

"They may call it a newspaper, but I don't think paper is involved anymore. A lot of dead-tree publications can be found only on the Net these days." He turned to the window, putting Janie at his back. "It's nothing to bother you with."

"You are certainly popular with the ladies."

He spun back around. "What?"

"Did you look at all your messages?"

Morgan scooted closer to the monitor and

149

saw the name "Candy Welch." He groaned, then hoped Janie hadn't heard. "That's tonight. I forgot all about it."

"She must be a special girl to be forgotten so easily."

"Come on, Janie. I've been out of town, and I have a few things on my mind."

Janie grinned. "Just not Candy Welch."

"Don't be cheeky, Janie."

"Was I being cheeky? I didn't mean to be."

"Now my sarcasm alarm is going off."

That made Janie grin. "Then my work here is done. Do you want me to make reservations? Are you picking her up?"

"No. I'll think of a place."

"You should take a gift. I'll pick something up at lunch."

"You're the best, Janie."

"Tell me something I don't know." Janie moved to the door that led to her private office. "You know where to find me."

"That I do."

Morgan turned his attention to the stock market and commodities and tried to focus. For some reason, Lisa Campbell kept coming to mind.

CHAPTER 12

"I have something for you."

Quetzal opened his eyes, raised his designer sunglasses, and squinted against the late afternoon light glinting off the expansive pool. "I was napping."

"I'm sorry to have to awaken you, your majesty, but while you've been baking yourself in the Atlanta sun, I've been working."

Quetzal raised the back of his lounge chair and took a long sip of iced tea. "Don't sound so put upon, Charles. You live in comfort and have more money than you can spend. Take a load off and enjoy a day. We're paying enough rent for this place."

"That's not why I do this. You know that."

"You're out to save the world. I get it. I'm doing my part. Just because I'm not a computer and science whiz like you doesn't mean I don't contribute. Now, did you bring me something important, or should I go back to napping?"

Quetzal saw Balfour roll his eyes but said nothing. The thin man moved to a lounge chair adjacent to Quetzal. He held a manila folder. "I found something — or, should I say, I found someone."

"You've been mining data again, haven't you?" Quetzal took the envelope and opened it, removing several sheets of paper and photographs. He went right to the pictures. "I don't recognize him. Should I?"

"His name is Andrew Morgan. He's the CEO of Morgan Natural Energy in Oklahoma City. As you know, we took photos of everyone who came to the Roswell presentation."

"Yes, I know that was going on. I believe it was my idea."

"If you say so, but it wasn't." Balfour shifted his weight. "Because tickets were purchased in advance, we have his name."

"Who's that with him?"

"A reporter. Her name is Lisa Campbell."

Quetzal grunted. "Pretty little thing. It's a shame she's a reporter."

"If it's all right with you, maybe we can return to Morgan. You might not recognize him, but I do. I did some cross-checking. He's one of our supporters. Not big-time, but he's poured a few thousand into our nonprofit."

"I like this guy already."

"I've done some research on him. He started contributing about six months ago. Sometime before that, his family was killed in a plane crash."

"Pity."

"Your grief moves me." Balfour, always too nervous to sit for long, rose and began to pace in front of Quetzal. "The guy is worth billions. And that's him personally. His company has huge resources."

"Do you think you can turn him?"

Balfour frowned. "Don't you mean, 'Can *we* turn him?' "

"Isn't that what I said?"

"No it isn't." He stopped pacing. "Look, the guy has money and he can use our help. Together we might make this work."

"So how do we make contact?" Quetzal lowered his sunglasses.

"I'm working on that."

Quetzal then lowered the back of the lounge chair to the horizontal position again. "Work harder."

"Parakeet die?"

"Huh?" Lisa looked up from her cell phone and into the pleasant eyes of her editor, Rodney Truffaut.

"Your parakeet. Did it die?" He pulled a worn, straight-leg chair next to her desk.

"I don't have a parakeet."

He nodded as if in solemn thought. "If you did, and if it died, I bet this is what you'd look like."

A moment later, Lisa got the implication. "I'm that transparent, am I?"

"You are to me. What's bugging you?" He leaned back and crossed his legs.

She turned in her seat. "I can't reach Andrew Morgan for an interview. If didn't know better, I'd say he's avoiding me."

"Sure you got the right number?"

She nodded. "I did a little investigating. The corporation number was easy. Getting his cell phone was tough."

"You got his cell phone number?" Truffaut laughed. "How'd you do that? Nothing illegal, I hope."

"You know me, I'm a stickler about staying on the right side of the law. It's a bad Christian witness for me to bend the rules to fit my purpose."

"No matter how tempting it is."

Lisa smiled. "It is tempting, I'll admit that. I tried the usual channels and then resorted to the direct approach. I called the hotels in Roswell, asked if Andrew Morgan stayed there. I told them we had met while in town, and I said I needed to get in touch with him. Believe it or not, the front desk had his cell number and gave it to me as if I were Morgan's mother."

"The clerk shouldn't have done that." Lisa saw the corners of his mouth dip.

"I'm a little conflicted about it myself, but it's not as if I'm stalking the guy. And he did give me a lift in his jet. I thought we hit it off. Besides, the interview could be good for him."

Truffaut cocked his head. "That a fact? How can an interview with a Christian publication be all that good for him? From what you told me, he's a touch prickly about Christianity."

"A touch? A cactus would avoid him. I came on a little strong. Maybe that's why he's avoiding me."

"Strong? You?"

"Sarcasm is beneath you, boss."

"Not at all. Sarcasm and I have been friends for years. So are you going to give up?"

"I don't give up. You know that. I'm hoping he's just busy. I'll find a way to make contact. Maybe a text message."

"That should do. He doesn't answer your calls, but he's bound to answer a text message."

She huffed. "There's that sarcasm again." Lisa paused. "You're right."

"Well, of course I am. That's why I get the big bucks." He stood. "Give him time. What's Garrett up to?"

"I went over my research with him. I have him reviewing it again and writing a quick five hundred words of background. I want to see his skill level."

"Good for you. Go easy on him at first. The kid has talent and more creativity than he knows what to do with, but he's raw. Mother him when you have to, but don't hesitate to apply your spectator pumps to his rear end if he gets mouthy or lazy."

"What do you know about spectator pumps?"

He grinned. "I've been married for over thirty years. My wife has more shoes than a Payless store."

"Yeah, but you love her anyway. Besides, how many tools do you have in that shop of yours?"

"I think I hear my phone ringing." He winked and walked away.

Lisa considered calling again. It was her nature. More than once someone had called her pushy and aggressive. She always denied it, saying she was "assertive, not aggressive." But she knew she could be annoying. Her father once said journalism was the only career that would pay her to be nosey.

She set the phone down and wondered what Andrew Morgan was up to.

Morgan's head hurt. Probably because his neck hurt. The ache in his back contributed to his general discomfort. McNair had been right — he was overdoing it at the gym. Still in his late thirties, Morgan was far from old, but there were days when he stayed up too late, got up too early, worked out too hard, and worried so much that he felt the AARP sneaking up on him.

He left the conference room proud of the new ideas his engineers had come up with for extracting shale oil. That was the part of the business he enjoyed most: creativity, engineering, and geology. Sitting behind a desk wearing a suit and tie sapped him of joy. He once threatened to do away with casual Friday and make the whole week casual dress. He never did. If he were the head of an Internet company or some Silicon Valley software company, then he could kick around in sandals, jeans, and T-shirts with witty sayings on them.

The oil business, however, was many decades older, and some traditions refused to die. His father always wore a suit, white shirt, and tie, so Morgan wore business attire. By ten in the morning, his feet longed for sneakers.

Outside his window wall, the sun was setting, something he normally welcomed, but not this afternoon. He had more work to do, although some wouldn't call an evening with a beautiful woman work.

He had spent the day reviewing reports from the CFO's office, reading a stack of papers written in the foreign language of lawyers about new testing standards, trying to analyze the fluctuating price of a barrel of local crude oil, and watching a CNN report on the Mexico eruption. He shook his head. The numbers of people dead, injured, and displaced grew by the hour. The video filled him with dread, concern, sorrow, and — he hated to admit this — pleasure. One more sign that the Mayans were right.

"Just the beginning." He spoke to his empty office. "One more proof."

"Did you say something?"

Morgan turned to see Janie enter the room. "Just thinking aloud."

Janie moved to his desk and set a stack of correspondence on it. They were smaller than letter-size and printed on heavier, ivory stock.

"Oh, man. Is it that time again?" He sank into his chair.

"Some people like sending birthday and anniversary wishes."

He grunted. "Yeah? Well, let them sign these things. Do we have to do this every week?"

"No, we could do it once a month, but the stack will be four times larger. Besides, this is an easy week. Just four senators, six congressmen, and one president."

"Our president or someone else's?"

"This week, it's ours. You know he opened up some offshore drilling again?"

Morgan pressed his lips. "Of course I know that, Janie. It's my job to know such things."

"Yes, sir. Of course, sir. Anything you say, sir."

Morgan did his best to look imposing, but it never worked with Janie. She was as funny as she was loyal. It was one of the reasons he hired her. He didn't want an administrative assistant who was afraid of his every move. He needed just what he got with Janie: professionalism, honesty, and a quirky attitude.

"Just leave them. I'll sign them before I leave."

"Blue."

"What?" He shifted the stack to the side.

"Wear your blue blazer. It shows off your eyes. No tie. Go with the gray slacks —"

"I'm fully capable of dressing myself for a date, Janie, but thanks for the coaching."

"But I haven't told you what color socks to wear."

Morgan rose. "And you're not going to."

She raised a hand. "Okay, okay, just trying to help my boss out. By the way, your girlfriend called again."

"This is my first date with the woman. It's a little premature to call her my girlfriend."

"Not her. Lisa Campbell. Are you going to call her back?"

"Why should I? I did the gentlemanly thing by helping her get home. That doesn't obligate me to long phone messages."

"You sure you don't want me to tell her to get lost? I'm good at that. It's part of my skill set."

Morgan had no doubt of that. "No, she'll stop soon enough."

"I doubt it. She doesn't seem the type." Janie raised an eyebrow. "If you know what I mean." She walked back to her office.

Morgan had no idea what she meant.

CHAPTER 13

Candy Welch was tall and curvaceous with raven hair and permanently puckered lips boasting a red lipstick the color of a stop sign. She slipped into the back of the limo like she had practiced it a hundred times. Perhaps she had.

Morgan smiled, complimented her on her little black dress, and held out his hand. She brushed it away, leaned close, and kissed him on the cheek. Fire rose in his face.

"Oh, look, I left a lip print on you. Let me get that." She removed a white, initialed hanky from the Gucci clutch she held, licked it, and began to rub his skin.

"No, please, let me. I can get it." He pulled away.

"I don't mind."

I do. He tried to pull away again. There was no stopping her. Morgan looked forward, through the opening in the glass divider that separated the front seat from the back. He saw Donny, his chauffeur and bodyguard, glancing in the rearview mirror. He raised an eyebrow and let slip a thin smile.

"Let's get going, Donny." He couldn't conceal his frustration, not that Candy noticed. He was sure Donny had.

The limo pulled away just as Candy finished scrubbing away the top layers of Morgan's cheek. "There, all better. Wow, this is a beautiful limo. How many do you have?"

"How many what do I have?"

"Limos, silly. Isn't that what we're talking about?"

"I don't own the limo — my company does."

Candy looked surprised. "Really? I would have thought you would have a fleet of limos."

Morgan blinked several times. "Why would I want several limos? I only need one."

"Oh, if I had your kind of money, I'd own several, all different colors. So where are we going?"

A dozen harsh comments buzzed in his mind, but he swatted them down. "Do you like Indian food?" Morgan asked.

"You mean like maize and stuff?"

A chuckle rolled back from the driver's seat. "How about a nice steak?" Morgan offered.

"I love steak." She leaned back and crossed her legs. Morgan guessed the shoes ran a couple hundred easy.

As the car pulled onto the freeway, Morgan wondered how long an evening could last. Albert Einstein once quipped that a minute spent sitting on a hot stove passed much slower than time spent with a pretty woman. Albert hadn't met this woman.

Benito's Italian Steakhouse was upscale, uptown, and a favorite haunt for people who didn't mind dropping at least a hundred dollars a plate. She asked for wine, and he ordered a San Pellegrino sparkling water.

"Don't you like wine?" She shifted in her seat, her eyes scanning the crowd as if looking for someone famous.

"Alcoholic."

"Excuse me?"

He had gained her attention. "I spent a short time living inside a bottle of booze."

"Really?" Her eyes widened.

"I mean that I was a drunk for a short time."

"Most men would never admit that, especially on the first date. I'm honored you

163

trust me so much." She reached across the table and patted his hand.

"It's not a matter of trust. I'm just honest about it. I spend a portion of each day reminding myself how far I slid."

"You know, it's genetic." She nodded as if she was revealing a hard-to-believe secret.

"I've heard that, but genetics had nothing to do with it."

"How do you know? Did a doctor tell you that? Because I wouldn't believe that unless a medical doctor told me."

"Yeah, I'm sure." He took a breath, afraid to speak the words. "So tell me about yourself."

Candy perked up. What followed was the longest monologue Morgan had heard. She was thirty-two, which she didn't mind mentioning like some women do; she was the only daughter of a man who owned several car dealerships but nearly went broke in the last recession and soon died after that; a hefty insurance payment kept her and her mother fed and clothed, but not at the level she'd like; fortunately people (which Morgan took to mean boyfriends) liked to give her gifts . . .

Morgan stopped listening. He wasn't ready to date. He told Aunt Ida that when she called. "You'll love this woman. She's pretty and witty and different from . . . you know."

"My wife?"

Aunt Ida, his mother's sister, had crossed the threshold of her seventieth birthday and had left all sense of decorum behind. "You need to get out, Andrew. You've had plenty of time to grieve. It's time to get your life back."

Morgan hadn't wanted to argue. Now he wished he had. He removed his smart phone to check the time and thought of the unanswered messages from Lisa Campbell.

The thought of her surprised him. He felt warm inside.

Lisa reclined on her bed, her stomach full of frozen lasagna, which she had heated in the microwave. She was tired. She was frustrated. She was angry with herself. And she couldn't stop thinking of Andrew Morgan. How could she reach him?

In the world of boxers, there are heavyweight champions and "the other guys." In the universe of actors, there are A-list names and "the supporting cast." In the world of private detectives, there is Jasper Kinkade and "the wannabes." That's how Jasper saw the world. Jasper Kinkade, Jaz to his friends,

165

Mr. Kinkade to everyone else, was the head of the largest private detective and security firm in the country. If those who calculated such things knew of his other less visible operations, they would have to find a new designation.

His clientele included the upper echelon of the Fortune 500. His fees would cripple smaller firms. Kinkade Investigations had offices in most major cities in the Western world. Over two decades of operation, he had built a stellar reputation for confidentiality, speed, and unquestionable results.

Looking under stones was his specialty. His team worked efficiently and honestly. If dishonesty was required, he did it himself.

At twenty-one, he joined the San Francisco Police Department. Ten years later, he wore a detective's badge. He hated the work. In traditional police work, it was the cops who wore handcuffs. Laws, regulations, and procedures left many crimes unsolved. He also hated the city. Too crowded. Too cramped. And just too weird for his liking.

He realized all this early in his cop career and started law school at night. It took him six years to finish the three-year degree, but he finished at the top of his class. Along the way, he lost his desire to be a legal eagle.

166

The thought of drawing up contracts, fine-tuning wills, or defending guilty people turned his stomach. Tort law was even less interesting. He couldn't imagine his face plastered on the back of a bus-stop bench advertising personal injury.

His goals were simple: freedom, a business that used his skills and training, and a way to make more money than he could count. A California private detective license later, Kinkade Investigations was born. He hired a PR firm and began making contacts. Five years later, he was on the speed dial of twenty city police departments and had worked as a consultant to Homeland Security. He had also earned his first million.

He could sit in a large office and direct his empire, but that held no interest to him. This was the twenty-first century. He could lead from anywhere in the world, including his car.

Jaz motored slowly along Burlington Drive in the Nichols Hills section of Oklahoma City. The houses were huge and set on acres of manicured land. Each property sported a security fence. No surprises there.

He kept the speed of the Acura Sedan slow, but not so slow to draw attention. He had selected the luxury car to blend in. Most rich people had fancy, classic, or bank-busting cars, but generally also had midrange luxury vehicles that provided comfort and gadgets that made them feel pampered but didn't scream "I'm loaded — carjack me." Nothing caught the eye like a silver Rolls-Royce or a red Lamborghini.

Jaz picked up his iPhone from the leather seat of his car and keyed it to life. The iPhone was off the shelf, but a few hacks later, it was a much-improved device. By entering a simple code, Jaz could erase all sensitive information it held. If he were stopped by the police, or if a TSA agent in an airport wanted to see what the phone held, he could turn it on, don an innocent expression, and hand it over, knowing that nothing but a handful of contacts and documents, all designed for this purpose, would be seen.

Yes, Jaz admitted, he was paranoid. To him, being paranoid was an essential attribute. Paranoid people were people with all the information.

The satellite photo on the phone showed the house he was looking for. He had the address, so locating the structure wasn't the issue. Seeing if anything had changed since the photo was taken was.

Andrew Morgan's estate was well-kept and large enough to house several families.

His intel told him the man lived alone. Jaz imagined the guy knocking around in the place all alone. If Jaz still had normal emotions, he would have felt sorry for the guy.

He slowed the car, raised his phone, and snapped several photos. He also took note of the small blue sign that read ALL ALERT SECURITY — Jaz recognized the company name. It was a decent firm with some of the better hardware in the business. Breaking in would be difficult for anyone, but Jaz had no intention of sneaking in.

He planned to walk up to the front door and ask for a few minutes.

And he would get it. Not tonight. Tomorrow would be soon enough. He still had a few more things to learn.

After dinner, Morgan had taken Candy to a nightclub that featured standup comics. Candy laughed a lot. She also laughed loudly. With every Appletini, she laughed louder; with every new comedian, she laughed longer. Three times she offered him a sip of her drink; three times he reminded her that he was an alcoholic. By midnight, he was seriously considering relapsing.

"I'm having the best time."

Morgan looked at her and conjured a smile. "I'm glad. Just let me know when you're ready to call it a night."

Her smile became lascivious. "You are a bad boy, aren't you? I can tell you have plans."

Morgan hoped the dark room masked the blush in his cheeks. "No, that's not what I meant."

"No need to lie to me. I'm a big girl. I understand such things. A man has needs. A woman has needs —"

"Please stop. I didn't mean that at all."

Her smile broadened. "Maybe I mean it."

A new comedian stepped to the microphone, interrupting the conversation. Morgan touched the phone in the pocket of his blazer and wished it would ring.

Two hours later, a weary Morgan walked Candy to the lobby door of her condo. She paused and moved her body close to his. He could smell the alcohol on her breath. Her speech was slightly slurred. She ran a finger around his ear and along his jawline.

"Sure you don't want to come up? I can make it worth your while."

Morgan shuddered. She was beautiful, sexy, shapely, and willing. For some reason, he found that repulsive.

He leaned forward. She closed her eyes, lifted her face, and puckered her lips. Morgan kissed her forehead. She pulled back.

Anger flashed in her eyes.

"Thank you for the evening." He had intended to call it a "lovely" evening.

She worked her lips, but nothing intelligent came out. That didn't surprise him.

He moved to the limo and crawled in the back. Donny, who would normally have been waiting with the door open, had stayed in the driver's seat, giving Morgan the privacy he needed.

The moment the door closed, Morgan felt the car pull from the curb. Two blocks later, Donny pulled to the side of the road.

"Is there a problem?" Morgan leaned close to the opening in the privacy divider.

Donny slumped sideways to the seat.

"Donny!"

The driver's body shook as he convulsed in laugher.

"Great. Just great." He tried to sound angry, but a moment later his own laughter filled the car.

Garrett Vickers knocked back another can of Red Bull and waited for the sugar and caffeine to do their work. It was three in the morning, his usual bedtime. Now that he had a job, he had committed himself to hitting the sack earlier, but that was before Lisa hooked him on 2012. He was a believer. Truth was, he believed in very little beyond his own doggedness and skill with a computer. What grabbed his attention was not a date, but a person: Robert Quetzal.

"How many of those are you going to drink?" Ned "Necco" Birdsong didn't look up from his laptop. His eyes were half-closed. Just two years ago, he could have done back-to-back all-nighters, but he wasn't that young anymore. He passed the quarter-century mark two months previous. Next to him rested three rolls of Necco candy wafers, which had given him his nickname. He popped a green wafer in his mouth. "That stuff will kill you."

"Really? Unlike candy?"

"These don't have a barrelful of caffeine. You know, that drink is banned in parts of Germany."

"Are we in Germany?"

"No."

"Then admit it, you want me to get you a can." Garrett rubbed his eyes.

"If you insist. It would be impolite of me to refuse."

"You have a girlfriend. Make her get it."

Necco pulled his eyes from the monitor and glanced at the thin woman with straight dark hair asleep on Garrett's sofa. He turned to Garrett. "Your jealousy is show-

172

ing. I can't help it if I'm irresistible to the fairer sex. Besides, how much are you paying me for these little trespasses?"

Garrett rose, went to the small kitchen in his economy apartment, and snatched another Red Bull. When he returned, he set it by the rolls of candy. "You used to do black-hat stuff for the thrill — for the challenge."

"I'm here, aren't I? What more do you want?"

"I want to crack the firewall of Quetzal's group."

"First things first, laddie."

"That's the worst Irish accent I've ever heard."

"Whatever. Okay, here's what we have so far: Quetzal has a nonprofit called Maya2012. It's chartered in Georgia with offices in Atlanta. He's got a valid 501(c)(3) —"

"Which means?"

"Nonprofit organizations are classified by the kind of work they do. Religious education groups get 501(c)(3)s."

"This guy has a church?"

Necco popped the Red Bull and took a long draw. "Nah. Not like we think of churches. He lists his work as religious education. Any religious group can do that,

173

and there are hundreds of thousands of them. It allows them to use volunteer labor and receive tax deductible contributions."

"Can you find out how much he's raking in?" Garrett moved behind Necco and stared at his computer screen.

"That's impossible. That information is held only in their corporation and the IRS. It's not like theirs is a public corporation that has to report its profits to stockholders."

"Impossible, eh? So how much did they rake in?"

Necco smiled. "I called in a few favors. I know a guy who knows a guy who has access to IRS passwords and codes."

"Really? Who is this guy?"

"Forget it. You work for the man now. A news organization at that."

"You don't trust me?" Garrett clutched at his chest.

"Of course I do, but I'm still not telling you."

Necco popped three sugary disks in his maw, and Garrett could hear them crunch and crack between his friend's teeth. He had never seen the man without at least one roll of the candy on him.

"Your confidence moves me. Just hit me with the numbers."

"Okay, the *Reader's Digest* version is this. Quetzal started the group five years ago. He pulled in half a million the first year; two million the second, and so on. Last year it was close to fifteen million."

"That's a lot."

"Not really. Some nonprofits bring in much more. Remember, this is IRS info."

"Meaning?"

"Meaning it's info provided by Quetzal to the IRS. Actually, it's probably a guy named Charles Balfour. He seems to be the guy running the organization. The best I can tell from online news reports, blogs, and journalistic search engines, Balfour is the man behind the curtain; Quetzal is the Wizard."

"You know how suspicious you sound?"

Necco smiled. "I spend my spare time breaking into computer systems of major corporations and military groups around the world. I'm afraid of people like me."

"You are a walking conspiracy theory."

"Thanks, Garrett. That's the nicest thing anyone has ever said to me."

Garrett sipped his energy drink. "So you think he's hiding funds?"

"Sure. Wouldn't you?"

"I refuse to answer that on the grounds that the answer may tend to incriminate me. How much do you think he's hiding?"

"It's hidden, man. How should I know? Based on his online itinerary, Quetzal is a world traveler. He's spoken in twenty-five cities over the last sixty days, and he'll be doing more than that as the big day arrives. He could have bank accounts all over the world, and some foreign banks know how to hide big deposits."

"Can you learn more?"

"Hey, this is me. I can always learn more, but it will take time."

"How much time?"

Necco shrugged. "With my busy schedule, it could take a little time."

Garrett knew when he was being worked. "Does she know about Tina?"

Necco snapped his head around to the woman on the sofa. She hadn't moved. Necco jerked his head back around. He spoke just above a whisper. "Hey, that ain't cool, man."

"Just asking a question. And as far as your schedule goes, you live with your mother, watch soap operas by day, and hack the Net by night."

"I'll make it a priority."

Garrett grinned. "You want another Red Bull?"

"I think I'm gonna need it."

176

CHAPTER 14

Robert Quetzal was more night owl than morning person. He preferred, whenever possible, to rise at the crack of noon. Today, however, noon would find him on the West Coast, or at least near the West Coast.

The Bombardier Challenger business jet banked sharply to the left, leveled, then banked to the right.

"Is the pilot lost?" Quetzal grumbled. The flight had been unusually bumpy, and he was having trouble keeping his breakfast down.

"I doubt it." Balfour kept *The New York Times* held up in front of him. On the flight from Atlanta, Quetzal had watched him devour *The Wall Street Journal,* the *Los Angeles Times,* and the electronic versions of several overseas newspapers. The man's brain was a sponge.

"Then what's with all the twisting and turning?"

"We're near Edwards Air Force Base. They do a lot of test flights. The place is the secondary landing site for the shuttle, although not many of those are flying anymore. Anyway, flights in this area are strictly controlled."

The aircraft banked again, and Quetzal could feel it shed airspeed. He hated that feeling. It was as though the craft had lost power. Instead of plummeting, the business jet began a slow descent.

A no-nonsense voice came over the intercom system. "Please prepare for landing."

Quetzal raised his seat back up and finished the coffee in his cup. He stowed the cup in a holder next to his seat, then gazed out the window. Below, brown ground dotted with Joshua trees, juniper plants, and scrub brush scrolled past. "We had to pick a place on the moon?"

"You know it's not the moon. We're over California's High Desert."

"Could it be any more desolate?"

"That's what makes it desirable."

The business jet set down on the rough runway of a private airport in the Mojave Desert. As it taxied to the tarmac and onto a large World War II-style half-pipe hangar, Quetzal scanned his surroundings through the window by his seat.

178

"It's a graveyard."

Balfour unfastened his lap belt and leaned to the side to look out Quetzal's window. "In some ways, I suppose it is."

"In what way isn't it?"

"We've been over this, Bob. This airport is known for many things, but for years it has been an aircraft storage facility. Commercial airline companies park aircraft too old to remain in their fleets here. Some are scraped, some are sold to movie producers for films, and others are renovated."

"It just seems that we would use a more sophisticated company to do this." He slipped his own seatbelt loose and leaned closer to the window. "You sure you didn't make a mistake?"

"How many mistakes have I made so far?" The words carried some heat.

"Ease up, Charles. I'm not calling your intelligence into question. It's just that I had a different image in mind for such important work."

"Between us, Bob, I'm the bigger believer. I chose this place and created the company to keep things under wraps. There are more contemporary-looking places, but they are far more crowded. More people means more eyes and ears."

"Wait. You created the company?"

179

The aircraft slowed, and Balfour stood. "I thought it best. I hired top project managers, engineers, and craftsmen. Each has signed a NDO, and I've done complete background checks."

"Did they gripe about the nondisclosure agreement?"

"I'm paying them close to double to leave their firms for a short-term project. There were no complaints."

The aircraft stopped with a small lurch. Quetzal stood, retrieved his suit coat, and slipped it on. Balfour straightened his collar.

"Time to get your act on, Bob."

"I'm always on, friend. Always."

"I know, but let me do the talking. We should be out of here in less than an hour."

"Okay, time for you to impress me."

Balfour's cell phone chimed. "Yes? When? For how long?" There was a long pause. "Tell me you can trace it."

Quetzal cocked his head to the side. "What's wrong?"

Balfour held up a finger while he listened. He spoke to the caller. "You're certain the trace is good?" A moment later, "Okay, someone will call you soon. He won't identify himself, but he will say 'Eleven.' Tell him what you told me." He switched off the phone.

"Trouble?"

Balfour nodded. "Someone has been looking for information about you."

"Not unusual. I am a public figure."

Balfour bit his lower lip. "I don't care if people Google your name or search online news sources, but when they break into our servers, it becomes another matter entirely."

"They did what? How could anyone do that? You said it was impossible."

"I know what I said. I believed the system could not be breached. I was *told* it was impossible."

The sound of the pilot opening the cabin cockpit door then opening the air-stairs of the cabin rolled back to Balfour and Quetzal. Balfour lowered his voice. "Whoever it was has some pretty serious skills."

"You sound like you admire him?"

"Or her. Hackers come in both genders. And it's not admiration, really. I just appreciate intelligence."

"But what he did was illegal."

Balfour raised his gaze. "You didn't just say that."

Quetzal felt his face warm. "You know what I mean."

"Look, hackers have breached military sites, NASA, the CIA, credit card compa-

181

nies, and the FBI. It's not easy, and it usually doesn't last long, but it happens."

"Do we know who did it?"

"It's been traced through a score of false locations, but our people are the best. Half of them used to be hackers. They got a valid trace. It's being taken care of."

"How?"

"It's being taken care of."

"What does 'eleven' have to do with it?"

"It's a simple code."

"Eleven?"

"Total the individual digits of 12-21-2012. Nothing sophisticated. Just a way for my man to identify himself without using his name."

"You should have been a spy."

"Who says I wasn't?" Balfour turned and started for the passenger door, punching numbers into his cell phone as he did.

Jaz hung up and pocketed his phone. That matter would have to be dealt with later. He needed to focus on what would happen in the next few minutes. He pulled the rental car into the guest parking area of the Morgan Natural Energy building and exited. He walked leisurely to a uniformed security guard behind a wide curving desk.

"How ya doing?" Jaz leaned over the

counter. Beneath the counter, he saw the glow of security monitors. He recognized the system. It was one of the best closed-circuit systems and had redundant over-the-air transmission capabilities in case of power outages or some wise-guy thief who thought he could defeat the system by cutting cables. Television and movies, Jaz long believed, made criminals all the more stupid.

"Can I help you, sir?" The guard was tall with a thick neck and a thicker accent. Jaz guessed he had been a terror on the junior college football field but lacked the talent to go pro.

"My name is Mark Davidson." Jaz removed a gold-plated business card case. "I'm with Jacob Davidson Security. It's my father's firm."

The guard raised an eyebrow.

Jaz chuckled. "We handle overseas executive — not building — security."

The man seemed to relax. "How can I help you?"

"I have an appointment with Mr. Andrew Morgan. He's expecting me."

"I'll have to call."

"I would hope so." Jaz took the edge off the comment with a grin. "I would be disappointed if you didn't. You know, one security guy to another."

The guard picked up his phone and punched in a number on the keypad. A moment later, he hung up. He raised a handheld radio to his mouth, his eyes fixed on Jaz. Beneath his coat, Jaz's muscles tensed. "Rick, I need you at the front desk." He set the phone down.

A thirtysomething man with a build that reminded Jaz of a two-by-four rounded the corner. "What's up?"

"I have to escort Mr. Davidson to The Top."

The Top. Jaz assumed it was the pet name for the CEO's floor.

"Sure. Don't take too long, I go on break in fifteen."

"You won't miss your break, Rick." The guard turned to Jaz. "Please follow me."

"A private escort. I wouldn't have expected less. You guys seem to have it going on."

"We take our work seriously."

Jaz looked at the man's metal name tag pinned over his left breast pocket: Clower. "I can see that, Mr. Clower."

Clower removed a smart card and swiped it through a reader mounted to the elevator's front wall. A man and woman tried to slip through the doors, but Clower held up a ham-sized hand. "Sorry folks. You'll have to take the next one." The two looked put out but said nothing.

The doors closed, and the elevator began to rise. Judging by the buttons on the control panel, the elevator went to every floor, but a card key was necessary to access the top three.

A short time later, the cab doors parted, and Clower motioned for Jaz to exit first. Smart man. Should something go wrong, being behind a man was a tactical advantage.

Jaz exited into a large but empty lobby. To the right was a pair of large wooden doors. A man in a black suit stood in front of the doors. His shoulders were as wide as a 1950s Buick.

"Donny, this is Mr. Davidson. He has an appointment with Mr. Morgan."

"I'll take it from here." The man identified as Donny stepped forward and held out his hand but didn't move his eyes from Jaz's. Jaz took it, and gave it a firm handshake. Donny's hand felt as if it were made of iron, and Jaz knew the man was sizing him up too.

As soon as the elevator door closed, Jaz smiled. "I hope I haven't kept Mr. Morgan waiting."

"Your call got his attention. Do you mind telling me what this is about?"

"As a matter of fact, I do."

Donny raised his chin. "I can send you back down the elevator, you know."

"What I know — Donny — is this. I have an appointment with Mr. Morgan. He told me so himself. If he has changed his mind, I wouldn't be standing on this floor. So now that you've done your best to let me know how intimidating you can be — and because our conversation is being relayed to Mr. Morgan over the pinhole camera just above the door — perhaps we can dispense with the posturing and stop wasting an important executive's time."

One of the massive office doors opened, and a shapely woman with intelligent eyes crossed the threshold. "Mr. Davidson, I'm Janie Horner, Mr. Morgan's personal assistant."

Jaz gave a small nod. "A pleasure to meet you, Ms. Horner." He saw a twinkle in her eyes. Something he saw in the eyes of most women he met.

"Mr. Morgan is eager to meet you."

Donny didn't move. Jaz stepped around him and approached the woman. He didn't have to turn to know Donny was close behind.

186

The office was massive and beautifully appointed, but it failed to impress Jaz. He had been in palaces. It took more than an overpaid interior decorator with an unlimited budget to make an impression.

A tall, trim, solid-looking man stood behind a wide desk and in front of an antique desk chair. He wore an expensive suit but looked uncomfortable in it. The suit hung as an expertly tailored suit should, but it couldn't hide a well-developed body. Jaz had done his homework and knew Morgan was an exercise fanatic. That made him strong, but it didn't make him tough.

"Mr. Morgan." Jaz moved to the front of the desk. Moving to the side would be considered a hostile motion by any bodyguard worth his salt. He held out his hand. "Thank you for seeing me on short notice."

"When a man tells me Robert Quetzal has a special message for me, well, it grabs my interest."

"What I said was the truth. At least that part was."

Morgan's eyes narrowed, Donny clenched a fist, and the woman looked puzzled.

"Maybe you should explain yourself," Morgan said.

"May I sit?" Jaz motioned to one of the guest chairs in front of the desk.

Morgan nodded.

"What I have to say, Mr. Morgan, is private."

"I trust these people. Ms. Horner is my confidential assistant."

"I imagine they are very trustworthy, sir, but this conversation can only take place in private. Mr. Quetzal made that very clear to me."

Morgan sat. "Let me see if I have this right. You come to my office on short notice and then tell me who I can have present?"

"Mr. Morgan. These are sensitive times, and, as you know, events are already in place that make the future doubtful."

"Oh, come on —"

Morgan cut Donny off with a hand.

Jaz continued. "Mr. Quetzal is doing a great deal to help people, but he must also be selective to whom he shares his plans. I have not been cleared to share this with anyone other than you. At least here. I have several other people of distinction to visit before my time in your state is done."

"What did you mean about being partly truthful?" Donny had moved two feet closer.

"Sometimes my work requires the withholding of information, or — like a good magician — the misdirection of attention. I'm a bit of a liar."

"So you're not who you say you are," Morgan said.

"No more than Donny here is just a chauffeur."

"We did an investigation on you and Davidson Security." Donny clenched the other fist.

"I'm sure you did. I wanted you to do so. But I assure you, all the information you have is wrong."

"Maybe you should leave." Morgan rose.

"Please Mr. Morgan, you are in no danger from me. I carry no weapons, but you know that. You have a metal detector in the door-frame of the elevator. At least on this floor. Please sit down, sir. All I ask is a ten-minute private conversation with you. If you want to tell your friend everything later, well, that's up to you. I can't prevent it, nor would I try. Still, I'm obliged to follow my client's orders. I'm sure you understand."

"What did you lie about?" Morgan took his seat again.

"My name is Jasper Kinkade. I'm the owner of Kinkade Investigations. Davidson Security is a dummy corporation. I have a dozen or so of those to help keep my enemies at bay."

"You have enemies?" Morgan leaned back and seemed to relax a little.

189

"Don't you?"

"Not really."

Jaz sighed. "I tell you what . . ." He reached into his pocket and retrieved his phone. Before he could activate it, Donny was at his side. Jaz ignored him and looked at Janie. "Do you have a secure e-mail address I could use?"

She looked at Morgan, who nodded. "Yes," and she recited it.

"I assume that it goes to an independent sever. If not, it should." He waited for a second. "Hey, Skip. Do me a favor, and e-mail the Morgan/Morgan Natural Energy file to this address." He repeated what Horner gave him, then signed off, returning the phone to his pocket. "In a few moments, you will receive a large file. It contains everything I've learned about you and your company, as well as your operations. You will find a document in there of great interest. It will change your mind about whether you have enemies or not."

Morgan looked at Horner, who disappeared though a side door.

"Please, Mr. Morgan. A private moment."

Morgan looked to Donny. "It's okay."

Donny's face reddened. "I'll be just on the other side of the door." He traced Horner's steps.

Jaz leaned forward. "Do the security monitors have audio?"

"No. I don't like people listening to my conversations."

"Good for you."

"I also don't like being worked, Mr. Davidson — Mr. Kinkade. So maybe you should get right to the point."

CHAPTER 15

"Okay, we have the room to ourselves, and I've given you my word that no one is listening — that is, if my word is good enough for you." Something about the man across the desk made Morgan uneasy. Morgan had always leaned to the suspicious side anyway, but the cryptic message about Robert Quetzal and his visitor's free admission that he had lied about a few things gave Morgan a reason to be suspicious.

"Of course, your word is good enough for me, Mr. Morgan. I have not been sent here to give you grief, but I have been directed to limit my contact to just the essential people. In this case: you."

"So you win people's confidence by lying to them?"

The man smiled. "The only people I've lied to today are your security people. I have been straightforward and honest with you about everything else."

"And that will continue?"

"Yes. We are, after all, on the same side."

"Are we?" Morgan watched Jaz's eyes, attempting to detect any indication the man was lying again.

"We are. Let's get down to cases, shall we, Mr. Morgan?"

Morgan answered with a sharp nod.

"I told you on the phone that Robert Quetzal sent me. I am here to make an offer, one you are certain to appreciate."

"We'll see."

"First, let me level the playing field. You have been following Mr. Quetzal's work for some time. You have visited his oganization's website many times, both from your office here and from your home."

"And how do you know that?"

"Any time you go online, you leave a traceable trail. It's not unusual or even that complicated. All visits to the website are recorded."

"That sounds a little like Big Brother."

Jaz shook his head. "Not at all. It's true for all websites. Call the people that manage the websites for your corporation. They'll tell you the same thing. In fact, if they're any good, they will find the number of times I check out your sites."

"Okay, so you know I've visited Quetzal's

193

site. So what? That's what it's there for, right?"

"Absolutely, Mr. Morgan, but there's more. We also know you were at his presentation in Roswell."

"I want to know how . . . The tickets I purchased."

"Yes. You gave your name and address. In your case, you gave a PO box within your firm. Your name, the business address, and the video of the audience we took helped us nail down the fact that it was you, the CEO of Morgan Natural Energy, sitting in one of our seats."

"You videotape the audience?"

Jaz raised a hand. "Don't read too much into that. It's used to judge the effectiveness of Quetzal's methods so he can improve his delivery and content, but occasionally we can use it to identify the special people."

"Special people? What makes me so special? Wait, let me guess: my money."

"That's a big part of it."

"Well, at least you're keeping your promise to be honest."

Jaz shifted back in his chair and crossed his legs, as if he were sitting with a friend talking sports. "Don't read into that. There are many nonprofits that will do almost anything to get into the pockets of their supporters. The fact that you are rich isn't why I've been sent here."

"The offer."

"Yes, Mr. Morgan. You have shown a keen interest in the truth being told by Quetzal and the Mayan 2012 organization. We think you're a believer. Are you a believer, Mr. Morgan?"

"In what?"

The smile on Jaz's face melted. "Mr. Morgan. I'm a busy man, and I have several more people like you to visit. If you're not going to take this seriously, then I'll just tell Quetzal that you are nothing more than a curious seeker and to give your spot to someone more — committed."

"Are you asking if I believe the world is going to come to an end in 2012?"

"That's exactly what I'm asking."

"I'm undecided."

Jaz looked sad. He stood. "I'm sorry to have wasted your time. Have a good day." He started for the door and then stopped. "Do I need an escort to leave?"

"No."

With a nod, Jaz started for the door. Morgan waited until the man's hand touched the doorknob before calling him back.

"Mr. Morgan, we're talking about the end of the world. I'm a betting man, and I'd lay my mortgage on the table that you have been researching this for a long time. Am I right?"

"You are."

Jaz returned to his seat. "Let's cut through the nonsense, shall we?"

"That's an odd tone coming from a man trying to recruit me."

"I'm not attempting to recruit you. I'm trying to save your life."

Lisa had been nervous about this request all morning. She had come into the office early to begin the research needed to write the article on the wealthy and influential 2012 believers, but she was hitting a dead end. The only real contact she could come up with was Andrew Morgan, and he wasn't returning her calls.

The phone on her desk buzzed. She answered, listened, hung up, and made her way to the boss's office. She knocked on the door then stepped in.

Rodney Truffaut sat behind a desk that had seen many years of use. He loved to tell all new employees how he had bought the desk from the *Chicago Tribune,* where he first worked. The desk had belonged to a famous reporter Lisa had never heard of. At least the man was famous in Truffaut's mind.

"No luck with Andrew Morgan?" Truffaut put his feet on the desk as Lisa sat in a worn chair next to the worn desk. She had to move the chair to see around the editor's feet.

"I've tried calling, texting, leaving messages, and even badgering their public relations office. I'm starting to think he might not want to talk to me."

"Ya think? What did you do to get his knickers in a twist?"

"Knickers? Really? No one uses that phrase anymore."

"I think it's a keeper. Now answer the question."

Lisa sighed and slumped back in the seat. "I poked my nose in where it didn't belong. But isn't that what a good reporter is supposed to do?"

"Were you gathering info for a story?" He raised a bushy eyebrow.

She pursed her lips. "Not really. Sometimes I can't tell the difference."

Truffaut nodded slowly.

"What? You're just going to sit there and agree with me?"

"Truth is truth." He followed the words with a broad smile. "Since you asked for this little meeting, I assume you have an idea percolating in that devious mind of yours."

"I do. I want to fly to Oklahoma City to see if he can turn me down in person."

"I don't think he'd have a problem doing that."

Lisa straightened. "I think he'll see me."

"You'd better explain that to me." Truffaut retrieved a pencil from his desktop, held it near the pointed end, and tapped the eraser against his leg, something he did when he was warming to an idea. Lisa had his attention.

"Look, we met in Roswell and sat next to each other for Quetzal's presentation. I got the sense then that he was a gentleman. You know, a man who grew up in a home that emphasized Southern civility. When he saw me in the airport, he was polite enough to make conversation, and then when he learned I was stranded, he offered to fly me to San Antonio, even though it was out of his way and would cost his company money."

"If I follow your logic, you think he's too much of a gentleman to ignore you if you're standing at his door."

"Yes."

"You know how big a stretch that is?"

198

Lisa cut her eyes away. "Yes, but I think it's a possibility we should pursue. Besides, he's my only lead at the moment. I'm stuck trying to find wealthy people who have signed on with Quetzal. It's not the kinda thing people announce with banners and PR releases."

"Okay."

"If I can interview him, it might open doors to . . . what did you say?"

"I said, 'Okay.' We don't have much of a travel budget, not like the big news outlets, but I think I can scrape together enough for a flight to Oklahoma City. Coach, of course."

"You know what I heard the other day? People choose their airline based on who abuses them the least. Not who provides the best service, but who is the least bad of the worst."

"Coach. Take it or leave it."

Lisa smiled. "I'll take it."

"Good. Now tell me how Garrett is doing."

Lisa hesitated.

"What? Don't tell me he's already made a mess of things. This is just his second day."

"No, it's not that. It's . . . he hasn't shown today."

Truffaut jerked his feet from the desk and

sat up straight. "Did he call? Why isn't he here?"

"I don't know, and no, he didn't call."

"Did you call him?"

"No, sir. I don't have his number." Lisa tried not to wither under her boss's stare. "Besides, it's not my place."

"Did you say something to offend him?"

Anger rose in Lisa. "Oh, come on. I'm not that bad."

Truffaut raised a hand. "No, of course not. I'm sorry. I'm just a little miffed. I apologize."

"Apology accepted, and if it's all right with you, I'm going to leave before your head explodes."

"That might be a good idea."

"How do I know this isn't some joke or scam?" Morgan was doing his best to appear detached, but what he had just heard was too much to swallow.

Jaz looked serious, as if offended by the question. "I deal with doubt like this all the time. I don't blame you. It is too much to believe, but I'm asking that you open your mind to the possibility. The offer is for you and one other person. We're talking about a horrible end becoming a new beginning."

"But you can't guarantee success."

"Nothing in this life comes with a guarantee, Mr. Morgan. You of all people should know that."

Me of all people. Does he mean my family? "What is this going to cost me?"

"A lot, Mr. Morgan. What Quetzal is doing is extremely expensive, and time is short. To be ready by mid-December is going to take round-the-clock work. It's close to impossible, but still possible."

"How long do I have to decide?"

"The end of the day. Once you agree, Charles Balfour or Quetzal himself will contact you. You were at the Roswell presentation, so you know who Mr. Balfour is."

"The end of the day! That isn't much time."

"Mr. Morgan, let me be blunt. As of this morning, there are 3565 people who want your spot and can pay for it. You won't be the first to say no. You won't be the last."

"Who else signed up? I know many of the movers and shakers in the business world."

Jaz looked disappointed. "I can't tell you that. We won't tell anyone about you, and we won't tell you about them. At least not for now. Things will change as we get closer to Threshold."

"Threshold?"

"December 21, 2012. Join us, Mr. Morgan. Be one of the few still alive on December 22."

CHAPTER 16

Charles Balfour's chest swelled with pride, and he did his best to hide it. By plan, Quetzal was the center of attention, not him. That didn't matter. His was and would be for some time a secret pride. He stood at the front of the refitted 747's passenger cabin. Everything he could see looked new, and the sixty-year-old bald, beer-bellied engineer standing next to him was explaining what else was new. The man, like engineers everywhere, wore a white shirt with a pocket filled with pens, pencils, and, to Balfour's utter surprise, a small slide rule. The engineer, Ron Presnell, explained that the rule had belonged to his grandfather and had been passed down to him. "It's a great conversation starter."

"As you can see in this prototype, the interior has been gutted and replaced with seats in a first-class style. That lowers the aircraft's passenger capacity but allows us to carry more fuel, just in case we need to stay airborne longer than expected."

"Seems wise," Quetzal said. "Of course, that also means —"

"What else?" Balfour interjected quickly before Quetzal could say something stupid like, "— fewer paying customers."

"Well, we've updated the galley and food storage, so no one is going to go hungry while airborne. The forward heads as well as those aft have been enlarged for greater comfort. The aisles are wider so people can move around to stretch their legs. All the seats recline like those on overseas business class flights."

"Very good, very good." Quetzal seemed genuinely impressed.

Presnell seemed to stand a few inches taller. "Thank you. We've also made structural improvements. We've been very selective in the planes we've chosen. It's one thing to replace fatigued metal skin, but it's an entirely different thing to rebuild a wing. Did you know the wings of commercial aircraft are the most intricate things on the plane?"

"I didn't know that," Quetzal said. "We are blessed to have someone so knowledgeable." Presnell grew another inch. "We can't be too careful."

Now that's the Quetzal I know and love. Balfour kept his smile to himself.

"I agree. I've set up a triple-check system in which foremen inspect the work of craftsman and technicians, and two engineers check them."

"How does that impact the production schedule?" Balfour touched one of the purple-fabric seats. Each headrest bore the logo of a phoenix, the mythical bird that rose from its own ashes and the universal symbol of new beginnings.

"It slowed us at first, but we have it down pat now. Since the work is largely repetitious, we have been able to speed up production. Every worker has become practiced in his or her personal activity. We gain time with each refitted aircraft. For the most part."

"For the most part?"

"Big birds like these are very complicated machines and each presents its own challenge. Some engines require more work than others; some hydraulic systems need to be replaced while others just need maintenance and new fluids. Every beast is different."

"Avionics?"

"We've updated crucial electronics and hardened the indispensables against electromagnetic bursts. If the sun shoots an EMB our way when we're aloft, the avionics will be unaffected."

"Now the big question." Balfour waited until Presnell had made eye contact. "Are you on schedule?"

The man didn't hesitate. "No."

"No?" Balfour clinched his jaw. "How far behind are you?"

"I didn't say we were behind." Presnell's smile revealed a smoker's teeth. "We're a week ahead. You'll have your planes, and if I have anything to say about it — and I do — you will have them early, fully tested and ready to fly."

"You don't know how good that is to hear." Balfour set a hand on the engineer's shoulder.

"I'm highly motivated, Mr. Balfour. The money is good; the challenge is noble; and my family and I have seats on one of these babies." He paused. "We do have seats, right?"

"Absolutely, Ron. Absolutely. We couldn't do this without you. We will not leave you and yours behind. Just remember, we can't take everyone, so keep that to yourself."

"My lips are sealed."

Balfour followed Quetzal into the Bombardier. Before one of the cockpit crew closed the door and entered the flight deck, Quetzal quickly found his seat, pulled a glass tumbler and a small bottle of Chivas Regal from a side compartment, and poured two fingers' worth. "You want a hit?"

Balfour grimaced. "You know I don't drink."

Quetzal raised the glass to his lips and sipped the golden fluid. "That makes me suspicious of you. I don't trust men who don't drink."

"Yet here we are, linked at the hip."

Quetzal chuckled and raised his glass. "To destruction and fear."

"I hope you'll put that away before takeoff. I'd hate to see that glass flying around the cabin."

"If this is flying around the cabin, then we have bigger problems. Not to worry. I'll put it back where it belongs. I have time for one drink."

Balfour studied his partner. The problem with him was that one drink led to several others.

The cell phone in Balfour's pocket sounded. He retrieved it and pressed it to his ear. He listened for a moment, then said, "Details." He listened carefully. "Thank you, I'll be in touch." He returned the phone to his pocket.

"Problem?" Quetzal swallowed the last of the Scotch.

"Nope. Good news, really."

"Judging by the cheesy grin plastered to your face, it must be fabulous news."

"It is. A killer asteroid is headed for Earth. It could impact our planet in December of next year. Now that's worth smiling about."

"You are one sick puppy. You know that, don't you? You're the only guy who could be happy about that kind of news."

"Why not? It proves the Mayans were right. It also proves I'm right — again."

Dr. Michael Alexander hung up the phone, looked at the office door he had closed a few moments before, and gazed through the door's window. No one was watching him, but that gave him no relief.

He moved his gaze to the customized BlackBerry he held. Charles Balfour had given him the phone and told him to use it if he learned anything interesting. Although he hadn't said so, Dr. Alexander assumed it was encrypted. He hoped so. He might be the director of the European Space Agency's Near Earth Orbit Laboratory, but he wasn't free to discuss his discoveries without permission of his superiors. He had been faithful to keep secrets, but three million euros had a way of dissolving an underpaid scientist's commitment. Besides, all he did was make a phone call.

He swiveled his chair so he could face the large computer monitor on a side desk and reviewed the frightening discovery again.

Finding objects in near-Earth orbit — NEOs — was not unusual. There were nearly two million objects near the earth. Most were small, and the majority would never come near the planet. Still, some did come uncomfortably close as they sailed through space at high rates of speed. Small objects — ten meters across or so — came within a quarter million miles of Earth on a weekly basis. Larger objects were another matter.

One such object, an asteroid called 2010 GA6, passed within the moon's orbit in April of 2010. In astronomical terms, 200,000 miles was a close flyby, but it presented no danger to the planet.

Every once in a while, an unexpected object, previously unseen, made an appearance and gained the attention of scientists who monitor such things.

One of the prospective end-of-the-world scenarios described by scientists and doom-sayers is that of a large body from space hitting Earth. It had happened in the distant past. But no such major event had occurred in recent history.

The last thought made him pause. He knew better than that. Eugene Shoemaker of the US Geological Survey estimated that a space object large enough to release the amount of energy given off by the atomic bomb dropped on Hiroshima hits Earth about once a year. These go largely unnoticed because they occur in unpopulated areas or the ocean.

He thought of the reports of impacts that took place in historical times. In 1490, 10,000 people in China's Shanxi Province were killed by stones falling from the sky; most likely fragments from the breakup of a large asteroid. Many scientists dismissed the number of fatalities as an exaggeration, but that didn't matter. People died.

A twenty-kilometer-wide ocean crater on the New Zealand shelf southwest of Stewart Island was most likely caused by a large impact. Ice core samples place the event in 1143.

Of course, the most famous recent event occurred in the Tunguska region of Siberia. In 1908, an asteroid or comet — scientists still argue about this — exploded three to six miles above the ground. The airburst felled eight million trees over an area of 850 square miles.

Such events happened, and there was nothing to say it couldn't happen again. The fact that a cataclysm had yet to occur over a populated area meant nothing. It was, to Alexander's mind, just dumb luck.

On his screen were several telescopic photographs showing white dots in the background. One dot was larger than the others, and when compared to photos taken later, the dot showed that the object it represented was moving — and moving fast.

The calculations were early, and many things could happen in the days ahead, but if the early numbers were right, 2012 GA12 would smack Earth right on the nose.

Alexander opened his desk drawer, removed a plastic bottle, and poured a half-dozen Tums into his mouth.

To Andrew Morgan, the only thing keeping this from being the "third degree" were hot lights and threats of a jail term. Donny and Janie entered the room from Janie's office before Jaz Kinkade had finished closing the office door behind him.

"You okay?" Donny looked concerned.

"I'm fine. Why, don't I look okay?" Morgan stood and stretched his back.

"You know what I mean. Did the guy threaten you or try to extort money or favors —"

"No. You'd be the first to know, and the cops would be the second."

"I was worried." Janie rocked from side to side, something she did when nervous.

"You guys worry too much. I'm a big boy. I can take care of myself."

"So . . . what? I'm not needed anymore?" Donny feigned hurt.

"You know what I mean. What was the guy going to do to me in my own office?"

"He could do plenty." A muscle in Donny's neck twitched. "You shouldn't have sent me from the room."

"You can't attend every meeting." Morgan sank back into his chair.

"Your other meetings are planned, and you know the people around you. This guy was a stranger, and I'll bet a year's salary he's up to no good."

"You might lose."

"I doubt it, boss. I doubt it."

"Well, aren't you going to tell us what he wanted?" Janie stopped swaying.

"Nope. It was for my ears only."

"That's not fair." Janie paused. "Okay, I know it's none of my business, but it's all so mysterious."

"Sorry, Janie, I trust you with almost everything, but some things have to be kept under wraps for now. Just know that I'm not in danger or being blackmailed or being forced to sell plastic kitchen products."

"Pity," she said. "I could use a new spatula."

"You need to fill me in, boss, and not me only, but the rest of security."

"Why?"

"You know why: Oil execs like you get kidnapped all the time. Colombia. Russia —"

"We're in the US, Donny."

"I know, but we're also in the age of homegrown terrorists. CEOs make great targets. I don't know what this guy said, but he could be setting you up for something unpleasant."

"Feel free to investigate him. He gave us his name and that of his real business."

Donny ran a hand over his head. "After he lied to us." He hesitated. "Besides, I did a quick check on him."

"And?" Morgan leaned over his desk.

"No criminal record. His company seems to be real. He does have a police record —"

"He's been arrested?" Janie raised a hand to her chest.

"I didn't say that. He has a police record

213

because he used to be a cop in San Francisco."

Morgan lifted an eyebrow. "And how did you learn that?"

Donny shrugged. "I know a guy who knows a guy who —"

"— who knows a guy. I get it. Ask you no questions so you'll tell me no lies." Morgan pulled at his lower lip. "So no criminal record. That's good."

"That doesn't mean anything. There are thousands of criminals with no record."

"I suppose so. Well, it was only a meeting — nothing more. And there's nothing for you two mother hens to worry about."

"I've got a bad feeling," Janie said.

Donny agreed.

Morgan turned to Janie. "Anything new on my schedule?"

"No."

"Okay, I need to do some thinking. Cancel the rest of my day."

Janie looked surprised. "Things are starting to back up."

"I'll work late tonight. For now, I need to noodle on a few things. Let's go, Donny."

"Where we heading?"

"The gym. I think best when I'm sweating."

"Eww." Janie grimaced.

Morgan snickered, rose, and started for the door.

"Oh," Janie called after him. "I almost forgot. That Lisa Campbell called again."

"Did you take a message?"

"Yes."

"Good. Now shred it."

CHAPTER 17

Garrett Vickers strode into the offices of the *Christian Herald* like a man with no cares.

"Oh, you had better have a good reason for showing up three hours late." Lisa cast a stern look at the young man and crossed her arms. Red rimmed his eyes.

"Late? Am I late?" Innocence hung on Garrett's face like a mask.

"You know you are. Your second day, and already you've ticked off the boss."

"I'm related to the boss, remember?"

"I wouldn't play that card right now if I were you. He might make you put salt on it and eat it."

"Did you just use a poker metaphor?"

Lisa tried to remain stern. "There are many other card games, you know."

"Yeah, I know. Anyway, this is the age of technology and information. Just because I'm not physically present doesn't mean I haven't been working. Truth is, I've been working all night."

"You look it. Aren't those the same clothes you wore yesterday?"

"Maybe."

"No maybe about it. You do have other clothes, don't you?"

"Yeah, I got plenty of gear. Not to worry."

"You might want to worry. Your uncle didn't look too pleased when I told him you hadn't come in."

Garrett looked aghast. "Why would you tell him that?"

Lisa frowned. "First, because he asked, and second, because — well, you were missing in action."

"I just told you I've been up all night."

Lisa could believe her ears. "News I could have used when this day started. How am I supposed to know you're working from home? In fact, who asked you to?"

"I'm showing initiative."

"Is that what you're showing?" Lisa stood. "If I were you, I'd pay a visit to your uncle. And don't blame me for you choosing to pull an all-nighter. I know I gave you a lot of material to read, but I didn't give you that much." She moved out of her work space.

"Wait, where are you going?"

"Away."

"What? Why?"

"Because I take my job seriously." She started for the lobby.

"I take my job seriously. Why do you think I stayed up all night? I have stuff to show you."

She looked over her shoulder. "Later, kid. I don't want to miss my flight."

She heard him say something but didn't bother to process it. Her mind was already in Oklahoma.

Every stride on the treadmill made Morgan's back ache a little more. He wasn't worried about injury. He knew himself well enough to differentiate between pain caused by injury and pain caused by tension. Some people carried tension in their necks, and others got headaches. Morgan's lower back tightened whenever the weight of life pressed him down. Exercise was his elixir.

He read the red display on the treadmill. He had put in only two miles. He was dogging it. But then again, his mind was racing. At least something was working at speed.

Even though it was the middle of the workday, the Rockpoint Fitness Gym was busy. It was always busy. Many execs struck deals on the golf course. Others, especially the younger junior execs, preferred to exchange ideas while sweating.

The emotional stew bubbling inside him decreased to a simmer. What was happening?

A meteor strikes an Arizona mechanic's workshop, a volcano erupts with unexpected force, and now I get an unsettling visit from a man who seems to be more than he's telling.

Morgan glanced at Donny, who stood to the side, his suit perfectly aligned and covering a well-muscled body. Sometimes he threw the iron around with Morgan, but today he declined the offer. He had made several passes through the open expanse of the gym and the upper floor. The guard/chauffeur was edgy. Morgan could sense it on the drive over. Donny fidgeted in the driver's seat, changed lanes more frequently than usual, and checked his mirrors every few seconds. Morgan also noticed that Donny took a different route. Paranoia seemed to reach a new high.

Morgan increased the treadmill's speed so he was jogging faster than normal. The pain in his back finally gave way and he could enjoy the exertion.

He wondered about his sanity. Yes, he thought there was something to the 2012 date. Yes, he believed the Mayans had somehow been able to make astronomical observation well beyond the skill and technology level of their time. He had no idea how they did that, but the evidence was clear. The fact they had done what no other people of their time could do was compelling enough for him — so *how* they had done it mattered little to him. And the fact that other indigenous people separate from but living in the same region had made similar predictions only made the whole concept more reasonable.

He stared at the glowing red numbers on the treadmill's console but read nothing. His mind had charted a course of its own.

How things had changed. Some would suggest his interest in the Mayan predictions stemmed from the loss of his family. It didn't. He had always been interested in those concepts that bordered science. It was true that his interest increased in the months that followed the tragedy. It gave his mind something else to focus on other than this blazing grief.

Still, he had changed. He loved his work less and loved being gone more. He had to force himself to come into the office, make himself listen during meetings, and mentally whip himself to lead his company. More and more, he found himself longing for his days in the field, working for his father as a geologist. Those days were gone. And if the Mayans were right, they would be gone forever.

The image of Jasper Kinkade came to mind. Morgan was an astute judge of character. He could spot a liar across a crowded room. He knew within moments of meeting someone if he wanted to do business with him. Kinkade struck Morgan as honest . . . or at least someone who believed the story he was telling.

Not long ago, he would have refused to meet with someone using Kinkade's approach, and once the person admitted to lying, Morgan would have chucked him from the office. He was a man who loved his privacy, and knowing that people had been investigating him made him furious. But at hearing Quetzal's name, Morgan had set aside his usual caution. Quetzal was going out of his way to help people see and prepare for the coming cataclysm. Morgan admired that.

Still, it was an odd way of making contact. He didn't imagine that Quetzal could make personal visits, not with the scores of speaking engagements Morgan had seen on the man's website.

It felt so real. Would Quetzal really call

him? What would he say? *Why me? Didn't Kinkade say there were thousands who wanted my seat? So let them have it. Whatever a seat meant.*

Morgan couldn't let go. He had until the end of the day to decide, but decide what? Kinkade hadn't given him enough information to make a decision. That made the man more believable. A truthful man never laid everything on the table all at once. Deceivers never stopped talking. Kinkade acted as if he didn't care if Morgan warmed to *him* or the *idea.* That made everything all the more intriguing.

Sweat soaked Morgan's shirt. His lungs burned. His calf muscles complained. He was having a great time.

Jaz Kinkade returned the rental at the airport and walked to the terminal serving charter flights. One hour later, he was airborne and on his way to Texas.

"So what'd she say?"

Necco's voice sounded distant and sleep-deprived over the cell connection.

Garrett paced the employee break room. "Nothing. I didn't get to talk to her. She told me I was late and that I should go see my uncle. Then she took off for the airport."

"Where's she going?"

"How should I know? She tossed me off like I was a dirty shirt."

Necco chuckled. "Sounds like my boy is in love."

"Yuck, dude. She's old. Gotta be mid-thirties."

"It's a wonder she doesn't need a cane."

"You know what I mean, man. She's too old for me . . . still, she is pretty hot." Garrett heard keyboard keys clacking over the phone. Necco never gave up.

"What'd your uncle do to you?" More tapping keys.

"Nuthin'. He never yells, but he can make you feel like three-week-old garbage with just a glance. He looked disappointed. That's what bothers me the most. He's a good guy."

"But you still have your job?"

"Yeah, but I'd better not screw up again, or I'll be baggin' groceries. Jobs are still hard to find."

"Tell me about it."

Garrett laughed. "You live with your mother. When was the last time you held a job, or even looked for one?"

"I'm not a cubicle gofer like you. I need my creativity — my space."

"The FBI has another name for what you do."

"I don't know what you're talking about. I'm just a pure-hearted geek . . . Oklahoma City."

"Sure you are — what?"

"Oklahoma City. That's where your new girlfriend is going."

"I told you she's not my girlfriend. She's old enough to be my — older sister. Besides, I've only known her a little more than a day."

"Love at first sight is always the best. Why would she go to OC?"

"That's where that Morgan guy lives."

"The guy you had me research last night."

"Yeah."

"You know you owe me big time, right?"

"I fed you and gave you a place to crash."

"Yeah, right," Necco said. "I haven't had a chance to crash yet."

"Since Lisa is gone, you might as well get some sleep."

"I came up with a few more things. I e-mailed them to you. This Quetzal guy has got it going on. He's got several offshore accounts. Is that legal for a nonprofit?"

"I don't know. I'll find out. Now get some sleep. I may need you later."

"Nighty night."

CHAPTER 18

Lisa spent the time at the airport and in the air thinking through her approach. The cramped seating on the airbus jet made her wish for the comfy leather seats she enjoyed on Andrew Morgan's private jet. Fortunately, it was a short flight.

Once on the ground, she rented a small sedan, drove to the Morgan Natural Energy building in downtown Oklahoma City, and circled the block several times. There were two main entrances to the underground parking. One was marked for the public, and the other had no signage but a lift-arm barricade. She hoped it was the private entrance used by upper management. Six more trips around the block, and she found an open parking space next to the curb that afforded an unobstructed view of the entrance.

It was all a gamble. She had no way of knowing if Morgan was in the building or elsewhere. She didn't even know if he was in the city. Nonetheless, her gut said this was the way to go. She had depended on her reporter's intuition many times, and it had often paid off. Of course, it had let her down a few times as well.

She pulled a protein bar from her purse and took a bite. It was nearing five in the evening. Hopefully, Morgan kept banker hours.

At 5:30, a black limo pulled from the private parking area and onto the street. Lisa hesitated. The windows were tinted. How could she know if it was Morgan in the back? Then again, how many execs rode in limos? For all she knew, they all did.

Lisa started the rental and pulled from the curb. She allowed two cars to pull in front of her. That was how they trailed people in the movies and on television. If it was good enough for Hollywood, it was good enough for her.

A glance in the mirror showed another limo behind her. Lisa wasn't prone to swearing, but she decided that if she were, this would be a good place for expletives.

Now what? Am I following him, or is he following me?

She took another look at the trailing limo. A Crown Vic, just a large sedan. The vehicle in front of her was a stretch limo. CEO quality. She decided to stick with it.

The car moved through the sluggish streets until it reached the 66. Then it headed north on the highway. Lisa kept a discreet distance, often driving in a different lane. She found the chauffeur's manner of driving interesting. He often changed speeds, switched lanes, and kept plenty of room between him and any vehicle in front of him. She guessed he had been trained in evasive driving. He might also be trying to determine if someone was following them. It seemed a tad paranoid, but since she was tailing them, she had to let the matter go.

She dropped back another car length.

So far, so good. Unfortunately, this was the easy part. She worried about what happened once the limo left busy freeways and surface streets behind.

She didn't have to wait long. The limo pulled from the freeway and continued north on a wide, well-maintained road. Several cars followed in its wake, as well as a produce van. Lisa stayed in the shadow of the delivery van. It blocked her view, but that also meant it blocked the chauffeur's line of sight.

One by one, the traffic between her and the limo peeled off onto side streets. Fortunately the van remained between them.

The taillights of the delivery van came on, glowing red in the dimming light. Lisa had to hit the brakes to prevent ramming the large truck. That would put an end to her plan.

A second later, she saw why the truck slowed: The limo was pulling into a long driveway leading to a beautiful home. "Must be nice." Lisa thought of her large apartment and fought off the wave of envy that threatened to drown her.

A moment later, the truck picked up speed, and Lisa followed past the house. She took in as much as she could through the corner of her eye. She saw a professional landscape behind a wrought-iron gate. No one stood by the gate, so she assumed it opened automatically, probably activated by a remote.

Using her rearview mirror, she watched the limo disappear behind the wall that separated the property from the street.

She drove another mile, then turned around, slowly returning the way she came. In the distance, she saw the limo pull back on the street.

"Oh, no. He's leaving again." *It's only been a few minutes.* Maybe he just had to pick up something. There hadn't been enough time for him to even change clothes. Unless . . .

Unless he didn't own the limo. Perhaps the company hired a service. If she were lucky, the driver just dropped Morgan off. If it was Morgan. It was possible that she had followed the wrong guy.

It was time to be sneaky.

Lisa parked on a side street and walked the remaining distance to the house she hoped belonged to Andrew Morgan.

Jasper Kinkade pulled from the freeway and made his way along the San Antonio residential area just west of the State 87 highway. The GPS app in his iPhone guided him through older streets crowded with apartment buildings. He found the building easily enough — a white stucco structure designed to look like an old Spanish villa. Its walls wore dirt, showed wear, and the landscape needed attention. Older, cheaper cars lined the street and filled the small parking lot. Jaz had no doubt this was a low-rent district.

He tapped the icon that activated his phone and placed a call.

"Yep?" The voice was young and male.

"Still at it?"

"Oh, yeah. Big time. Guy went quiet for a few hours. My guess is he was grabbing some Zs. Traffic shows he'd been at it all night and most of today."

"But he's back?"

"Straight up. He's pounding keys as we speak. He's changed the routing several times, but I got the runt nailed. He can chart a new course every five minutes if he wants, but I'll be breathing down his neck."

"Is he still lifting info?" Jaz stared at the apartment building. A young girl sat on the walkway playing jacks. It made him smile. Nothing in the world cuter than a five-year-old girl.

"Oh yeah. He's positively klepto. You want me to shut him down?"

"No. Not yet. Just keep monitoring him. Give me a call if he drops off."

"Will do."

Jaz rang off and removed a small pair of binoculars from their case. One of the advantages of flying charter was his ability to bring equipment with fewer questions. Too much electronics tended to draw the attention of the Transportation Security Administration.

He looked in each window but saw nothing of interest. He settled in, preparing for a few hours of doing nothing . . . when his cell phone sounded. It was the young Internet security guy he had just spoken to.

"He's gone offline."

Jaz thought for a moment. "Maybe he's in the head."

"Nah. You don't go offline for that. He's signed off."

I got here just in time. "Thanks."

"I've got something else for you. I recognize this guy."

"What? How can you recognize someone over the Internet?"

Jaz heard laughter. "We hackers are an arrogant bunch. Some can't resist putting little touches in that reveal their identity. The guy behind the keyboard goes by the name Necco."

"Like the candy?"

"Exactly. Charming, isn't it? I met him at a black-hat hacker's conference. The guy has no life."

"Is he tall, super thin, with ratty hair?"

"Yeah. How do you know that?"

"Gotta go." Jaz hung up and watched Necco walk from the building. Next to him was a twentysomething girl with sad eyes and Goth makeup.

He wished Necco had been alone.

The gate was close to ten feet tall with vertical members too narrow to pass through — even for a person Lisa's size. Each wrought-

231

iron pole on the gate stood upright and ended in a spear-shaped design that looked deadly.

A short distance from the gate was an intercom system. She could see a camera lens behind a protective plastic pane. Another camera was mounted to the pilaster, where the security wall met the fence. Perfect. She pressed the TALK button and waited.

"Yes?" The voice was less tinny than she expected. Before she could respond, she heard, "I don't believe it."

Bingo.

"Mr. Morgan, I presume." The wind picked up and mussed her hair. It was cold, and she shivered. She couldn't have scripted it better. "I was hoping I could talk to you." She wrapped her arms around herself, fending off the cool breeze.

"There's a reason I didn't respond to your calls."

More wind. The large security camera at the top of the wall moved from side to side. She guessed he was scanning for her car, which she hoped he would not be able to see.

"How did you get here?"

"I promise not to be so abrasive this time. I want . . . I want to apologize. And then, if it's all right with you, we can chat for a while."

"You didn't answer my question."

"I'm being evasive."

"I can see that."

The camera moved.

"I'm also being honest, Mr. Morgan. I've come a long way."

A full thirty seconds of silence passed, and then the gate began to move. She was pretty sure his Southern gentlemanliness wouldn't allow him to leave her standing at his front gate. Still, it had been a gamble, and the last thing she wanted to do was return home and have to explain why her idea failed.

She kept her arms folded, her purse hanging over her left shoulder. Although she knew better, the driveway that led to the front of the mansion seemed the length of a football field. She estimated that it was a third of that. The drive had a gentle slope, making the walk a little more challenging.

As she neared the massive wood door, it swung open. Andrew Morgan looked different. Before, he had been dressed in stylish, casual clothes; now he wore an old pair of jeans, dirty New Balance sports shoes, and a gray sweatshirt with the sleeves cut off. His hair was mussed, and a sheen of perspiration covered his face, forming a V-shaped stain over his broad chest. He didn't step outside.

Lisa smiled and looked down at the driveway as she transitioned to a walkway of gray pavers. Her heart stuttered, and she wasn't sure if it was from fear, embarrassment, or . . . something else.

"Good evening, Mr. Morgan."

He gave a slight nod, but he didn't smile. "You look cold."

"The breeze has picked up. It's chilly."

He stepped aside and motioned for her to enter. As she brushed past him, she could smell the musky-sweet odor of sweat. Her heart picked up speed.

The moment she was in the wide lobby, he closed the door and locked it. She looked up and saw an expensive-looking crystal chandelier over her head. Beneath her feet, marble tile covered the floor. She stepped deeper into the foyer.

"It's very kind of you to see me. I'm sure my presence is a little unexpected."

Along one white wall hung a dozen or so photos. Family photos: white-water rafting; a teenager playing in a high school basketball game; a trim, beautiful woman in a strapless black evening gown. Fingerprints marred the glass of every photo. Lisa could imagine Morgan touching the photos over and over again. Her stomach clinched into a knot.

"I should be surprised, but I'm not." He moved past her. "This way, please. We'll sit in the living room."

She could hear tension in his voice. "Thank you. Wait, did you just say you're not surprised?"

He led her to a living room the size of her apartment. The assessment was probably an exaggeration, but not by much. The marble tile gave way to a carpet so thick and lush that she wanted to lie down on it. Furniture that would cost her a year's salary populated the space. Paintings — fine reproductions of paintings by well-known impressionists — in wide, ornate frames hung on the walls. At least she thought they were reproductions.

"You strike me as the kind of person who doesn't take no for an answer."

"I did call." A blanket, pillow, and a couple of paperback books cluttered a large sofa next to the wall. Two glass tumblers with a film of their dried contents rested on the floor. Was he sleeping down here?

"Yes, you did. Let's talk in the sitting area. It's cleaner." He motioned to a pair of sofas with flowery print fabric in the corner. His wife's choice, she assumed. A round, glass coffee table sat centered in the space. It struck Lisa as odd that there would be a "room" within a room, something she had seen only in magazines. "I should apologize for the mess. As you know, I'm a bachelor now."

A weak joke.

"No need to apologize to me. I showed up unexpectedly. I seem to have got you mid-workout."

If being dressed the way he was embarrassed him, Lisa couldn't see it.

"My second workout of the day. I was at the gym earlier."

"A light workday?" She regretted the words the moment they left her mouth. His frown made her guilt worse. "Sorry. I still have control issues with my mouth."

"Which is why I didn't call you back."

"I didn't think I had been that rude." She sat on one of the sofas. He sat on the sofa across from her.

"Rude enough."

"I did apologize."

"Yes, you did, and I know I'm overly sensitive, but the more I thought about our conversation, the more it ate at me."

"I apologize again. I shouldn't have pried into your personal business or offered counseling I'm not qualified to give."

A slight, polite smile appeared, the kind a man who has been offended gives the one who had offended him. "I work out a lot. It's how I deal with stress, and I have a great deal on my mind."

"I pace. I've ruined my share of carpet by logging miles and miles of pacing."

"So where is it?"

The question caught her off guard. "Where is what?"

"Your car. I live off the beaten path. I doubt you walked here."

"Maybe I took a cab."

"Maybe, but I doubt it. You seem like the kind of person who plans well. I need to know if I should call a taxi for you. Do I?"

"No. I parked down the road, on one of the side streets. Then I walked here."

"I figured it was something like that. Clever in its own way, but a bit manipulative, don't you think?"

"You're kind to say that it's just a 'bit' manipulative."

His smile turned genuine. "By 'bit,' I meant 'way over the top.' "

"Oh."

He leaned forward, resting his elbows on his knees. "Lisa, why are you here?"

"First, I wanted to apologize again for being so nosey and pushy when all you did was go out of your way to get me home."

"You've already done that, and you could have done that on the phone."

Lisa raised an eyebrow.

"Okay, you got me. You could have done that on the phone if I had returned your calls. What's the second reason you're here?"

Lisa had seen video of the members of the Polar Bear Club — people who, every winter, jumped into freezing water with nothing but a swimsuit on. She felt as if she were about to do the same. She inhaled deeply and held it for a moment. Then she let it out. "My editor wants me to do a story on people who believe the world will end in 2012."

"There are tens of thousands of people who believe that. Why me?"

And there it was: the question she didn't want to answer. "Because you're rich."

He straightened. "What's that got to do with anything?"

She bit her lip. "Okay, cards on the table. You're not like the others. Let's face it. Some people will follow any wild-eyed cultist."

"Wild-eyed cultist?"

"You know what I mean. You're different than most people. It's not just your wealth, but your education, your success in business, and your intelligence. I want to do a story about people like you who — it seems — would dismiss the 2012 theory in favor of . . ." This time she caught herself.

"In favor or something more logical?"

"Well . . . yes."

Morgan sighed and rubbed his face. Before he could speak, his cell phone rang. He retrieved it from his jeans, looked at the screen, and closed his eyes. "Excuse me." He stood and raised the phone to his ear. "Hello, Candy."

Candy? She looked around the room, trying to appear disinterested. She saw nothing, but she heard everything Morgan had to say.

"Actually, I'm kinda busy." He listened. "I know I haven't called, but I've been swamped with things. I apologize." Another pause. "No, I'm sorry, I'm not available tonight." He began to pace faster. "I have a meeting tonight . . . Yes . . . No . . . Yes, there's a woman here, but . . . Candy . . . Candy, let me talk. It's not like that. She's a reporter. Then I have a video conference soon, and . . . Candy, listen to me . . . Yes, I enjoyed our dinner, but . . . Candy? Candy?"

Morgan lowered the phone and returned it to his pocket.

"Should I ask?"

"Probably not." Morgan stared at her for a moment. "Let me ask you a question. Do you like Indian food?"

"Are you trying to curry my favor?"

"Oh, a punster."

"The pun's the thing."

His smile broadened. "And Shakespeare too."

"To answer your question, I love Indian food."

CHAPTER 19

"No she didn't!" Lisa laughed louder than she intended, drawing the attention of several of the patrons in the Star of India restaurant downtown. "She said, 'Indian food like maize?' " She laughed again, holding her sides. "That's rich. That's . . . I don't know what it is."

"Apparently you think it's pretty funny." Morgan was grinning. "I didn't see the humor in it at the moment."

"I'm sorry. I shouldn't laugh. It's rude —" Another belly laugh erupted.

"My chauffeur found it amusing too." He raised a glass of water to his lips and took a sip. He gazed at her through the clear glass. Her laughter was as contagious as it was loud. Her normally slightly pale face was reddened.

Lisa raised a hand and dabbed at the tears forming in her eyes, careful not to touch her eyeliner. Morgan found it endearing.

He straightened the napkin on his lap, spreading it over the fresh pair of jeans he had donned. He wore a gray long-sleeve shirt and a dark blue sports jacket.

"Did things get better from there?" She took several deep breaths.

"No, the whole thing started off slow and then bogged down from there. I'm afraid one drink after another didn't improve her any."

"That's cold."

"But accurate. She did, however, invite me up to her place. She made it clear she had, um, intentions."

Lisa's smile evaporated. "Oh, really? Well . . ."

"This is where you ask if I accepted her offer."

"That would be impolite." She picked up her glass of sparkling water and took a long sip.

"Come on. I know you know how to be impolite."

Lisa snapped her head up. "What's that supposed to mean?"

Morgan didn't reply. He did broaden his grin.

"Okay, okay. I had that coming. So, did you take her up on her offer?"

"Nope. I kissed her on the forehead and

ran like a scared Cub Scout."

"I bet she liked that."

"Not so much. If looks could kill, you'd be dining with a corpse."

"Oh, yuck. Woman trying to eat here." A moment later, she chuckled. "At least you're not sitting around the house feeling sorry for yourself." Her own words shocked her. "I didn't mean —"

"No problem, but who's to say I'm not sitting around moping?"

"I just assumed . . ." She pursed her lips. "I don't know what I assumed."

"Everyone and their dog is trying to get me back into the dating scene. I was never good at that. I met my wife in college. She's the only one I've dated . . . well, until Candy."

"People are really pressing you to date?"

He nodded. "My aunt, three vice presidents, four of their wives, my personal assistant, and my chauffeur."

"Are you going to see her again? I mean, she did call you."

"She's called me a dozen times. Okay, I may be exaggerating, but she has called several times. Apparently my aunt Ida gave Candy my number."

"Between me and Candy, you may have to get a new phone number."

"I may do that."

"So you're not interested in dating."

He folded his hands on the table. "What's the point? I can't get over my wife, and besides . . ."

"Besides what?"

"You know. December 21, 2012. Who knows if any of us will be around?"

"And you really believe that?"

Morgan said he did. "Don't you Christians believe the rapture is coming? You know, that event when believers will be caught up in the air to meet Jesus?"

"Yes, but that's different."

He leaned back in the chair. "Not in my eyes."

Morgan watched her, waiting for a sharp retort. Instead, she looked sad but said nothing.

The waiter appeared and set down a plate of Tandoori chicken in front of Lisa, and a plate of lamb curry before Morgan. The sight and smell revved his appetite. That and two challenging workouts in one afternoon had left him in need of sustenance.

Morgan seized his fork and was about to stab a cube of lamb when he noticed Lisa sitting with her head bowed. His son had started praying over meals a few months before his death. The sight of the silent conversations drew sad memories from the well of his soul. He waited for her to finish. When she raised her head, he took his first bite. The spice made his eyes water and threatened to cause his tongue to combust. He wouldn't have it any other way.

"How much time do we have left?" Lisa asked as she pulled the chicken from the bone.

He glanced at his watch. "About an hour-fifteen. We have time." When she had agreed to join him for dinner, he told her that he had to be back home by eight. Jasper Kinkade had sent him a text informing him what time Quetzal would call. He also received an e-mail from Charles Balfour sharing his excitement about the upcoming chat.

"So, how much can I ask you about the video conference?"

"That's an odd question."

She shook her head, took a bite, closed her eyes, and moaned with satisfaction. "This is fabulous." She chewed for a few moments. "I asked the question because I know I've pushed the envelope with you. I'm surprised you didn't leave me standing at your gate."

"No, you're not. You're working me, and I know it."

"Then why invite me to dinner?"

He shrugged. "I was hungry. I'm not as upset with you as you imagine."

"Really?"

"No, I'm upset with you, but I believe in new beginnings. That and I want to have dinner with a woman that has a brain."

"Now, now, Candy has a brain. Let's not be cruel."

Morgan shoveled another bite into his mouth. "I'm a cruel man."

"No you're not. You're firm, you're determined, and you're your own man, but you're not cruel. A cruel man would have called the police on me for trespassing and maybe apply for a restraining order."

"And you're determined, a tad pushy, overly religious, and results-orientated."

"Does that mean I can't ask you about your meeting?"

"Maybe over dessert."

"Dessert. This day just gets better and better."

Morgan wondered what he was going to do with the bulldog sitting across the table from him.

Candy Welch — Meredith Roe on her birth certificate — paced her condo. Things hadn't gone according to plan, and no matter how hard she tried to regain her footing, she couldn't. Jaz wasn't happy, and if she couldn't turn things around, she would be on the bad end of his wrath.

She swore at herself and then at the absent Jaz. She had never failed a mission before. It was why she was the highest paid operative in Jaz's empire. That, and she was called upon to do what other operatives wouldn't do. Some were good at surveillance, but she was good at seduction. That is, until Andrew Morgan came along.

Where had she gone wrong? The man was ripe for the picking: a lonely widower with a high-pressure job. She had taken scores of such men to bed.

She stepped into the bedroom and let her eyes drift to the two hidden video cameras.

"What a waste."

Her cell rang. "Oh great." She took a deep breath. "Hello, Jaz."

Jaz tossed the phone onto the front passenger seat. He wanted to throw it through the windshield of his rental car, but that would serve no purpose. He would have to deal with Meredith and her failure later. He had gone through a lot of trouble to orchestrate a plan that would involve Morgan's aunt. He had drawn several scenarios, but the easiest was to take the *real* Candy Welch out of the picture. That was easy enough. Aunt Ida was one of the last of Morgan's family still living. On a hunch, he had placed an operative on her, tapped her phone, and followed her. They hit gold early. His company did all the background checks on anyone who Balfour and Quetzal thought might be interested in their organization.

Sifting through thousands of IP addresses of those who visited the site had been made easier by a custom software application. The website recorded the Internet addresses of everyone who visited the site. A computerized search of the information led to a name and other data. If the physical location was in a wealthy area, that information was gathered and passed to a worker who did additional research. They had been on Morgan's trail for some time. When he showed up in Roswell, he became a prime target.

Jaz pushed those thoughts to the side. He had another problem. He was tailing a young man and woman. Tailing a car was easier. Following pedestrians while in a car was nearly impossible. It would take only a few moments for the subjects to notice a slow-moving vehicle behind them.

He had let them get a block away before

pulling from the curb, but once he was moving, he had to drive past them and turn onto a side street. If he saw that they hadn't caught a glimpse of him, then he could drive by again. Normally, a successful tail like this required several operatives spread out along the subject's anticipated path, but he didn't have the luxury. In fact, he hadn't anticipated following anyone from the apartment.

He assumed the couple lived nearby; otherwise, they would have driven or taken the bus. Jaz drove down the street, made a right on a side street, turned around, and pulled back to the intersection. He parked near the corner and raised his binoculars. Wherever the couple was headed, they were in no hurry.

They made a left and continued down the sidewalk. Jaz looked at his GPS unit and identified the street as Beech Avenue. He had done his research. There were no apartments on that street, just older homes that looked as if they had been around for more than fifty years. He pulled into the street and drove a parallel course to the one on which his prey was walking. He felt a wave of anxiety. If he was too slow, and if one of the old homes was their destination, then he would have to stake out the street until they reappeared.

He made the first left he could and drove slowly across the intersection, gazing down Beech. His timing was perfect. He saw the couple walk to an olive green bungalow-style home.

Jaz parked again, giving the couple time to enter the home. Only then would he risk driving down the street to scope out the house.

Garrett returned to his apartment with a bag of burgers and fries in one hand. He also carried a mind full of frustrations. Two days on the job, and so far he had managed to tick off his uncle and watch the reporter who was supposed to be training him fly off to Oklahoma, leaving him to help with obituaries, photocopies, and filing. He was a reporter, not a secretary. He should have been allowed to go with Lisa. How else would he learn?

The apartment was a mess, but Garrett gave it little thought. It was always a mess. Necco hadn't made it worse, nor had he improved it. He set the burgers down on a battered coffee table, turned on the television, and went to the refrigerator. Necco had nearly cleaned it out. For such a skinny guy, he ate like an alligator. At least he had left a can of Coke. There was no food.

Garrett had anticipated that. It was why he had picked up fast food on the way home.

He returned to the living room and glanced at the desk where he and Necco had set up their respective computers. Necco's laptop was gone. A sticky note hung from the desktop monitor: *Thanks for the challenge. You owe me.*

Garrett was beat. He had been up all night, worked all day, and now he was too tired to look at Necco's latest research. He turned to the television and then back to the computer. Snatching up the fast-food bag, he turned off the television and switched on the computer. He had finished the first bacon cheeseburger by the time the machine booted.

After unwrapping the second cheeseburger, Garret studied his desktop. An icon caught his eye: a roll of Neccos. Garrett shook his head. His friend was definitely weird.

He double-clicked on the icon, and a document filled the screen. It was a single page with blue links to web sites, and notes arranged in short sentences. The last note read: *I could be wrong, but I think they may have sniffed us out. I cleared your Internet history. Destroy this.*

"Oh great, so much for you being Mr.

Invisible."

Someone knocked on his door.

CHAPTER 20

Lisa shifted in the front seat of the Mercedes SLK Roadster and then shifted again. The sleek car looked like it could outrace a missile, but that wasn't what made her nervous. As sporty and fast as the car appeared, Morgan drove slowly over the surface streets. She couldn't decide if he was being gentle for her sake or if he was just a cautious driver.

Maybe he just wants to spend a few extra minutes with me. She jerked her head to the side. Where had that thought come from? She wasn't here for any other reason than to get the interview. She told herself that several times.

"Are you okay? Doze off? I have that effect on people."

"No. I'm fine. I just . . . I have no idea what I was doing. Daydreaming, I guess."

"About what?"

She looked at him. The sun, which was

now low in the sky, nevertheless illuminated his handsome features. Lisa shrugged. "Nothing. My mind tends to run off on its own."

"I know that feeling. My mind is seldom where my body is." He exhaled noisily, started to speak, but she cut him off.

"Let me guess — you're trying to decide whether to give me the interview."

Their eyes met for a moment. "I don't see how I can do that."

"I promise to not make you look like a wacko."

"Oh, so you plan to lie."

She grinned. "I'll have you know, Mr. Morgan, I'm addicted to the truth."

"Isn't 'truthful reporter' an oxymoron?"

"Watch it."

"I can't do the interview."

She expected that. "What can I do to change your mind? After all, I came a long way."

"Which was your decision." He checked the rearview mirror. "In some ways, I'm a public man. I'm not movie-star famous, but I head a publicly held company. That means I have thousands of stockholders to answer to. If the CEO looks flaky — and, let's face it, believing the world may come to an end in 2012 will strike some people as flaky —

they may think I'm unfit for this job."

This was going badly. Morgan struck her as the kind of man who digs his heels in deeper when pushed to do something he didn't want to do. "Do you really believe the world will end eighteen months from now?"

"I believe something dramatic — probably catastrophic — will happen."

"Then what does it matter if some of your stockholders will think you've gone 'round the bend'?"

"It doesn't mean anything to me personally, but I won't do anything that will negatively impact the firm. I have a duty to thousands of workers."

"Okay, how about this: We do the interview, but I never mention your name, Morgan Natural Energy, or even the state you live in. I could just call you a high-ranking executive who wishes to remain anonymous. I don't know if my editor will go for it, but he might."

He stared through the window and Lisa felt a moment of hope. At least he was thinking about it.

"Why is this important?"

"Because the 2012 flap is going to increase in the months ahead. It has to. Do you remember all the Y2K hubbub? In the end, a couple of microwaves quit working, but the claims of power outages, loss of personal information, the digital crash of hospital electronics, the suspension of credit, and cars no longer able to start turned out to be nothing but the fruit of imagination."

"I remember. It might interest you that I thought all that was nonsense."

"You see, that's what I want to write about. Why do you believe the 2012 theorists now, but before the year 2000, you dismissed the doomsayers then?"

She caught him glancing at the clock on the dash. She felt the car speed up.

"I've done my research. Let's just leave it at that."

War broke out in Lisa's mind. Her impulse was to tell him that she couldn't leave it at that, but the thinking part of her brain reminded her that the night had gone a long way to heal the rift between them. To spout off now could upend the progress.

She spoke softly. "I might as well lay it all on the line. I know you're thinking of dropping me off at my car, but I'm going to risk being forward. I want to go back to your place."

He turned to her, his forehead furrowed with confusion. "Are you going Candy on me?"

"Going Candy — no. Not at all." She felt her face warm. "I didn't meant that. Boy, do I need to rephrase that."

Morgan laughed. "Okay. Rephrase."

"I want to listen in on your video conference."

"Well, that was straightforward."

"I'm running out of road. We'll be to your place in minutes. I can't think of a clever way to ask."

He drummed his finger on the steering wheel. "You know, it's supposed to be a private meeting."

"Listen, Andrew. I'm sensing a strong disconnect between what you say you believe and how you act about your belief. It's confusing."

Too direct?

"Confusing how?"

"If you truly believe the world is going to be negatively impacted in December of 2012 and that lives will be lost, then I'd think you'd want to do something about it. Save whomever you could."

"Maybe I'm a selfish jerk. Maybe I'm out only to save myself."

Lisa shook her head. "You told me earlier that you're a good judge of character. Well, so am I. It's a required skill in my profession. I need to be able to judge if someone is jerking me around. My gut tells me you're one of the good guys."

"You could be wrong."

"Of course I could, but I'm not."

Morgan slowed the car as they approached his home. Lisa felt a moment of hope.

"I don't have time to give this proper consideration." He pulled into the drive but stopped at the closed gate. He parked the car and pinched the bridge of his nose.

Lisa let him think, fighting the swelling urge to pressure him to acquiesce.

"You said you were addicted to the truth. Is that the truth, or just Christian hyperbole?"

"I meant it. For me, it's part of my faith. I let my yes mean yes and my no mean no."

Morgan turned in his seat. "I don't have time to debate this. I'm cutting it thin as it is. Here's the deal: You can listen in. You will say nothing. You will stay out of sight. You will publish nothing without my permission. I will give you the interview, but my name, position, firm, and location will not be revealed."

"No reporter makes her article contingent on the approval of anyone but her editor —"

Morgan dropped the car into reverse and began to back onto the street.

"Wait."

He stopped.

Lisa stared at the dashboard, but her mind churned with other images, primarily those of an angry editor. "Maybe we could —"

"No. That's my deal. It's my way or nothing."

"But —"

"No. Is it a deal?"

"I need a minute."

"I don't have a minute." Again, he put the Mercedes in reverse.

"Okay. Deal."

"You sure?"

She frowned. "What alternative do I have?"

"Go home and forget the whole thing."

She shook her head and wondered if it was really the story driving her decision.

Morgan pulled forward again, pressed a button on the remote control for the gate, and pulled to the house.

Garrett was uncertain of where he was. For the first few moments, he thought he was snuggled in bed, but the mattress was too hard and the sheets didn't feel right — too rough. He rolled onto his back and opened his eyes. Only one opened. There was no ceiling light above him. His bedroom had a ceiling light with an ancient-looking glass diffuser populated by dead bugs. This ceiling was familiar, like the one in the living room of his apartment.

He turned his head, an act that sent lightning bolts of pain down his neck and into his back. The tables at the side of the living room that held his computer equipment stood bare. A tangle of computer cords rested on the floor. The place was lit by the light from the five-foot-by-five-foot foyer.

He tried to sit up, but the pain was too much. With each new awakening moment, the pain grew. It hurt to breathe, and his legs refused to respond as they should. As his pain grew, so did his awareness. Several facts competed for his attention. He struggled to sort them out, and with each new realization, his agony grew more excruciating. Every inhalation told him his ribs were broken; every effort to sit up let him know that one arm was busted. A few seconds later, he came to understand that both legs were broken just below the knees.

Shock. He decided that he was still in shock. It was the only reason he wasn't screaming. His mind remained muddled. He couldn't recall what happened, but enough brain cells were firing for him to realize he was in big trouble.

Turning his head to the left, he saw his cell phone, or what was left of his cell phone. He tasted blood, and the left side of his shirt was wet.

He forced his head to move to the right — to the computer center. A phone lay on the floor, but the cord had been cut.

Garrett began to weep from pain, fear, and frustration. With the one arm that still worked, he touched his side and saw blood. A flash of memory returned. He recalled being stabbed. If he didn't receive help soon, he would die.

He couldn't make it to the door, but he might be able to do something else. He used his working arm to push his way to a small set of plastic drawers beneath the table. To reach it, he had to travel three feet. It felt like crawling three miles. Every movement stabbed him with pain. Darkness hovered at the edge of his vision, threatening to flood his eyes forever. Another inch brought another million volts of electric pain.

He cried.

He groaned.

He whimpered.

Sweat drenched him by the time he had inched his way to the plastic drawers. Half of his mind prayed for death. The other half refused to listen.

With two fingers, he pulled open the bottom drawer. Although just a few inches deep, it was too tall for Garrett to reach in. He pulled more until the storage drawer slipped from its home. It took three tries, but he managed to upend it. Computer and video cords tumbled out. He ran his hand through the tangle, struggling to keep enough of his wits to distinguish one cord from another.

Moments passed like decades until he found the one that felt right. He lifted it and saw the business end of a phone cord, an extra he had from when he upgraded to DSL service.

After taking several deep breaths, Garrett inched to the wall. He tried to stay focused. It took eight tries to slip the plastic connector into the phone jack. He gave himself a thirty-second break, and then he forced his trembling fingers to search for the other end, hoping that it wasn't hopelessly intertwined with the other cords. He wished he were a neater person.

He found the plug and brought it to his mouth, slipping it between his teeth. There was a copper taste in his mouth he knew came from blood, not the phone cord.

He swept his arm along the floor, hoping

he was close enough to the fallen phone. He didn't have the strength or endurance to move along the floor another inch. His hand hit the knot of loose cables, the plastic drawer, then the cool plastic of the phone. Tears coursed down his cheeks.

Moving the phone was like moving a concrete block. His strength was fading. He pulled it close, lifted it, and set the base on his chest. Fingers probed the back of the device until he found the port. Removing the jack from his teeth, he made several attempts to connect it. Finally he felt the gentle click he was praying for.

The handset lay next to him. He lifted and dropped it in the cradle. One second later, he lifted it again and placed it next to his ear, hearing the sweetest sound ever: a dial tone.

"Second row," he whispered to himself, "third button — no . . . third row, third button."

Nine.

"Think, think." Gray fog swirled in his blood-deprived brain. "First button, first row." He ran his fingers on the keypad.

One.

"Again."

One.

Ring. Ring.

"Nine-one-one, what is your emergency?"

"Hurt . . . attacked . . ."

The gray fog turned black. As Garrett slipped into the dark waters of oblivion, he heard, "Sir? Sir? Are you hurt? Sir?"

Jaz drove at a leisurely pace along the freeway headed to the San Antonio airport. He rubbed his jaw and looked at his skinned knuckles. The kid knew how to throw a good punch. Caught him right on the left side of the jaw. It had been a long time since someone hit him hard enough to make him see stars.

"Stupid runt." There was a big difference between landing a lucky shot and putting up a good fight. True, the computer freak landed two or three punches that got Jaz's attention, but all it did was infuriate him.

That last realization bothered him more than his sore jaw and swollen knuckles. Jaz was a professional, and professionals remained in control at all times. Perhaps it was all the travel he had been doing lately. Maybe it was this stupid idea that the world was coming to an end, a concept he couldn't bring himself to fully dismiss. He had only slept a few hours in the last few days, and that put him on edge.

He also had to confess that he hadn't

expected the kid to be in the apartment like he should have. That was a blunder.

Still, he had done what he needed to do. True, he didn't have to pummel the kid as much as he did, but the pain sent gallons of adrenaline speeding through his veins.

In a suitcase in the trunk were several hard drives taken from the computers found in the home of the skinny kid with the girl-friend, or as it turned out, the home of his mother — and Garrett Vickers' apartment. He had taken the time to check the kid's ID to make sure he had beaten and stabbed the correct man. The name matched what he had been told by the team that tracked the hacker back to that apartment.

A moment of remorse passed over him. It always did on jobs that required extreme action. He gave it sixty seconds and then forced it from his thoughts. There were other things that needed his focus.

He keyed a number into his cell phone. When he heard someone answer, he said, "Done," and then hung up.

CHAPTER 21

Andrew Morgan's home office was upstairs and over the kitchen. It felt odd to lead a woman through his home and upstairs to the bedroom wing. No female had crossed his threshold since the accident, let alone make her way into the deep, private areas of the home.

Lisa followed quietly as if she knew that her presence was breaking a concrete rule. He had asked her to concede points reporters seldom gave up. Although he had backed her into a corner, giving her the choice between a story he controlled or no story at all, he appreciated her flexibility. Could he trust her? He didn't know, but he couldn't explain why he agreed to let her listen to the video conference. It was a gut decision.

"That is the bedroom wing." He pointed down a wide hall to his left. "There's a bathroom three doors down if you need it."

"I'm good." She smiled. "I don't want to

miss anything."

"We've got five minutes." He turned right down the hall. Three steps down the wall to the left opened to a large game room. Morgan glanced in. It had been weeks since he had shot a game of pool or watched a game on the big-screen television.

"Wow. I could fit all of my furniture in there."

"It's not as big as it looks."

"Maybe not to you."

Morgan didn't respond. He pushed open a pair of pocket doors that disappeared into the side walls and stepped in to the large space. Although it held his computer and printer, he considered it more of a retreat, a den where he could escape the pressures of the corporate world. Red oak bookshelves lined two of the walls. Three-dimensional, white plaster panels textured to look like waves covered the other walls. A large dormer with mullioned windows looked over the front landscape. At one time, he felt proud of the space. Now it was just a space.

He glanced at Lisa and saw her wide eyes. "You did all this?"

"Me?" He laughed. "No. My wife got a restraining order to keep me away from power tools. She insisted instead that her husband have all his fingers."

"Some women are picky that way. Well, whoever did the work did a great job."

"I suppose she did."

"Suppose?"

"Things change a man's perceptions."

She nodded and had the good sense to keep quiet. Morgan admired that.

Stepping to a long glass table with arching chrome legs, he pushed the power button on the computer tower beneath the desk and sat in a contemporary-looking ergonomic chair. The chair cost several thousands of dollars, and he'd never been able to feel good about the purchase. He bought it because he could — and because it was stylish. Those seemed like foolish reasons now.

A wide monitor dominated the center of the desk. It came to light moments after Morgan turned on the device. He glanced at a small lens built into the top frame of the monitor. A blue light next to it blinked on and then off. The video camera was working.

A few key strokes later, he was on the Internet in the remote "meeting room" he had been told to visit. The "room" was a service provided by a company that served businesses by providing servers that allowed businesses from all over the world to conference with each other.

"Please turn off the light."

"You just turned it on."

"I know, but a dark room will help keep you hidden."

Lisa did as he instructed.

"Okay, close the doors and stand a little further to your left. You're still in frame."

"I won't be able to see from there."

He turned to her. "Lisa, if you can see them, then they can see you. I'm pretty sure that will end the conversation."

"Maybe a mirror." She closed the doors.

Morgan shook his head. "I repeat, if you can see him, then he can see you. Would reflect your image as well as Quetzal's."

"I have an idea." She approached Morgan, glanced at his image on the screen, turned, then sat on the floor behind and to the side of his chair.

"Lisa, that's not going to work." He faced the monitor and saw only himself and the wall behind him. "Okay, maybe it will."

A popup window appeared on the screen, stating that someone else had joined the meeting.

"Promise me you won't move or speak."

"What happens if I start choking to death?" He heard the humor in her voice.

"I insist that you die quietly."

"Sheesh. What a nice guy you turned out to be."

"I am what I am."

"Thanks, Popeye."

Morgan snickered, donned his business meeting face, and clicked the link.

Emotions ran through Lisa like a train through a tunnel. At one moment she was thrilled with her reporter skullduggery — the next moment she was a basket of nerves. Those emotions were followed by the warm flow of joy she experienced over dinner. She had not laughed so much or so hard in years, and she certainly had not had a better time. Still, she was not so naive as to ignore the underlying tension broadcast by Morgan.

Still, here she was, invited into his home. All right, she was sitting cross-legged on the floor behind him like Labrador retriever, but she was here.

While she waited for the video link to connect, Lisa took another look around. She noticed that things seemed orderly, but there was a thin layer of dust on almost everything. The living room sofa was disheveled from where Morgan had obviously been sleeping at night. She guessed that he spent very little time in here and perhaps had even fired the maid.

The monitor flashed, and the image of Robert Quetzal appeared on the screen. Seated behind him — and to one side — was the thin man Lisa had seen at the Roswell presentation: Charles Balfour. For some reason, Lisa thought of a ventriloquist and his dummy.

"Mr. Morgan, it is a pleasure to speak to you. It's an honor." Quetzal's grin was almost Cheshire-Cat quality.

"I think I'm the one who should feel honored."

Oh brother. A mutual admirations society.

"I understand that Mr. Kinkade paid you a visit."

"He did." Morgan leaned back, and his chair squeaked. "I wasn't sure what to make of him. To be honest, he made me uncomfortable."

Quetzal's smile disappeared. "Really? Did he say anything to offend you? He's normally a very polite man."

"Oh, he was polite, all right. I just don't like being investigated."

Lisa realized what Morgan was doing: He was setting the tone for the meeting, putting the other man on the defensive.

The smile returned. "Oh, that. Yes, he is

thorough. If he wasn't, he wouldn't be working for us. Our operation requires . . ." He seemed to struggle for just the right word. "Discretion. These are times unique to history, Mr. Morgan. We must be very cautious about the people we invite into the Circle."

"Still —"

"Still, nothing, Mr. Morgan." Quetzal's words were sharp. "Please, let's stop posturing. You've spent a fair amount of time investigating us."

"Not with a paid investigator."

"Granted. Look, I know you're the CEO of a large, multibillion-dollar business and that you're used to running meetings your way. You want to lay down ground rules and choose the tone. I recognize the technique and appreciate it. It increases my admiration for you. I know the tricks, but I'm not a junior executive made to sit in a chair lower than yours so you can have the psychological advantage. I don't have time for gamesmanship. I have to fly out of the country, and my plane leaves in twenty minutes. Now we can spend that time jockeying for control, or we can get down to business. Which do you prefer?"

This guy's good. Lisa gently pulled a notepad from her purse. She would have preferred to use her smart phone for note taking, but she feared the glow of the screen might give her away. She would have to do this old-school with pen and paper.

"I'm ready to listen." Morgan straightened in his seat.

"I'm going to make an offer. It will sound outlandish, and maybe even impossible, but I assure you, everything I say is the gospel truth."

Odd choice of expression for a so-called Mayan priest. Lisa studied the background behind Quetzal but saw nothing but a blue backdrop. Was he hiding something behind the screen or just using it to make himself more visible over the video? She had no way of telling.

"Okay," Morgan said.

Quetzal hesitated as if he sensed something was wrong. Lisa looked at the window on the monitor that showed Morgan. She could see him and the bookshelves behind him. She did not see herself. "What's that behind you?" Quetzal cocked his head.

Oh no.

"Excuse me?" Morgan turned and looked at shelves along the wall. "Do you mean the bookshelf?"

"Yes. Are those books about 2012?"

Morgan turned again, nodded and faced

273

the monitor again. "Yes. As you know, there's a new book a week. I try to keep up on all of them."

"So you are a believer, then?"

"In the coming 2012 event? Yes."

"You didn't hesitate."

"Should I have? I've not let it be known because of the business implications."

"Which theory do you ascribe to?" Quetzal steepled his fingers.

"I'm open to them all. I'd like to think that December 21, 2012, will usher in a new age of reason."

"You'd like to believe it, but do you?"

"There's no way for me to know."

Quetzal's head bobbed, but Lisa doubted it was from agreement. "I know. In a few moments, I'm going to let you in on something known only to a handful of people. It will be news soon, but right now, it's still under wraps. But first, I want to know why you believe."

"Why? It's not enough that I do?"

"No, it's not. Your answer will tell me if I should let you into the Circle." He paused a moment. "Look, the sad truth is, I don't have room for everyone."

"Room?"

Quetzal's smile turned sad. "Space is limited. I'll explain later, but for now, I need to hear why a wealthy, successful, university-trained man like yourself believes in all this nonsense."

"Nonsense?" Lisa saw Morgan tense. "Are you telling me it's a sham?"

"No, I just wanted to gauge your reaction, and I like what I see. So, why do you believe?"

Lisa couldn't believe what she was hearing. Quetzal was doing her job for her, asking questions she had asked but Morgan had sidestepped.

Morgan took a deep breath and let it out. "Because I don't believe in coincidence. I can't bring myself to believe that a group of people who were so accurate in their astronomy and architecture could be so wrong in their calendar. The fact that people groups hundreds of miles away have similar calendars without ever having contact with the Mayans indicates that ancient people had an insight we don't today.

"I cannot believe that we can pass through an alignment with the galactic center and not experience some kind of influence. Recent Earth events have leant credibility to the Mayan prophecies. Because . . ." Morgan drifted off. Lisa could hear a change in his voice.

"All good reasons, Mr. Morgan. Judging

by the books behind you, I have no doubt that you can give me a hundred reasons, but I need to hear the real reason. I need to hear the reason of your soul."

"I've always been interested in such things —"

"The reason of your soul, Mr. Morgan. The real reason."

Lisa watched Morgan reach for the mouse on the pad next to his right hand, the device he used to click on the Internet link that made the meeting possible.

He's going to disconnect.

A second later, he drew his hand back. "I believe for all those reasons, and a hundred more, but most of all, I believe because my . . . because my wife believed, and she was the smartest person I've ever known."

"That's the first time you've admitted that, isn't it?" Quetzal's words were soft.

"Yes, but you need to know that —"

Quetzal raised a hand. "I know your belief goes beyond that of your dead wife's. I've seen such things before. Her belief was the catalyst for yours. Was your son a believer?"

Morgan shook his head. "No, he was a Christian. A new Christian."

"There's nothing to keep Christians from accepting the truth of the end. They have many prophecies that match those of the

Mayans."

Lisa bit her lip.

"I suppose so. All I know is that God let me down. He let my family die."

"I understand." Quetzal glanced at his watch. "I can see this is an emotional time for you. Would you rather we talk at another time?"

"Every day is emotional for me. A later meeting won't be any different."

"All right, then. I'll need to be brief. I and my supporters have been creating scenarios and palaces of refuge."

"*Palaces* of refuge? Don't you mean *places* of refuge?"

The Cheshire-Cat grin returned. "No, I said it correctly. Our plan is this: One, save as many worthwhile people as possible. Two, create a place for them to live comfortably. And three, create a new society."

Oh, simple. Lisa was finding it more and more difficult to keep quiet.

"What do you mean by 'worthwhile people'?"

"It's an unfortunate phrase, Mr. Morgan, I admit. I'm not certain how else to frame it. I don't mean to indicate that some people have more value than others. We are all equal in the eyes of the god."

A shiver trickled down Lisa's spine.

Quetzal leaned closer to the camera. "We can't save everyone, Morgan. Not even if we had the resources of several nations, but we can save some: people who can bring something to the new society. The people in the Circle are folks like yourself . . . successful, educated, determined, and capable of making a significant contribution to the New World. Your curiosity, adventuresome spirit, education —"

"And my money."

"Absolutely. What we have underway is very expensive — unimaginably expensive. To join us will cost a great deal of money. I'm not trying to trick you or extort you. I'm being up-front."

"How much money?"

"Close to a hundred million before all is said and done."

Andrew Morgan's image on the monitor blinked several times.

"You were expecting me to say more, weren't you? After all, you're a billionaire several times over. I could ask for a billion or two."

"But you know I don't have a billion stuffed in my sock drawer."

Quetzal laughed. Balfour remained quiet and still. "I know a man like you has much of his wealth tied up in stocks, bonds, property, and other businesses. We've dealt with quite a few people in your position, many of them with much greater wealth."

"And what does such a fortune buy for me?"

"Life, Mr. Morgan. Life and opportunity."

"And just how are you going to save my life?"

Quetzal moved his head from side to side. "We have made very careful and exacting plans, but I can't discuss them now. This connection is secure, but Mr. Kinkade thinks I should be a little more paranoid. If you agree, I will send you information for a private meeting. I will say this: Think global. This isn't a movie we're scripting. It's real life, and I want to save yours and anyone else you want to bring with you."

"I can bring someone else?"

"Yes. Some are bringing their immediate families, others are bringing their significant others. Think Adam and Eve."

"You'll fill me in on the details at this meeting?"

"That I will. I will also —"

A cell phone's ringing filled the room.

Oh, no. Lisa reached for her purse and retrieved it. It sounded again.

"Excuse me," Morgan said to Quetzal. He pulled his cell phone from his pocket, punched a button, and said, "Hello."

Lisa silenced her phone.

"I'm sorry," Morgan said, "I'll have to call you later." He listened. "I'm sorry. I'm busy right now." He set the phone down. "I apologize. I meant to turn that off."

"You're a busy man. I understand."

"When will I hear from you again?"

"So you're interested?"

"Very interested."

"Good," Quetzal said. "You'll hear soon. Right now, I have a flight to catch."

"Wait, you promised to tell me something that would be in the news soon."

"Ah, I did. There's an asteroid headed for the earth. It will pass well within the moon's orbit and will probably strike the planet. The European Space Agency and NASA plan a joint press conference soon."

"How do you know this?"

"I have connections, Mr. Morgan. I have many, many connections."

The monitor went black.

"I'm so, so sorry —" Lisa never finished the sentence.

"Give me the phone. Quick! Now."

"You're not going to break it are you? Meant to turn it off —"

Morgan yanked the phone from her hand.

"Hey!"

He dialed. A moment later his own phone rang. He answered but didn't raise it to his ear.

"Why'd you call your own number?"

"These guys have been investigating me, and I don't think they've stayed within the law. That crack about having many connections makes me nervous."

"You think they might look at your phone records?"

"Yeah. As soon as the phone rang, that Balfour guy started dialing his phone. If they do check my cell phone records, they'll see this call near the time your phone rang. It won't be exact, but it'll be close."

Lisa rose. "But it will be my number. They might be able to figure out I'm a reporter."

"How many times have you called me over the last few days? They'll think you're still being annoying. At least I hope they do."

"But you never answered those calls."

"Doesn't matter. You left messages."

"You are a quick thinker, Mr. Morgan."

He looked at her and smiled. "You forgot to say good looking."

Lisa felt herself blush.

He handed back the phone and she scanned the missed-calls register. "My editor. It's kinda late for him to be calling."

She dialed his number.
His words made her stomach burn.

CHAPTER 22

Lisa laid her head back against the seat rest and closed her eyes. Her mind raced like a Formula 1 car, and she did her best to let off the throttle. The voicemail had rattled her. The phone conversation that followed had unraveled every strand of her strength.

Breathe. Slow. Easy. Breathe.

Images flashed on her mind with strobe-like intensity — not memories, but images her mind conjured up. Each mental picture was more garish than the previous.

Shut down. She wanted to shut down her brain, if only for a few minutes. Lisa tried tricks she used when she couldn't sleep: Name all the remaining contestants on this year's *American Idol.* List the main characters in the classic TV show *Star Trek.* Name the presidents of the United States. Usually she fell asleep within minutes, bored by the mental exercise.

It wasn't working.

She felt Morgan's plane bank as it continued its climb. So much had happened in so little time. One moment she was sitting on the floor of Morgan's office, hiding in the shadows just out of range of the webcam on his computer. The next moment she was airborne in one of Morgan Natural Energy's corporate jets.

Of course, things had happened in-between time.

"What's wrong?" Morgan's voice was strong but worried.

"It's . . . it's . . ."

He placed his hands on her shoulders. "Look at me." She didn't. "I said, 'Look at me.' " Lisa looked up from the phone. "What has happened?"

"A young man — a new reporter I was working with — has been attacked. He may die."

Morgan straightened, his face changing from confusion to concern. "He's a friend of yours?"

"Yes . . . well, no, not really. I only met him yesterday. He's the nephew of my editor. I'm supposed to be showing him the ropes. He wanted to come here with me, but I brushed him off." Tears scorched her eyes. "If I had let him come —"

"You can stop that right now." His tone was firm but not harsh, like a father talking to his teenage daughter. "No one wins the what-if game."

"I know . . . I just . . . Oh, I can't even think."

He led her to a guest chair in his office and made her sit. What she really wanted to do was pace for a while and then scream until her lungs came out.

Morgan moved to his desk.

Lisa inhaled deeply and dabbed at her eyes. "I don't know why I'm so upset. I barely know the kid."

"You're upset because you're a good person, and you know violence wounds more than the victim." He picked up the phone and dialed. The moment he tapped the last key, he motioned to her. "Give me the keys to the rental."

"I can't. I need to get back to San Antonio. I want to be there for Rodney."

"Rodney is the name of the reporter?"

"No. He's my editor. Garrett is the nephew."

He nodded several times as if sealing the names in his head. "Bring me your keys."

She rose and did as he said. Her normal pigheadedness had gone missing. Just as she reached him, he spoke into the phone:

"Donny, it's Andrew. I need your help." He explained about Lisa and the rental parked a few streets down. He then said he was headed to the airport. He listened for a few moments and then hung up.

"He'll be here in fifteen minutes. We have a half-hour drive to the airport."

"You're taking me to the airport? My flight doesn't leave until tomorrow afternoon."

"A gentleman always takes his date home."

"We didn't have a date. I came here to wrangle an interview."

He smiled. "Did we or did we not just have a pleasant dinner together?"

"Yes, but —"

"I declare it a date." He started for the office door. "Let's go."

"Wait — you don't have to do this."

He stopped at the threshold. For a moment, Lisa thought she had angered him.

"I know. Now are you coming or not?"

Downstairs, Morgan dropped the keys on a narrow table in the massive foyer and proceeded to lead her through a wide kitchen — one that could make an international chef weep — and into the garage.

The garage held four cars. She saw a red sporty job she couldn't identify, and it looked extremely expensive. There were two luxury sedans, a Cadillac SRX Crossover, and a slick, small SUV. It was the same car he had driven her to the Star of India in.

"Get in," he opened the driver's door.

"Didn't you call your driver?"

"He can't return your rental and drive a limo at the same time. Donny's off duty. I'm not going to ask him to drive us to the airport, then come back for your car, then —"

"He can chauffeur you, and I can drive the rental. You don't even have to go. I'm a big girl."

"Fasten your seatbelt."

"What did your chauffeur say about this?"

"Donny? Well, Donny is a very conscientious man."

Lisa looked at him as the overhead light poured through the windows and painted his face with shadows and light. She swallowed hard.

Morgan punched a button, and the garage door rose behind them. He started the car and backed out.

"What do you mean by 'conscientious'?"

"He's my bodyguard when I allow it. He doesn't like me going into heavily populated areas alone."

"So he's a little angry?"

"A little. Yeah, that's it. He's a little

angry." He turned on the headlights and slowly pulled down the drive. "When I went to Roswell, I insisted on going alone. For a moment, I thought I saw him hanging onto the wing."

The image made Lisa smile. Guilt wiped it away.

As they pulled up to the gate, Morgan tapped the remote, and the gate slid open. Just as it reached its stop, headlights blinded them. The driver had the brights on. Before Lisa could think, Morgan hit the brakes, followed by the automatic door locks. "If I tell you to duck, do it."

"But —"

"Don't argue!"

The lights dimmed and went off. It stopped on the other side of the gate. Morgan had already triggered the gate's remote, and it was closing.

The Cadillac's beams shone on an Acura sedan. The driver's door opened, and a shapely figure emerged.

"I don't believe it." Morgan rubbed his eyes.

"What?"

"It's Candy."

Lisa started to make a wisecrack but decided against it.

Again, Morgan opened the gate and pulled

forward. As he did, he rolled down his window. He stopped by the woman. "Candy, what are you doing here?"

"I want to reconnect. I feel we got off on the wrong foot. I may have been a little too . . . Who is that?"

Lisa felt like she was in a lineup. The woman was about Lisa's age but was far more . . . ample. Night had fallen, but there was enough of a moon to see her features. She was a beauty with angry eyes.

"Candy, this is Lisa. Lisa, this is Candy. Lisa's a reporter."

"A reporter? Right."

Morgan leaned toward the window and spoke in a low voice. "Candy, she is a reporter."

"A reporter who just happens to be interviewing at night . . . and after you turned me down for a date."

"Oh, brother." Morgan made no attempt to hide his frustration. "Candy, she was one of the meetings I told you about."

"I just bet she was."

Lisa decided that a wise woman would just stay out of it. Morgan didn't have that option. She saw his right hand tighten on the steering wheel.

"I'm sorry, Candy. Did we get married on our *one* date, and I missed it?"

"No, I just thought we — you know — connected."

"I'm sorry, Candy, but we didn't, and this little display of yours has made certain we won't."

Lisa heard the gate close behind them.

"Don't say that, Andrew. I didn't mean anything by it. I was just a little hurt that we haven't gone out again."

"It's only been a couple of days, Candy. I don't want to be cruel, but I don't want to be suffocated. Now, if you don't mind, I need to drive Lisa to the airport."

"Of course, I'm sorry. Let's do try again. Let me show you I know how to behave."

When Morgan didn't answer, Candy leaned forward. "It was nice meeting you, Ms . . . Ms . . ."

"Campbell," Lisa said. She didn't return the compliment. There had been nothing nice in meeting Candy with the Claws.

Morgan pulled away, and for a moment Lisa wondered if she shouldn't have given the woman her last name.

Morgan sat in the rear-facing seat opposite Lisa. She had said only a handful of sentences since they boarded the Cessna Citation Sovereign. She appeared to be asleep, but he knew better. Her eyes were closed —

not because she was tired, but because she was shutting out the world. He knew the technique. He still practiced it. An ostrich was no safer when it hid its head in the sand, but at least it didn't have to look at what was coming.

He caught himself smiling. For some reason, staring at her — annoying as she could be — brought him joy. The Indian cuisine dinner they shared had been his attempt at civility. In truth, he hadn't wanted to go, but he didn't want her leaving so angry that his name appeared in publication under the headline BIG OAF IGNORES LOVELY REPORTER. He guessed she was too professional to stoop that low, but it made an easy excuse to justify his action.

Still, he hadn't expected to have a good time. Of course, she turned tenacious again, and he caved to her request to observe the teleconference. *You're slipping.* He looked out the window and gazed at the rhythmic flashes of the aircraft's beacon reflecting on the clouds below.

His eyes drifted back to Lisa again. When she heard of her fellow employee's condition, she had shown real emotion, even though she had known the young man for only a day or two. Anyone would have been shocked by such news, but few would continue to show concern for a near stranger. Morgan didn't want to, but he admired that.

The plane bounced through some clear-air turbulence and settled again into a smooth flight. Lisa didn't budge. A moment later, her lips began to move. Had he not been studying her face so intently, he would have missed it.

Dreaming? A twitch? A few seconds later, he knew what he was seeing: Lisa was praying.

Meredith Roe had watched Morgan drive off with the woman. Lisa Campbell — a reporter, he had said. That could be trouble. Real trouble.

She slipped back into her car, retrieved her cell phone, and made a call.

A short time later, she pulled a backpack from the trunk of her car, slipped her arms through the straps, and climbed the gate.

CHAPTER 23

Lisa hated hospitals. She imagined that was true for most people. Everything about a hospital seemed designed to make people uncomfortable. Privacy was limited to a thin gown that refused to stay closed in back, leaving — at best — one's underwear-clad bottom showing, or — at worst — one's bare fanny hanging out. In an effort to get the most money and use out of each square foot of floor space, strangers were made into roommates. Lisa had been a patient only once, having received the gift of a swollen appendix, and she spent most of the first night listening to an obese woman in the bed next to her alternate between snoring so loud the diffusers in the overhead lights rattled and moaning from pain.

Walking on polished floors, bracketed by depressing green walls, Lisa fought to ignore the smell of disinfectant, hospital food, and odious odors wafting from some rooms —

odors she didn't want to identify.

Her heart fluttered, and her stomach turned. They had parked at the front of the hospital and made their way to the ER. Morgan had insisted on accompanying her. She drove them in her five-year-old Ford Taurus. She wondered when the last time was that Morgan had sat in any vehicle costing less than fifty thousand.

A thickly built male nurse with massive arms in the ER informed them that Garrett Vickers had been moved to ICU. He eyed Morgan and gave him a nod in what she assumed was one gym rat's secret salute to another. He gave them the barest directions on how to find their way to the ICU.

"Can you tell us how he is?" Lisa knew the answer before he spoke it.

"No ma'am. They will be able to tell you more in ICU."

"But —"

"Come on." Morgan took her by the arm. She didn't resist. His touch seemed to pour strength into her.

Down two more shiny halls and a four-floor elevator trip put them next to the Intensive Care Unit. A set of metal doors with a small portholelike window in each marked the boundary between the realm of the healthy and that of the critically ill.

Somewhere beyond those doors lay Garrett Vickers. A white sign with red letters read, No admission. Please check in with the nurse's station.

Lisa's first impulse was to push through the entry and deal with the gatekeepers later, but she reigned in the urge. "How am I supposed to check in with the nurse's station if it's on the other side of the doors?"

"Here."

She turned. Morgan stood by a small metal box. It had a red button with the word call above it.

"Your friend's name is Garrett . . ."

"Vickers. Garrett Vickers."

Morgan started to press the button but pulled back. "Tell me again: What's his uncle's name?"

"Rodney Truffaut. Why?"

"Do you think he'll be in there?"

"Probably."

Morgan nodded. "If Garrett is . . . out of it, they might not let you in, but if family is there . . ."

He pressed the button, and a female voice poured from the tiny speaker. "Yes?"

"Lisa Campbell to see Garrett Vickers."

"Let me check with his nurse."

Morgan shrugged. A moment later, he heard, "Come in." The doors opened automatically.

A shiver raced up Lisa's spine, but her skin felt hot. She felt afraid of what she might see. Her feet stuck to the floor, and then a familiar hand on her elbow started her forward. Morgan led her into the unfamiliar world where the most fragile of patients lay.

No one looked up as they walked in. Lisa felt like a ghost, invisible to everyone around her. Not everyone. A voice to her left said, "Please wash your hands."

Lisa turned. A short Filipino nurse with bright eyes motioned to a metal sink. Yet another sign: ALL VISITORS MUST WASH HANDS BEFORE VISITING PATIENTS.

"Oh, of course."

Morgan leaned close. "This is the age of swine flu, bird flu, duck flu, and armadillo flu."

"Armadillo flu? Really? I didn't know." The moment of humor helped.

"Yup, thickens your skin and turns it a lovely shade of gray."

"Every girl's hope."

They washed, using the pink disinfecting soap that came from a reservoir mounted behind the metal sink. When they finished, the nurse pointed to a set of rooms. "Cubicle 212. Please keep your visit short."

"Of course." Lisa felt the urge to salute, but then she chastised herself. The woman was doing her job and protecting the patients. Lisa had to admit that her emotions were getting the best of her.

She inhaled deeply. "You don't have to be here. You've done so much already."

"I know." Morgan led the way to a glass wall that faced the nurse's staging area. Everything in the ICU was designed to keep the doctors and nurses aware of what was happening at all times.

Morgan stopped two steps from the open door. All the cubicles had doors, but none were closed. Lisa assumed they were shut only while medical personnel treated the patients.

Lisa hesitated at the threshold. Inside was a single bed. A figure she couldn't recognize lay motionless on the white sheets. Several monitors flashed lights and drew lines that meant something to doctors, but not to her. The patient's head was wrapped in thick gauze. Both legs were in casts and elevated above the bed by wires and pulleys. One arm also dangled from medical cables.

Lisa stared at the face. It was swollen and purple. One eye was covered with bandages.

Her hands began to quiver. Was that Garrett? Granted, she had only spent a day with him, but it was enough to know what the man looked like. Whoever it was in the bed barely looked human.

Her eyes moved to a figure seated at the foot of the bed. It was a man hunched over, his face buried in his hands. He didn't move or look up, but Lisa knew who occupied the chair.

Slowly, Lisa approached and whispered, "Rodney?" At work, she called him chief or boss. Here, those appellations seemed out of place.

Truffaut looked up. In the dim light, Lisa could see the man's red eyes. Over the years, Lisa had seen the man in many situations, and he always presented a tough, bulletproof exterior. Now he looked like a lost child — confused, scared, and without direction.

"Lisa." He stood. "I didn't expect to see you . . ."

Lisa took him in her arms and held him. He shook and then wept. Again, Lisa began to pray.

When they parted, Lisa's cheeks were wet. "I got here as soon as I could."

"I know. I didn't expect you to come at all. I just thought you should know." He looked up, and Lisa followed his gaze.

"Oh, I'm sorry. This is Andrew Morgan.

Andrew, this is my boss, Rodney Truffaut.

Morgan offered his hand and the two men shook. "I wish I were meeting you under better circumstances."

"So do I — *The* Andrew Morgan?" He looked at Lisa. "This is the guy you went to interview?"

"Yes. I was with him when you called. He arranged to fly me back."

"Again with the corporate jet? No wonder you got here so soon."

"I like showing off." Morgan moved deeper into the room. He glanced at Garrett. "How bad . . . How's he doing?"

"He's hanging in there." Truffaut seemed reluctant to talk. "Let's step outside for a few minutes." He moved to the only limb of Garrett that didn't have a cast and gently touched it. "I'll be back in a few minutes, Garrett."

They moved through the ICU past the double metal doors to a nearby waiting room. The room was empty. About fifteen Naugahyde-clad seats filled the space. A silent television mounted to a metal support hung from the ceiling. The window provided an unhindered view of one of the parking lots.

"How is he?" Lisa sat, hoping the others would too. They did.

299

"Both legs are broken, and so is his arm. His skull is cracked, one of his cheekbones is fractured, and his right eye socket is shattered. He may lose the eye. Whoever did this stabbed him . . ." Tears began to flow. "Stabbed him four times. He almost bled to death. It's only by the grace of God he didn't die."

Lisa felt sick, as if someone had poured acid into her stomach. "That's horrible. Do the doctors expect . . . I mean . . . I can't even ask the question."

Truffaut gazed at floor as if the answer might be there. "They don't know yet. His injuries could kill him, the shock could do it, and there's infection and a dozen other things to worry about."

"His parents?"

"Down in the cafeteria. The police are still investigating. They've already interviewed me. I was useless and clueless. I have no idea who would do this to him. The cops will probably want to talk to you too."

"Me?" Lisa sat back. "Why would they want to talk to me?"

"They're talking to everyone at the office. We were the last to see him before . . . the incident." He sighed and looked out the window. "You might want to let them know you're here."

"I'll see if they're still around when I leave." Lisa studied her boss. He looked as if he had been awake for a week. "I hate to ask, but is Garrett alert?"

Truffaut shook his head and wrung his hands. "The ER docs told me he had lost a lot of blood. He flatlined several times. Once in the ambulance and twice in the ER. When they got him in a room, they couldn't get a decent blood pressure. They pumped whole blood and whatever else they give a patient in his condition. He came to for a while, but all he could do was to utter one word — Necco."

"Necco?"

Morgan cleared his throat. "It's a candy company. They've been around since the mid-1800s. They make little candy hearts that you see at Valentine's. They also make Necco wafers and a few styles of candy bars."

Lisa stared at Morgan.

"What? My wife liked candy."

"You are a man of many facets, Mr. Morgan."

"Thanks — I think."

Lisa turned back to her boss. "Why would Garrett mention candy?"

"I don't know. Doctors think it was because he had lost so much blood. After what he's been through, it's a wonder he could speak at all."

"He hasn't said anything since?"

Truffaut rubbed the back of his neck. "No. He slipped into a coma. He may not come out of it."

"I don't know what to say, Rodney. I'm at a loss."

"Me too, Lisa. Me too." He rose and walked to the window. "Did he say anything to you? Anything that might explain all of this?"

Lisa leaned back and tried to think. That morning seemed like a month in the past. "No. He came in late — well, you already know that."

"Yeah, I feel bad about that. I really lowered the boom on him. Now I wish I hadn't."

"Don't beat yourself up, Rodney. You had no way of knowing this would happen."

"I know. I know." He began to pace the room. "Anything else?"

"Sorry, no. He came in late, and I gave him a bad time about it. Told him to go see you." She waited, hoping more memories would come forward. "He said he had been working from home and pulled an all-nighter."

"A party?"

"No." Lisa drew the memory forward. "I wasn't paying much attention. I was getting ready to leave for the airport — wait, he did say that he had been doing research for me and that he had something to show me."

Truffaut turned. "Like what?"

"I don't know. He didn't say, and I didn't ask. I just said goodbye and left." Guilt blanketed her. "I guess we both have regrets about today."

"Life is measured by regret," Morgan said softly.

"What?" Lisa turned to him.

"Nothing. Just talking to myself."

The police interview went quickly because Lisa had nothing to offer. She was out of state when the attack happened; no, she didn't know Garrett well — only one day. No, she didn't know where he lived, or if he had enemies, or if he was a drug user, or if he showed signs of being a troublemaker, and he didn't look nervous or frightened to her last time she saw him. No, she didn't know what kind of relationship he had with his family or his uncle Rodney. Lisa felt useless.

One question threw her: "Do you know Ned Birdsong?"

"Never heard of him."

The detective, a round man in a cheap sport coat, stared at her. "What about his girlfriend?"

"Still no."

"His mother?"

"Detective, I've never heard of Ned Birdsong, and I know nothing about him, his family, his work, or his pets. Who is he?"

"He, his girlfriend, and his mother were found dead not far from Mr. Vickers' home."

"That's horrible."

"We searched the house and found several photos in the home that showed Vickers and Birdsong together. You know, hanging out at parties and that kind of thing. We found a similar photo in Mr. Vickers' apartment. It had an inscription: Me and Necco, Spring Break, Ft. Lauderdale.

"Necco?"

"Yes, like the candy. The guy must have been a sugar addict. We found a case of the candy in his bedroom." The detective scratched his belly.

"Rodney told me that Garrett kept saying the name *Necco*." Lisa's brain chugged as it tried to make sense of things. "Who would kill three people and then try to kill Garrett?"

"That's what we're trying to figure out,

Ms. Campbell."

The interview ended, and the detective turned to Morgan, who raised a hand. "Don't bother. I've never met the kid or anyone else involved. I don't know the family. I'm just here to support Lisa."

The detective cocked an eyebrow. "You two a couple?"

Lisa and Morgan spoke simultaneously: "No."

■ ■ ■ ■ ■

PART 2

■ ■ ■ ■

CHAPTER 24

March 21, 2012

Shadows inched westward, cast by large, stone buildings and the bodies of a few thousand tourists. The air smelled of dust, plants, and sunscreen. Children, free of parents too weary to care, chased each other along a stone plaza, weaving between adults as if they were trees. The slight sound of digital clicking punctuated the spring air and mixed with the constant hum of conversation. Overhead, a few marshmallow-white clouds slowly drifted beneath a cerulean sky, amorphous creatures watching the action below.

Morgan wore a faded pair of jeans and a white T-shirt with the emblem of the Oklahoma State Cowboys emblazoned on the front. Next to him stood Robert Quetzal, dressed in ivory Bahama shirt, tan slacks, and leather sandals.

"Entire cities, pyramids, temples, even

houses were built with the cosmos in mind. The four corners of every house are set to the cardinal points of the compass. Did you know that?"

Morgan nodded. "As a matter of fact, I did."

Quetzal smiled. "That's what I like about you, my friend. You're not a follower because of fear, but because of knowledge. You've done your homework."

For some reason, that comment felt uncomfortable, like a poorly tailored suit. He wrote it off as the usual out-of-source feeling he experienced when traveling. Not an unpleasant one, just a sense he was a step or two off. He looked at his watch — a few minutes before 4:00 p.m. "It's almost time."

"Excited?"

"Yes. Maybe *fascinated* is a better word. I've been to many interesting sites around the world, but this is my first time to Chichen Itza. I've avoid it because it seems like a tourist trap."

Quetzal patted Morgan on the shoulder. "I know what you mean. Every year on this date, about fifty thousand people gather here. That's the size of a small city."

Morgan agreed. Somehow Quetzal had been able to have a 20-by-20 foot area near the Pyramid of Kulkulkan cordoned off.

Around the perimeter crowds had gathered into a suffocating mass. He had no idea what Quetzal paid for this privilege, but he was certain there were a few Mexican officials whose wallets were a little more padded than they had been in the past. Sharing the marked-off area was Balfour and a half-dozen men and women Morgan had met on the plane. Balfour spent his time rubbing elbows with the others. Morgan didn't know why, but Quetzal seemed to focus on him.

"Are you familiar with the term *cosmogram?*" Quetzal turned his gaze to the 90-foot tall, stone pyramid. He seemed proud, as if he had built the structure with his own hands.

"It refers to the pyramid's design; the way it reflects the cosmos."

"Exactly." He pointed at the structure. "We're looking at more than a building — we're seeing a centuries-old calendar. Each side has a set of stairs, and each set of stairs has ninety-one steps. Four times ninety-one —"

"Equals 364."

"Add the top platform as the shared, last step, and we have 365. Just like the number of days in the year. The Mayans divided each of the terraces into eighteen segments, which matches the Mayan *haab'* calendar. I tell you Mr. Morgan, no ancient civilization reached the mathematical and astronomical achievements of my people. Oh sure, the Egyptians and other cultures achieved great things, but nothing so precise, so forward-looking as what the Mayans have done."

Morgan felt the man's enthusiasm, which was multiplied the tens of thousands of tourists who filled the area, each one here to see the same event. In the three hours he and the others had walked around the ancient complex, Morgan had heard conversations held in Dutch, Spanish, French, Russian, and a dozen other languages. The words were different, but the sense the conversations carried was the same.

Some were tourists out to see something interesting. Others were worshipers. Morgan was certain he had seen every flavor of New Age adherent. Dressed for the warm first day of spring, the crowds moved from the famous ball courts where Mayan men competed to advance a heavy ball by bouncing it off their hips, attempting to propel the sphere through a large stone ring. The prize? Life for the winners — death for the losers.

"It's starting!" Someone shouted.

Morgan turned his attention from the

milling crowds and scampering, squealing children to the top of the nine-story structure. Every year, on March 21, the shadow of Quetzalcoatl began a slow, serpentine descent from the top of the structure to its base. As the sun set, the shadow lengthened until the leading edge met a sculpted, stylized snake head at the foot of pyramid. Quetzalcoatl the feathered snake god, sometimes called Kulkulkan, was center of Mayan mythology. And he was returning as a moving, undulating shadow. The designers and builders had been so precise in the placement of the large pyramid, and in the positioning of the stairs and terraces, that on this day, and only this day, Quetzalcoatl's shadow would appear along the side one of the four stairways.

"Amazing," Quetzal said. "I've seen it many times, but it never ceases to fill me with awe. My people knew more than any civilization of their day. Do you know what their real legacy is, Morgan? They were predictors, prophets of the future. They didn't have just a prophet or two as you find in the Bible. The entire race was committed to chronicling the past and predicting the future. This is proof of their skill, don't you think?"

"It is impressive."

"It's more than impressive. Other ancient civilizations were fixated on the heavens, but the Mayans went beyond charting the heavens to know when to plant. They predicted future catastrophes." He paused. "You do believe that, don't you, Mr. Morgan?"

Morgan didn't answer at first. He kept his eyes fixed on the descending shadow.

"I know you believe, Morgan. I can sense it. It's one reason I brought you here. I want you to experience the glory of the past so you will have no doubts about the apocalypse of the future."

"I don't need to be convinced. I may not agree with everything you believe, but I agree enough."

"That's good. That's very good."

Minutes passed quickly, and the body of Quetzalcoatl touched the stone snake head carved by people long gone but not forgotten.

Did they know they were changing the future? Morgan convinced himself they did.

CHAPTER 25

December 3, 2012

Morgan sat in the last seat of the Bombardier Challenger corporate jet as it cruised at thirty-three thousand feet. Whenever he traveled on commercial airliners, he flew first class, which put him at the front of the aircraft. Even in his business jet, he preferred being directly over the wings — less bounce that way. However, this was not a commercial jet or his beloved Cessna Citation Sovereign. It was a jet owned by Quetzal and the Maya2012 organization. As well appointed as it was, he preferred his own aircraft and pilots.

The cabin was a little over half full. In addition to himself, there were six other guests. Add Quetzal and Balfour to the count, and the number rose to nine in a cabin designed for fourteen. Each passenger had two things in common. First, every passenger was rich — personal wealth in the

315

top fifty of the United States. Second, each believed the world was about to undergo a dramatic and probably cataclysmic change. They believed it enough to spend millions of their billions.

Morgan knew there were others. Quetzal had been up-front about that, although he never divulged just how many people were taking out 2012 insurance policies. "We have followers the world over," Quetzal had said. "Each brings something special to the table. We will seed the new world with the best and the brightest that humanity has to offer."

Being one of the best and brightest didn't motivate Morgan. He was highly intelligent, but he held no illusions about being the sharpest crayon in the box. Although he studied the sciences, especially geology, he never thought of himself as a scientist. He was, at best, an engineer, and he took pride in that. Of course, his days of oil discovery were long past. The countless hours in the field, flying across the country and around the world, were over. Still, he considered them his best days. Now his greatest physical discomfort came from sitting behind a desk for too long.

He gazed out the small rectangular window and saw nothing but blue water and bobbing ice floes. Winter in that part of the country comes much earlier than it does in Oklahoma.

The trip began with Morgan's flight to Atlanta, where he stayed in the five-star Albert Lloyd hotel near Hartsfield-Jackson Atlanta International Airport. That night, Quetzal treated his guests to a banquet served by the hotel's top chef and staff. Nothing about the pending end of the world was discussed. Little more needed to be said. Once Morgan had signed on and sealed the deal with a ten-million-dollar "contribution," he received weekly updates about events around the world. As the months passed, weekly updates became daily. All information was routed through secure servers that only the "future-nauts" had access too.

Morgan hated the appellation. Someone had jokingly referred to the inner circle of supporters as "future-nauts," and the term stuck.

The next morning, he and the others boarded the Bombardier and took to the air. The aircraft was capable of flying over three thousand miles, especially with a passenger list just sixty percent full. Still, they made a stop in Vancouver to refuel and to clear customs. From there, they flew northwest over Canada and made one more stop in Anchorage, Alaska. They took time to dine and stretch their legs before starting the next leg of the journey. A little over three hours into the trip, the pilot's voice poured from the intercom system. "Lady and gentlemen, I thought you might like to know that we've crossed over the International Date Line. It is now yesterday."

The comment sent titters through the cabin. Morgan found it amusing but not worth drawing his attention from the rolling, ice-dabbled ocean below.

His mind ran to Lisa, as it often did. The last sixteen months had passed quickly, and their relationship had grown but had reached a stalemate. Like a fish kept in too small of an aquarium, it just refused to grow any larger.

Heaviness pressed on his chest, which was something that was happening more and more often. He wasn't looking for a new love, and he had made that clear to Lisa. She had made it clear that she could not love a man who rejected Christ. They settled on being friends.

"The party is at the front of the plane." The voice, nasal but confident, drew Morgan's attention from the window. Charles Balfour slipped into the rear-facing seat opposite Morgan. "We have champagne, beer, wine, and an exceptionally good burgundy."

"No thanks." Morgan hoped his smile came across as genuine. "I notice that you're not drinking."

Balfour chuckled. "Very observant. Alcohol doesn't agree with me. I have a sensitive stomach."

"Yeah, me too."

Balfour tipped his head to the right. "Really? I'm sorry. I forgot. You have a problem with — sorry, that's a lousy way to begin a sentence."

Morgan wasn't surprised that the thin man knew of his previous battles with booze. "That's all right. I'm not ashamed of it. Truth is, I describe myself as a sober alcoholic, but I was probably just drowning my grief. Some people do that. I may not be a textbook drunk, but I got close enough to see it."

"Well, that's one problem I'll never have. The stuff makes me puke."

Balfour had always come across as a refined gentleman. Hearing him use the word *puke* made Morgan smile. Balfour raised the corners of his mouth too. "I did plenty of that, but it wasn't until the morning after."

"As you can tell, Charles Atlas has nothing to fear from me. I'm a tad puny."

"Charles Atlas? That's an old reference."

Balfour shrugged. "When I was a kid, I read his ads about body-building. Even sent away for his material. Didn't work. My father used to say God gave me less body and more brain than He gave others."

"Your father was a religious man?"

"Not at all. He was a medical doctor and believed only in what could be measured and tested. For him, *God* was just another word to sling around." Balfour shifted his small frame in the leather seat. "What about you? You a spiritual man?"

"No."

Balfour remained quiet. Morgan suspected he was waiting for a longer answer. Morgan didn't feel obliged.

"I can't speak from firsthand experience, but losing loved ones can squash a man's faith."

"To be honest, Mr. Balfour, I didn't have much faith to begin with. Never saw much sense in it."

"We've known each other — albeit mostly over distance — for many months now. Isn't it time you started calling me Charles?"

"Sure. If you want."

"I insist. We are going to be partners in the New World, Andrew. We need to be comfortable with each other."

"It takes me a while to bond with others."

"Understandable. Understandable." Balfour folded his hands on his lap. The roar of the engines filled the silence between them.

Morgan wondered what the man really wanted. At first, he thought Balfour was just being a good host. Now, he sensed there was motive behind the visit. Morgan decided to wait him out.

Finally, Balfour leaned forward and spoke in low tones. "I'm wondering if you've chosen who you will be bringing with you. You know . . . when the time comes."

"No. I may not bring anyone."

"You're entitled to do so. Your contribution level makes space available for almost anyone."

"Almost?"

Again, Balfour leaned back. "By now, you should know that we are a . . . careful bunch."

"Paranoid comes to mind."

An ear-to-ear grin spread across Balfour's face. "Yes, just like you, we're paranoid. Considering what we've undertaken, paranoia is a requirement."

Morgan couldn't argue the point. It was one of the things that attracted him to Quetzal and Balfour. If they hadn't been

321

overly cautious, he would have doubted their sincerity.

Balfour drummed his fingers on the arm of the seat. "I would have thought you might want to bring Ms. Campbell with us, or perhaps Candy."

"How do you know about them?"

"We never interfere in the private lives of our people, but we do need to be cautious."

"You've been spying on me?"

"Of course. You're not really surprised, are you?"

Morgan's jaw tensed and then relaxed. "No, not really."

"We have too much at stake here, Andrew. For example: Suppose you wanted to bring with you someone with a terminal disease or a mental illness. How would we care for them? We have made provisions for some medical care, but some things will be out of reach. So, yes, we monitor — without invading privacy, mind you — our participants."

"Candy and I have dated on and off, but that's it." Morgan hated to admit it, but loneliness drove him to see the woman again. In subsequent dates, she showed herself to be more intelligent than she let on.

"Most men want a dumb woman, Andrew.

I made a mistake thinking you were like others."

Once he noticed that she had put away the airhead persona, Morgan found Candy to be more likeable. Still, there was one problem: Even in Candy's presence, his thoughts would run to Lisa. He hated that.

Balfour continued. "Have you spoken to Ms. Campbell about joining you?"

"She's not interested."

"Not interested in survival?"

Morgan rubbed his eyes. "She thinks it's all nonsense."

"Ah, we know the type, don't we?" Balfour bent forward, and Morgan wondered if the man was this antsy at home. "Well, you're under no requirement to bring anyone. There are several who are coming alone — some even have families." He shook his head. "I don't know what they're thinking, but I'm not a counselor. Anyway, it's all up to you. But time is running out."

Balfour stood. "I leave you to your thoughts. Perhaps you'll feel like joining the festivities. It's a great way to pass time. Did I mention there is shrimp?"

"No, you didn't."

"Come and spend some time with your fellow 'future-nauts.' "

Morgan fought off the urge to cringe.

Lisa watched Garrett work his way through the bullpen and felt a fresh wave of guilt sweep over her. Over the months, she had watched him slowly heal. It took three months before he recovered from the broken bones in his legs and one arm. The recovery process had been made longer by the dozen surgeries and weeks of physical therapy. Plastic surgery reconstructed his fractured cheekbone and eye socket. More than once, he had confided to her that he feared looking like Quasimodo, with one eye situated inches lower than the other. Medical science had saved him that fate. He looked very much as he did that day she sprinted from the office to the airport, leaving him behind to ponder what to do with his new information.

The swelling and casts were gone, but not the limp that required the use of a cane. Doctors assured him that he would not need the cane for much longer, but Lisa wasn't so sure.

Her guilt was misplaced. She knew that, but she had a hard time fighting it off. Morgan had told her several times that she felt guilty because Christians enjoyed the feeling. To feel lowly and useless made them feel spiritual. No matter how she argued against the claim, he stuck to his guns. It infuriated her, but she refused to give up.

Garrett hobbled down the narrow aisle formed by the bullpen's rows of desks. She watched him, turning her eyes away to disguise her gaze. Step, limp, lean on the cane — step, limp, lean on the cane. He held a file in his free hand. The clacking, clicking of computer keyboards filled the open space, something she seldom noticed. Today, it seemed unusually loud. Perhaps it was because business had been good over the past year, and the number of reporters had doubled.

Garrett pushed into Lisa's area and plopped down in the chair beside her desk. "Fine."

"What?"

"I'm fine."

"I didn't ask how you were doing." She pushed back from the desk.

"You were going to. You always do. If I walk away for an hour, you ask how I'm doing when I return. You're still fighting misplaced guilt."

"Now you're a psychologist?"

"Laugh if you want. It's just another defense mechanism."

"Ooh. Another big college word." Lisa softened the jab with a grin. "Fine, I'll never ask again."

"Good."

"So how are you doing?"

Garrett lowered his head and shook it like a father dealing with an uncooperative child. "I'm frustrated. Necco's killer is still out there, and the police aren't doing anything about it."

"I'm sure they're doing their best."

"Ha. The whole thing is about to become a cold case file. Necco deserves better." He paused. "So do I."

"You know I'm with you on that. That's why we're still poking around in things. Did the police talk to you today?"

"For about five minutes. It doesn't take long to say, 'Nothing new, kid. We'll let you know.' "

Lisa nodded. The story had been the same for months. They had run down every lead they could, tracked the case as much as the police would allow, and had no better ideas.

"So when do we let go?"

"Never." Garrett propped his cane against the deck. "We both know it has something to do with Quetzal and his crazies."

Lisa picked up a pencil and rolled it between her fingers. "We've been over this a hundred times since . . . ."

"My beating? Yes we have, and I'm sticking to my guns. I owe it to Necco, his girl, and his mom."

"Garrett, I don't know what else to do. We don't have the resources the police have."

"I may have something better."

"Is that a fact?" She set the pencil down. "What have you been up to?"

"Now that I'm up, around, and in my right mind, I've decided to take things in my own hands."

"Who says you're in your right mind?" Lisa lifted an eyebrow.

"Funny. You know what I mean. Between the trauma, the pain meds, and everything else, I haven't been myself."

"Are you telling me you're starting to remember being beaten?"

Garrett frowned. "No. Just bits and pieces, but nothing of use. The trauma, the coma, and the meds have pretty much obliterated that part of my brain. It's a blessing, I suppose, but it's also frustrating." He set the file on Lisa's desk and pushed it toward her.

Lisa pulled it close and then opened it. Her eyes darted over the contents. Her stomach dropped like a free-falling elevator. "Garrett, there's a good chance that this is what got you in trouble in the first place."

"I don't care. I have to get busy. Too much time has passed. Before, there was very little I could do. Now I can at least do brain work."

"I'm not sure I understand what I'm seeing." The file contained only five pages, but most of it was gibberish.

"I want it to look that way for a reason. To get this, I may have stretched a few laws."

Lisa looked up from the file. "Stretched or broken?"

"I think I'm still in the neighborhood of misdemeanors."

"Just what am I looking at?"

Garrett leaned toward her and lowered his voice. "Before I tell you, I need to know you're with me on this."

"Haven't I proven that to you over this last year?"

His expression softened. "You've been golden, but I need to know you're going to stand by me."

"That depends. Are your actions going to hurt someone?"

"If God is listening to my prayers."

"Garrett!"

"I'm serious. I don't mean physical harm. I want justice for Necco and me."

"I don't want to break any laws." Lisa felt

as if the moral ground under her feet was shifting.

"I'm not asking you to break any laws, but you will have to trust me."

"You know, they'll take away your cane in prison."

"I'm not doing anything prison-worthy."

"Is that opinion from you or the police?"

Garrett didn't answer.

CHAPTER 26

At this latitude and at this time of year, darkness came early and stayed. The moon was in its last quarter, well on its way to being a dark new moon. It cast very little light through the clear, cold air.

The Bombardier circled an airfield situated in a low-lying valley. Two snowcapped mountain ranges bracketed the field like bookends. Snow covered much of the terrain, reflecting the moon's dim glow spaceward. As the jet descended, Morgan could see its beacons washing the ground below. Not long before, they had passed from the North Atlantic over the Kamchatka Peninsula. The pilot dutifully announced the names of the volcanoes below. Morgan forgot the names as soon as he heard them. After Mexico, he was just glad that Quetzal had been wise enough not to set up shop near several potentially active volcanoes. They were headed across the peninsula.

The field below was not well known, at least to Morgan. He and the others had been briefed on their exact destination once they left Anchorage. Below was Sharomy, a former military base in Kamchatka Krai, Russia. Once it served two roles: one, as a traffic diversion airfield for the Petropavlosk-Kamchatsky Airport, and two, as a staging area for airstrikes against the United States. That had been during the Cold War, when Russia was the steering wheel of the former Soviet Union. When the Cold War had permanently warmed, such bases became useless and expensive. Especially expensive to a country in the throes of economic collapse, internal problems, failing infrastructure, and major crime problems. From the first pass over the field, Morgan could tell the runway had to be better than 10,000 feet in length. One didn't spend millions of rubles on a runway that length unless they were planning on landing big birds — like long-range bombers.

From the air, the pair of long runways with a three-sided tarmac and hardstands for aircraft formed a shape that reminded Morgan of a tomahawk — apropos for a Mayan priest.

Everyone had returned to their seat and

waited for the landing gear to touch down. The sooner the better for Morgan. He had grown weary of traveling.

Dr. Michael Alexander should have been happy. After all, the news was great. He had been up all night crunching numbers, talking to key astronomers around the world, and sifting data. The 2012 GA12 asteroid had become his baby to watch over — at least at the ESA. The leaders of the European Space Agency trusted him. His credentials were impressive, and his work was without blemish. They trusted him and his calculations. For the last year, he wished they hadn't. Every night, he took the knowledge that a rock the size of small mountain had the earth in its sights. Moving at speeds measured in hundreds of miles an hour, the prospective impact was quickly branded a world killer.

Of course, there had been other such objects that, for a short time, looked as if they were on target with the earth. Each of those had missed by a wide margin, never coming closer than a couple hundred thousand miles.

But Alexander was a pragmatist. He didn't believe in luck. He was a numbers man. Even so, he caught himself slipping into sloppy math, and one math myth kept percolating to the top of his mind, especially as he lay alone in his bed. If all the rest missed, then the odds were greater that the next space rock would hit Mother Earth right on the nose. In freshman statistics, he was taught that if a man flips a coin, the odds of it landing heads up was the same as it was for it landing tails up. If the man flipped the coin again, the odds did not change: They remained fifty-fifty. That was true for each individual flip.

But Dr. Alexander wasn't dealing with a fifty-cent piece. He was dealing with millions of tons of rock. In the face of that truth, fifty-fifty were lousy odds. Sooner or later, a near miss was going to become a direct hit.

What had amazed Alexander was the success of the conspiracy of secrecy. Although the asteroid was large, it could not be seen with the naked eye. Space and ground telescopes could locate it easily enough, but they knew exactly where to look. The populace had no clue, and no country was willing to tell its citizens. Why would they? There was still some hope that the thing would zip by and continue on along its very elliptical orbit of the sun.

Alexander and other scientists had exchanged heated views about what should and shouldn't be said. In the end, every head of government made it clear that a panicked population would not change anything. The US alone had 350 million people to worry about. The rest of the world approached seven billion. How does one safely shelter that many people? It couldn't be done, and therefore it was agreed that it shouldn't be tried.

Oh, heads of state would be fine. After all, the president of the US had his Mount Washington designed to protect him and the leaders of his country from nuclear attack and the nuclear winter that would follow. Millions would die, but the government would continue — even if it had millions fewer to govern. Other countries had similar arrangements. Those that didn't were just out of luck.

Keeping such a large secret required more than a polite request. The US and the European Union had made it clear that anyone who leaked word of the possible disaster would be held liable for any property damage, injury, and deaths that came about from a global panic. Thousands could die from such turmoil. That would be a lot of murder charges.

Then there was the bribery. Worried leaders had thought ahead and arranged safe bunkers for the people in the know who knew how to keep their mouths shut. It might be scientifically unethical, but that was a small deterrent when it came to saving one's spouse and children.

Some of his colleagues couldn't stand the strain. Over the last few months, more than a dozen astronomers, physicists, geologists, and meteorologists — all working to estimate the damage the impact would cause — had disappeared or committed suicide. At least, Alexander *hoped* it was suicide that had taken their lives.

Last year, shortly after he let his superiors know of the "Hammer of God" — a name taken from the science fiction book penned by Arthur C. Clarke in 1993 — Alexander began to suspect he was being followed. Like Mary's little lamb, wherever Alexander went, the dark sedan was sure to go.

He no longer trusted his phone. That's why the next call had to be made on a special device delivered by a man named Jaz. Inside the package was the latest Iridium satellite phone. Small scratches on the back casing told him the device had been modified. He was pretty sure it could call only one number, and it had been encrypted.

It was time to deliver the good news. He dialed a number he had committed to memory and waited. His stomach twisted, and his face grew warm. Why should he be so nervous? He was about to deliver good news. The Hammer of God would miss the earth by better than one hundred and fifty thousand miles. That would make anyone happy.

Right?

"Coming?" The only woman on the trip pulled on an orange parka so bright that Morgan felt the need for sunglasses. They were all wearing them — all but Morgan. He had yet to rise from his seat. The woman had long mahogany hair, which she wore in a style that would have looked good a few decades earlier. Her hair pooled in the hood of the parka. Morgan only knew her by reputation: She was known as the iron-willed woman who returned a faltering computer giant to a streamlined money-making machine. She had cut two thousand jobs, closed two overseas plants, and sued a half-dozen competitors until she achieved her goal.

"I'm coming. I'm old and slow."

"Yeah, right. I got fifteen years on you easy, and I don't mind it. Of course, it's not one's age that matters."

She lifted a suggestive eyebrow. Morgan looked away. Sonya Ballios, CEO of Ballios Computers, was known for aggressive personal habits as well as business ones. In the last years, she had led her company into the third spot in sales of all similar companies, and she made no secret that she would not be happy until the likes of Hewlett Packard, Dell, and Apple were her footstools. Still, she had time to marry three times, destroy those husbands, and move on to a chain of other men — each now bobbing in her wake. Morgan had no desire to join her parade.

Morgan gave a friendly smile he didn't feel, and he pulled on his parka.

"Don't you want to know what does matter?" She took a step toward him.

He had watched her hit on the other men, married or not. "No. I've got other things on my mind."

"Me too." The other eyebrow went up.

The booming voice of Quetzal rolled down the cabin. "Everyone suited up? It's a tad chilly out there. At the moment, it is a toasty twenty degrees."

A chorus of groans filled the space. Morgan understood the sentiment. During his junior year of college, he had traveled to be the best man at his friend's wedding — in Minot, North Dakota — in mid-January. He had traveled to many states, but none in the extreme north of the country. He had brought a light jacket, which he donned after the plane landed. He still remembered the amused looks on the faces of his fellow passengers, but he didn't understand it until he stepped from the plane and walked to the small, freestanding terminal. The wind-chill factor was thirty below. The event created a lasting respect for cold.

Quetzal spoke over the grumbling. "You won't be outside long. Just long enough to cross the tarmac to the waiting SUVs. We have about an hour's drive. The cars will be warm." He paused. "Ready?"

There were a few grunts.

The pilot and copilot moved from the cockpit, donned their heavy coats, and then the copilot opened the door. Cold air rushed into the craft and was greeted by several obscene remarks. One of which came from Sonya. The copilot deplaned.

"Watch your step, please." The pilot, a tall, narrow man with gray hair, was courteous and cheerful. Morgan imagined the man was looking forward to some time away from the cramped cockpit.

Morgan was the last to leave the warmth

of the business jet behind, and he stepped into a lively breeze that clawed at his face with icicle fingers. Before him, the passengers stepped quickly along the concrete runway lit by the landing field lights and toward a row of three large, black, foreign-made SUVs.

"They're Russian UAZ Patriot SUVs." Robert Quetzal stood just behind Morgan. "The Russians have a long way to go to match American or Japanese craftsmanship. Of course, considering the state of their economy, it's a wonder they can make anything. And a bad economy for them turned out to be a good thing for us."

Morgan faced the man and saw a gleam in his eye. "Sometimes the successful man must build on the broken dreams of another," Quetzal said.

"That's a bit harsh. Who said that?"

Quetzal grinned. "I did. And you're right, it is harsh. I didn't say the successful man should *destroy* the dreams of others. Just that he must, at times, build where others failed. The Russians need money, and we need something they have — which is why we're here. Shall we go?" He motioned down the stairway. "Parka or not, I'm cold."

"Must be that Mayan blood."

Quetzal nodded. "Must be."

Morgan had descended two steps when an electronic chiming caught his attention. He turned in time to see Quetzal pick up a thick phone. Morgan recognized it as a satellite phone.

Quetzal recognized the voice immediately. "This is an awkward time." He started to use the man's name, but the pilot and Morgan were still in earshot. He walked down the jet's aisle, his back to the pilot. He turned in time to see the pilot motion to the cockpit and then slipped into the control area, closing the door behind, giving his boss the privacy he wanted.

"I'm sorry, Mr. Quetzal, but I thought you'd want to know."

"Know what, Dr. Alexander?"

"We have new numbers on the Hammer of God. There is good news."

Quetzal doubted the news would be good. "Tell me and do it quick. I've got people turning into popsicles."

"Really? Where are you?"

"It doesn't matter, Dr. Alexander." The man was stalling. "What have you found?"

"Our early calculations about the asteroid were less than accurate. I mean, they were as accurate as they could have been at the time."

Quetzal closed his eyes. "It's going to miss us?"

"Yes."

"How far?"

"Most likely, it will slip by unnoticed, having come no closer than 150,000 miles. Still inside the moon's orbit, but far enough away to present no danger."

"I see. Who knows about this?"

"Just the inner circle of scientists assigned to this. Only my superiors here know. I can't speak for NASA or the Japanese space agency."

"When did you reach this decision?" Quetzal worked to keep his tone even.

"Earlier today."

"Keep a lid on it."

There was a long pause. "What?"

"Keep a lid on the information."

"How?" Quetzal could hear the tension in the man's voice. "I don't have that kind of influence. Besides, it will be a relief to the world."

"Don't be an idiot. The world doesn't know. And how do you think people are going to respond when they learn that their countries kept a potentially life-ending disaster secret? There'll be riots in the streets, and your picture will be on the protest signs."

"That might be an overstatement."

"Use your head, Dr. Alexander. The only reason you're calm about this is that you were in on the discovery and deception."

"I didn't deceive anyone."

"You withheld information."

The man stammered. "We let the proper people know. After that, it was out of my hands."

"Which makes you a coconspirator with them. Look, keeping it secret made sense. It still makes sense. I kept it secret. I didn't want to cause a panic any more than you did. I'm trying to save lives here — trying to assure that humanity has a future."

"What do you want from me? I've done everything you've asked — everything within my power to do. You were the first one I called when the asteroid was discovered and its preliminary track determined. What do you want me to do? Push the planet into its path?"

Quetzal tightened his jaw so hard that his teeth ached. The asteroid had brought in more money than he could have hoped for. Sure, the meteor in Arizona had helped, El Popo near Mexico City had drawn the attention of the fence-sitters, as did a half-dozen other disasters, but the Hammer of God was a godsend. Even those who had only moderately bought into the story had taken to that bit of information like trout to cheese. The one thing he wanted to avoid was a few dozen billionaires with banks of lawyers asking for their money back.

Quetzal inhaled deeply and forced his shoulders to relax. "Look, Dr. Alexander, I know it sounds like I'm blaming you, but I'm not. I've been traveling nonstop for months and am well beyond tired. I just don't want my people to get the wrong idea. The end is coming December 21, 2012. If not by asteroid, then by something else."

"We still have a deal, right?"

"Yes, Alexander, we still have a deal. On December 20, I'll transfer two million euros to your private account."

"It's three million euros, Mr. Quetzal, and considering things, I would like it a week earlier."

"You don't trust me?"

"No. I need a safety net. I don't want you disappearing on me. In fact, you'd better make it December 10. That gives me time to call all the people you don't want me to call if you don't deliver."

If the astronomer were standing in front of him, he would slowly crush the man's trachea. "Agreed. Say, how is that grandchild of yours? You call her Bluebird, right?

I hope she's been able to get the medical care she needs."

"Watch yourself, Quetzal."

"I always do. She lives in Trachoma, doesn't she?"

Dr. Alexander switched off the phone and stared at the photo of his four-year-old granddaughter, snuggled beneath white hospital sheets. Her smile was weak but present. She held the teddy bear he had sent. Next to her sat her mother. Even in the photo, he could see the moisture in her eyes.

Kidney transplants were difficult to find for children so young.

Morgan stood a short distance away from the aircraft stairs and watched Quetzal pace the empty aircraft. Even through the small windows, he could see the man was upset.

"This way, Mr. Morgan." Balfour appeared at his side. The parka he wore hung on his thin frame like a parachute. "You'll be warmer in the car."

CHAPTER 27

Morgan climbed into the backseat of the UAZ Patriot and reached for the safety belt. Before he could snap it in place, Balfour slipped into the front seat.

"Good evening." The Russian driver spoke English through an accent that made Morgan wonder how many marbles the man had in his mouth.

"Privyet," Morgan said.

The Russian turned and smiled.

"You speak Russian? I'm impressed." Sonya anchored the other end of the rear seat.

Between them was the very bald, very abrasive, and very brilliant Edward P. Rickman, president and CEO of E.P.R. Cellular, the newest cellular phone company. He was known to leave more debris in his wake than a category-five hurricane.

"I'm fluent in at least ten words."

The crack made Rickman laugh. "That's

more than me."

Balfour turned to face the three in the back. "All of our hosts speak English. In Europe and Asia, almost everyone is bilingual or trilingual. What's it say about our country that so few can speak more than one language?"

"That we're focused." Rickman didn't miss a beat.

Morgan saw the smile on the driver's face disappear. The one on Balfour's face remained but looked painted on.

Morgan didn't want to look at Rickman. He turned his gaze out the side window but saw only his reflection. He hadn't noticed when he entered, but the windows were opaque.

"I see you've noticed," Rickman said. "It appears that we're not meant to take in the sights."

"It's so dark outside," Sonya said, "we wouldn't be able to see much anyway."

Balfour's smile brightened. "We're still in secrecy mode. The windows are to keep people from looking in, not to keep you from looking out."

Rickman snorted. "We were just outside in full view of whoever wants to take a gander."

"The airport is secured, and security

swept it before we landed —"

"Then why the windows?" Rickman looked satisfied, as if he were the only kid in class who had seen the teacher's error. Morgan wished the driver would turn off the overhead light so he wouldn't have to see Rickman's face.

"Ease up, pal," Morgan said. "Let the man answer."

"What?" Rickman turned in his seat and leaned toward Morgan, invading his personal space. "Who do you think you are?"

Slowly, Morgan turned his head until his nose was just an inch from the bald man. "I'll tell you who I'm not, Eddie. I'm not one of your timid, browbeaten toddies. You might get away with intimidating your employees, but all you achieve with me is to make me seriously angry."

"Now children, no need to try and impress me." Sonya's voice was almost musical. "Try to remember that there's a lady present."

Rickman swiveled her direction and was about to speak, but she cut him off. "Careful, Mr. Rickman. The snide remark rattling around in your empty head is liable to get you slapped so hard your mother will scream."

The driver erupted with laughter. "Ha! I

love Americans."

Balfour maintained an even keel, and Morgan admired him for it. The man had to be as weary as he was, if not more. "As I was about to say, the airport is secured as is our destination. However, we will be passing through several small towns. Three identical cars might attract some attention. We don't want people taking photos. We promised to keep your identity concealed."

"What about Chuckles here?" Rickman pointed at the driver.

"He knows how to keep a secret, and we're paying him enough to make sure he does."

"No worries," the driver said, and started the car.

A moment later, they pulled into the darkness.

The road was smooth. For some reason, Morgan had expected a serpentine, pothole-plagued dirt path, as if they were traveling in the deep wilderness. He could see enough through the windshield to know that the road was narrow and paved in a new coat of macadam. Forward was the only view available, and the empty road soon bored Morgan. Even the towns they passed through were dark and the streets empty.

The trip had taken its toll. Rickman

slumped in his place and rested his head on the seat. Sonya leaned against the door, her hand serving as a pillow. She blamed the wine she consumed on the flight as the cause for sleepiness, but Morgan guessed that the stress of pending disaster and the long trip had drained her. It had certainly drained him.

Occasionally, he would glance over his shoulder and see the headlights of the other cars in the convoy. No one seemed to be in a hurry. In the front seat, Balfour sat erect, his eyes boring into the night.

Morgan had traveled abroad many times but never under these conditions. He was having trouble believing that he was at Kamchatka — having just landed at a former military field — and was now allowing himself to be chauffeured to an unknown destination. He knew something of his destination, but details were kept under wraps. He had come to trust Quetzal and Balfour, but each time he thought of that, a sense of disquiet swept through him. He comforted himself with the thought that scores of other people, each as successful and bright as he, had found the men and their organization trustworthy.

Something caught his eye. A light appeared in front of them. At first, Morgan thought they were driving head-on into an oncoming train. The driver continued forward and the light grew. Still, it seemed unusual.

"What's that?"

Morgan glanced at Sonya, who had awakened. He heard her smack her lips. Post-drinking aftertaste. Morgan remembered what that was like.

"A light." Rickman had come to.

"Ya think?" Apparently Sonya wasn't one of those people who woke up chipper. "Looks weird."

Balfour shifted to face them. "It's our destination. You're seeing a light in the entrance tunnel. The Russians placed it well back so it wouldn't draw attention from above."

"You mean God?" Rickman said.

"US bombers," Balfour explained. "Remember, Cold War and all that."

"I knew that."

Morgan chose to keep quiet.

The driver slowed, and Morgan leaned forward, looking around Balfour's head. "A bomb shelter."

"Oh, no, Mr. Morgan. We promised you much more than that. This is no bomb shelter, but it was designed to withstand a direct hit."

"So it is a bomb shelter." Rickman squinted at the light.

"It's a COG, Mr. Rickman, a 'continuation of government' facility. Just like the US has Mount Washington and several other places where government leaders can wait out an attack, so the Russians have theirs. This is just one such facility and was designed to harbor military leaders in the eastern part of the USSR — when there was a USSR. There are others, including one near Moscow. Those aren't available. The Russian government doesn't trust your government very much."

"The feeling's mutual," Rickman said.

"Then why have they let us use this one?" the driver asked.

"Money," Morgan said. "It's one reason we've been pouring millions into this."

"Well said, Mr. Morgan. You're exactly right. The end of the Cold War, the fall of the Communist government, and the economic upheaval of the last few years have put the Russians in a financial hole. I don't need to tell business leaders like you about the problems Greece, Italy, France, and our own country have endured when the global economy went belly-up."

"Cost me a fortune in stocks." Rickman shook his head. "That's money I'll never see again."

"You're not alone in that," Sonya said. "When money gets tight, computer sales go in the toilet."

Rickman nudged Morgan. "As I recall, only oil barons made money in those early years."

"Yup. My mattress is stuffed with hundred dollar bills." He let the sarcasm slip in. "We did okay. I lost a lot in the market as well, but oil held its value. I didn't miss any meals."

The car pulled into a concrete tunnel that reminded him of a large pipe. The headlights cast enough sidelight for him to see the heavy foliage that concealed the entrance.

The feel of the drive changed, and Morgan assumed they had pulled from the asphalt road.

Balfour pointed to his left. "The road continues around the mountain. Seen from the air, it would look like any other roads weaving through the area." A short distance into the tunnel, the car stopped.

"You'll want to see this." Balfour opened his door, and Morgan did the same.

The first thing Morgan noticed was the size of the tunnel, something he had trouble gauging from the vehicle. He estimated the tunnel to be a hundred or more feet across.

It was a half tube, which meant the ceiling was at least five stories over his head. A set of track ran down the middle of the floor. He assumed it had been used to move supplies and equipment deeper into the facility. Everything looked cleaner than it should.

The two other cars in the caravan pulled into line, and the others started to exit. Quetzal drove the third vehicle. Those in the car were laughing as they stepped onto the hard, bare floor. Apparently, he had been entertaining them.

He walked to the front of the first car, breezing past Morgan. His baritone voice echoed off the rigid walls. "Welcome, friends. Welcome to your salvation."

At first, no one spoke, then Rickman — who apparently couldn't leave any silence unmolested — said, "This? This is it? This is what I forked over millions of dollars for? A big, concrete sewer pipe?"

For a moment, Quetzal's smile faltered, then brightened. "Of course not, Mr. Rickman. If I were trying to swindle you, I wouldn't have traveled all this distance to lock myself away with the people I conned. This is just the entrance. Watch."

He stepped up to a metal switchbox about the size of a deck of playing cards and pulled away the cover. Inside was a keypad and five small glass plates. "Anyone want to guess the code?"

No one spoke. A few seconds later, Morgan said, "One-two-two-one-two-zero-one-two."

Quetzal let loose a laugh. "Right, Mr. Morgan." He entered the code.

Rickman looked at him. "How did you know that?"

"Think about it."

Sonya huffed. "December 21, 2012."

"Ah. Of course." Rickman seemed embarrassed. Maybe he was human after all.

The moment Quetzal hit the last button, the tiny glass panes began to glow. He placed the fingers of his right hand on the sensors, one finger per pane. A moment later, a massive metal door emerged from the floor at the front threshold and continued upward until it had sealed the party inside.

"Impressive, isn't it?" Quetzal pointed at where they had entered. "That blast door can withstand attack by bombs, missiles, and anything else you can imagine. Now watch." He turned, and the back wall of the tunnel began to move, descending into the floor just as the entrance door had risen. It took two minutes for the opening to clear.

"Now, my friends, prepare to be amazed."

Quetzal marched toward the opening.

They crossed the threshold into which the second blast door had descended. A narrow metal sill piece covered the gap in the floor. Morgan stepped over it. The room on the other side was two to three times as wide and twice as tall as the entry tunnel. Like the entrance, the foyer was made of concrete. On the walls hung plaster reliefs, depictions of Mayan iconography and life. The art was stunning but still seemed out of place for the environment. Track lighting was mounted to the wall above the three-dimensional cast, flattering light on the surfaces. A dozen life-size figures stood on two-foot-high pedestals, each wearing Mayan ceremonial dress. Morgan could have sworn the lifelike eyes were following them.

"Wow," Sonya said. "Who's your decorator?"

"Do you like it?" Quetzal seemed pleased.

"It's stunning," she said.

Rickman grunted. "I hope our money went to better use."

Quetzal faced the man, his face expressionless. "The art came from my pocket, Mr. Rickman . . . not yours. If you're unhappy with the way I'm running things, I can have one of the drivers take you back to the airport, and you can wait for us there. If you want to back out, now is the time to say so. Once we move on, there will be no turning around."

"No need." Rickman took a step back. "I'm just a little tired — a little grumpy. It's all very lovely. Carry on."

Morgan saw Sonya grinning.

Quetzal stepped up to Rickman. For a moment, Morgan expected their host to slam a fist in the man's face. Instead, he smiled broadly. "You're going to love the next part." He slipped an arm around the executive's shoulders. "This way, my friends."

Quetzal took the lead again and mimicked a museum docent. "And we're walking, walking, walking."

Several of the group chuckled.

Ten steps in, the blast door behind them began to rise, and the grinding of machinery rolled through the space. Morgan saw Balfour standing by a control panel on the wall by the door. It gave Morgan the creeps.

They reached another door. Again, Quetzal approached another panel. This one was less complicated. The door was fifteen feet high and looked like something that should be hanging in front of a Fort Knox vault. It swung open on massive hinges with very little noise.

Cool air rushed from the opening. High-pressure sodium overhead lights painted the next room in an eerie yellow glow. The art in this room consisted of ceremonial Mayan headdresses, each reproduced in detail and kept safe from dust in cases made of thick plastic.

To one side was a long row of electric golf carts. Morgan counted twenty. Quetzal turned to the group. "Your chariots await. I'll drive the lead cart. Mr. Balfour will drive the next. Any of you CEOs know how to handle a golf cart?"

This time, the laughter was loud.

Quetzal continued. "We have about a mile to go, and all of it is downhill. The walk down would be easy, but the return trip would be a little trying." He slipped behind the wheel of the first cart. Morgan sat behind him. Sonya quickly took the spot next to him. Rickman chose to sit in the front with Quetzal.

Quetzal raised a hand and motioned forward like the master of a nineteenth-century wagon train. "Tallyho!"

"Could we have just driven in the cars?" Sonya asked Morgan.

"Yes, but we'd be filling the space with exhaust. I'm sure the place is designed to scrub the air, but why tax the system?"

Quetzal glanced. "Absolutely right, Mr. Morgan. In the old days, the Russians hid many things down here, including aircraft. It's designed to exchange air on a regular basis, but we're not running everything to speed yet. No need to for our small group."

"Are we the first to see this place?" Sonya asked.

"Well, the first of our little group. We bring groups in every few days. This is the premium shelter. Less than one hundred people will wait out the destruction here. We have two years of food and water stored here. As I'll explain to everyone later, you can live here in full comfort for a long time without ever going above ground. The severity of the catastrophe will determine how long we stay here."

"We?" Rickman said.

"Yes. We. I will be with you. As you know, we have a few more of these places, but none as nice as this. We even have a sports area. There will be plenty to do."

"And if nothing bad happens?"

Quetzal cut him a glance. "If you believed that, you wouldn't be here."

The transit tunnel ended, giving way to a huge expanse. Quetzal exited the cart and waited for the others to do the same. He bounced on the balls of his feet like a child in front of a Christmas tree.

The small group surrounded him. He motioned. "Welcome, my friends, to Xibalba. The next time you're here, this area will be filled with furniture and an eating area. Think of a high-end cafeteria. Right now, you have to use your imagination."

He started for a hallway at the far end of the space. "For security reasons, I've sent the workers home. After we leave, they'll come back. We have teams working twenty-four hours a day." He paused. "But let me show you what you really want to see."

One hour later, Morgan wished he could spend a couple of hours sitting and contemplating what he had just seen. He was a difficult man to impress, but this had taken his breath away.

"Are you okay, Mr. Morgan?" Balfour was in the front seat of the Patriot again. Morgan and Sonya sat in the back. Rickman had decided to ride back to the airport in another vehicle. No one in this car complained.

"I'm fine. Why do ask?"

"You seem distant."

The driver backed from the entrance tunnel and into the night.

"Just thinking. I don't do it often, so I have to be careful."

Balfour grinned. "I enjoy your self-deprecating humor. Do you have concerns?"

"Just one."

"About what you've seen, or are you bothered that we will be spending the night in a hotel? It will be safe. We've rented all the rooms and have brought in our own staff. We need to vacate Xibalba to allow the workers back in."

"No, that's not it. It's the name."

Sonya perked up. "You don't like the name? I think it has high marketability. Of course, we're not marketing it."

"What bothers you about the name, Mr. Morgan?"

"Its meaning."

Sonya frowned. "What's it mean?"

Morgan faced her. "It's the Mayan word for the underworld. It means 'the place of fear.' "

CHAPTER 28

Lisa read the text message again as she had done twenty times before.

WANT TO SEE YOU. NEED TO SEE YOU. PLEASE COME TO OC ON FRIDAY. — M.

Over the last sixteen months, she had visited Morgan in Oklahoma City many times. He would pay her airfare and hire a limo service to pick her up. They would spend time chatting, visiting restaurants, and had even gone bowling. Morgan was athletic, but bowling eluded him. It was the only sport she stood a chance of winning.

She had attended professional and college basketball games, gone to movies and dinner theater, and even visited museums. When she stayed overnight, he put her up in a local Marriott. Had he invited her stay in his mansion, she would have refused. He never offered. He remained the perfect gentleman.

On several occasions, the conversation turned to Lisa's faith. He argued against it with logic, but he was never cruel. He never mocked her. However, her faith in Christ and his lack of it is what kept them at arm's length.

In her secret moments, when her mind and heart weren't too busy lying to her, she had to admit that she was drawn to the man. She felt this way only when she thought of him — and she thought of him constantly.

No matter how often she wanted to give in to the attraction, it was — as the Bible put it — an unequally yoked situation, a believer tied to an unbeliever. Could they live happily in such a combination? Perhaps, but Lisa knew too many who had tried and failed. Morgan had told her that he'd be out of town for a few days, but he'd get in touch when he returned. He kept that promise. The text message was time-stamped 3:15 a.m. Lisa didn't find it until she crawled from bed at 6:30.

She went to work, reporting on the mild 2012 furor oozing over the world. Many had predicted panic in the streets, but aside from radio stations specializing in para-normal events, and an unending cascade of documentaries on cable channels, most of the world viewed the pending end with boredom.

And why not? The world had been through this before. In 1974, the bestselling book *The Jupiter Effect* by Gribbin and Plagemann predicted catastrophic events caused by the rare alignment of the planets. Disastrous earthquakes along California's San Andreas Fault were to all but destroy the state. Nothing happened. Then there was Y2K, the heralded end of all electronics as the calendar changed from 1999 to the triple-zero of 2000. Aside from a few microwave ovens that refused to operate, less than nothing happened. Of course, many said the world would forever change at the dawn of the twenty-first century. They were over a decade into the new millennium, and all remained as it was.

She had written scores of articles on fringe groups that took the 2012 prophecies seriously, including groups that stored food and guns. Some were moving into caves and bomb shelters. Lisa had visited several such places.

There had been an uptick in the sales of guns, dried food, cases of water, and toilet paper, but most people treated the whole matter as a curiosity, some resorting to,

"Well, if it's my time, then it's my time."

Still, prophets of doom appeared by the dozens. Each claimed a special insight, a spirit guide, or an ecstatic vision. Some people purported to be able to read hidden prophecies in the Bible. Not one prophet agreed with another.

What Lisa had not been able to do was write the assigned article about wealthy business leaders like Morgan who invested time and millions of dollars following "the cranks." Of all the doomsayers, Robert Quetzal remained the "alpha prophet." No one could match his charisma or intellect. She lost count of the number of times the man had appeared on the talk-show circuit, yakking it up with Leno, Letterman, and every other nighttime and daytime host on the tube.

To Lisa's surprise, many mainline television news shows featured him as a "consultant." When she was with Morgan, she never failed to ask for new information. He never failed to refuse.

December 21 was just a few weeks away, and she had no idea what would happen. She wasn't worried about cataclysm. She was worried about Morgan. He never told her so, but she knew he had poured a steady stream of money to Quetzal's organization.

It was his money, and he could do what he wanted with it. What concerned her was how he would respond after he learned he and the others had been wrong all along. She put the question to him once, and his response was to turn the tables: "I'm worried about your response when all this proves to be right."

"Won't I be dead?"

He hadn't answered.

That evening, she returned home and packed a bag. She walked by the bedroom she used as an in-home office, stopped, then turned back. On her desk was a file folder: Garrett's file folder. The information was disturbing if it were all true. She had no way to confirm his conclusions and she couldn't use the material without exposing her news organization to lawsuits. Even a simple lawsuit could bring them to their knees. In such suits, even the innocent need barrels of cash, and the *Christian Herald* barely made payroll each month. No, Rodney Truffaut would never allow it.

Add to that the fact Garrett had used less-than-honest means to get the information. An investigation into the source of the information would expose others, perhaps lead to criminal charges and open the *Herald* to another flood of lawsuits. Even she was subject to legal action, and she definitely couldn't afford an attorney.

She stuffed the file in her bag. She might not be able to share it with the world, but she knew who she could share it with.

Garrett eased from the front seat of his 2006 Toyota Camry, and he slowly rose. He was glad to be driving again, but getting in and out of the sedan always caused him pain. The doctors said that would change, but not for a while. For now, he had to learn to live with the discomfort. He had motivation. Every muscle in his body hurt, and the thought of standing in a hot shower gave him the impetus to work through the stiffness. He missed the vitality common to a young man still in his twenties. He moved like a man well north of seventy.

The sun was close to the horizon, and the early evening sky had turned the color of putty. He hated the short days of late fall. Winter would only be worse.

A familiar wave of depression rolled over him as he shut the driver's door. The doctors told him depression was common among victims of violent crime. It, like his aches and pains, would pass in time. He had to learn to deal with it. One nurse said, "Act the way you want to feel, and you will begin to feel the way you act."

She had been right. It wasn't a hundred percent, but it helped. He straightened his spine and lifted his head and pushed his shoulders back as if he were a man with no problems, filled with confidence and determination.

He still felt depressed. His eyes began to burn. Many times he had burst into tears for no reason. The attack had injured his emotions as well as his body.

Garrett waited a moment until the despair passed and his legs ceased their shuddering. He took a deep breath and released it in a slow stream. He started around the front of the Toyota and toward the curb in front of his apartment building.

Before he reached the curb, a car pulled alongside his car. Garrett turned to see a silver Lexus. The front passenger window lowered.

"Excuse me. Are you Mr. Garrett Vickers?"

Garrett bent and looked at the driver through the open window. The man was smiling, and it gave Garrett the shivers. "Who are you?"

"Oh. Sorry." The man held up a leather case. Inside was a badge and an ID that read FBI. "Could I have a moment of your time?"

"Why? I didn't do anything."

The man smiled again, and it chilled Garrett's blood. "You're not in trouble, son. I'm here because we think we found the guy who attacked you."

"Really?" He paused. "Wait. The FBI doesn't investigate assault or routine murder cases."

"We do if the murder crosses state lines or is involved in a hate crime. You work for a Christian news outlet, right?"

"Yeah. So what?"

"I thought as a news guy, you'd know this, but there's been a rise in violence against Christians. It's sad but true. And to us, a hate crime is a hate crime. Besides, the local cops haven't had much luck, so we're helping out."

"What do you need me for? I told the police everything I knew over a year ago."

"I've read those reports. As I said, I think we have the guy. He's being held not far from here. We're hoping that you would try to identify him."

"You need to read those reports again, agent. I don't remember diddly about the attack. Traumatic amnesia."

The man nodded. "I know, and I know

this doesn't make much sense, but we need to have you try. If we don't, it will come up in court, and we'll look like a bunch of amateurs. You don't want this moron doing to others what he did to you and your friends, do you?

"Of course not."

"Look, Mr. Vickers. I know it seems silly. A lot of cop work does, but it is what it is. I can get you down there and back in less than half an hour, and then we both can start our weekend."

The last thing Garrett wanted to do was get in another car, but if they had captured the guy who ruined his life, and if seeing him could jog his memory, then it needed to be done.

"Come on, Mr. Vickers. I promised the wife and kids dinner and a movie. If I blow off another family date, I'll be sleeping in my car."

"I guess we can't have that." He started for the Lexus.

"Need help?"

"No. I got it." Garrett opened the door and slipped into the car. "You guys drive nice cars."

"It's my wife's. She's in real estate. My service car is in the shop." He pulled down the road. As he did, the driver removed a photo from the pocket of his suit coat and handed it to Garrett. The photo had been folded in half. Garret opened it, and his heart stopped.

"Know her?"

"What is this?"

"I asked you a question. I suggest you answer it." The friendly tone had disappeared.

He studied the photo. Lisa sat in a chair. Duct tape held her wrists to the arm of the chair and her feet to the chair's legs. Another piece of tape covered her mouth. Someone with his back to the camera held what Garrett guessed was a 9mm or .45 caliber handgun at her head.

"Yes. I know her."

"Okay, here's the deal. You give me any trouble, you try to escape, you scream, you do anything I find annoying, and the man holding the gun will put a bullet in the lady's pretty head. Do we understand each other?"

Garrett raised his eyes and studied the man behind the wheel. For months, he wished he could remember the face of the man who beat him and left him for dead.

Now he wished he could forget again.

CHAPTER 29

"You look invigorated." Lisa gave Morgan a quick hug. She was glad he had chosen to pick her up instead of sending a car. She understood that his schedule sometimes required that he delegate such tasks to others, but seeing him at baggage claim always gave her an extra thrill.

"Thank you." Morgan took her suitcase and carry-on bag. He wore beige pants, a white polo shirt, and slip-on loafers.

"You also looked exhausted." Lisa shouldered her purse and straightened the coat of her pale green pantsuit.

"Thanks again — I think." He pretended to stagger to his left, bumping into her.

"Too weary to walk straight, Mr. Morgan?"

"Just drunk on your presence, Ms. Campbell."

"Now you're just being silly. I'll give you an hour to knock that off."

They moved through the crowded airport lobby and into the cool night of Oklahoma City. As expected, Lisa saw a now-familiar limousine waiting curbside. Donny, dressed as always in black pants, a white shirt, and a black suit coat, waited by the rear door. He bowed slightly as they approached. Morgan had told her that he did that only when she was present.

"It makes me feel like royalty." Something Lisa enjoyed.

"I think he's about to make a move on you."

"I'm sure you'll protect my honor."

Morgan shrugged. "Maybe."

Once they were comfortably seated, Donny pulled into the thick of traffic. Lisa couldn't help noticing that the privacy divider between the front and the rear seats was up. Lisa couldn't put her finger on it, but there was something different about Morgan tonight.

"So what were you doing awake at 3:15 in the morning?" Lisa turned in her seat to face him.

"How did you know . . ." He raised his chin. "The text message had a time stamp. I forget that sometimes."

"You could just go on believing that I'm brilliant."

"That you are, and I'll fight anyone who says you're not."

"Really?"

He shook his head. "No. I don't like violence."

"I think I detect some rust on your suit of armor." She settled back in the seat. "So why the summons?"

"Invitation."

"Okay, why the invitation?"

"Is it wrong to want to see you?"

The comment made Lisa feel warm. "You know, this is the weirdest relationship I've ever been in."

"Didn't you tell me that you haven't been in many relationships?"

"Okay, if you're going to start listening to me, I'm going to have to be more careful about what I say. Now stop avoiding the question. Did something happen on your trip?"

"That's part of it. I want to run something by you." He didn't look at her.

"Okay. I'm listening."

"Not here." He looked out the window.

Morgan had never shown a reluctance to speak within earshot of Donny. Of course, most of their conversations were benign when the man was around.

"You never told me where you went," Lisa said.

"All things will be made clear soon, Ms. I'm-full-of-questions reporter."

"I'm the curious sort, Mr. I-got-millions-of-secrets businessman."

He opened the limo's wet bar. At one time, the minibar held Scotch, vodka, and other small bottles of booze, but Morgan admitted to having them all removed almost two years ago. Now it held sodas, juices, and bottled water. Lisa took a Cran-Apple drink and hoped she wouldn't spill any on her green outfit. The red of the drink on the green of her pantsuit would make her look like a Christmas tree. Morgan took a bottle of water.

The remaining minutes of the trip were spent in chitchat, which only elevated Lisa's hunger to know what was going on in Morgan's head.

Donny drove them to the Marriott where Lisa was staying while in Oklahoma City. Morgan carried her bags to her room and then escorted her back to the limo. A few minutes later, Donny dropped them at the front door to Morgan's spacious home.

"Hungry?"

"If I say yes, you're not going to start cooking, are you?"

"Nah, I like you too much for that. I have a plate of sandwich meats, cheese, fruit, pumpernickel, and sourdough bread. I thought we could eat by the pool."

"That sounds lovely."

The blanket of night had settled over the city, bringing out stars that decorated the ebony dome overhead with their sparkle. The night was cool, but not cold. A gas-powered heater stood near the picnic table, radiating warmth.

Morgan appeared with a wide platter of food, the kind provided by a caterer. He set it down and reappeared with a large bottle of San Pellegrino sparkling water and a small bowl of limes. He poured the bubbly water into two glasses and held out the dish of limes to Lisa. She took one and squeezed it into the glass. He did the same.

Lisa bowed her head and thanked God for the meal. She did so silently. Morgan never joined her in the ritual, nor did he ever interrupt or ridicule her for doing so.

"This is nice." Lisa looked around. Lights from the house shimmered on the pool's water, and she felt the tension in her shoulders melt away. She had been by the pool several times over the months since she first met Morgan in Roswell, but at night, it had a magical quality. She felt enchanted.

There was something new. She hadn't noticed at first, perhaps because it was on the other side of the pool, almost hidden in shadows.

"Have you taken up a new hobby?" She nodded to the large telescope resting on a solid-looking tripod.

"Ah, that. That is a Meade LightBridge Deluxe 16-inch truss tube Dobsonian telescope."

"Okay, if you say so. And why is it in your backyard?"

"You know I love the sciences. There's something I want to show you."

"Show me? What?"

"Not yet. I need to talk, and I need you to listen."

Lisa cocked her head. "I always listen to you."

"That's something we can debate later. What I mean is, I want to share a few things with you, and I want you to let me get through it. I've been practicing so that I don't mess it up, and interruption —"

"Who interrupts?"

Morgan stared at her for a moment.

Lisa felt she had crossed the line. Morgan had always been serious, but despite his joking, he was clearly carrying some additional emotional weight. Lisa apologized.

"Recently, I read a poll. Less than one percent of the population in the US believe something dramatic is going to happen on December 21. Only one in ten of those think the event will be negative, and about half of those think it will be a catastrophe. As you know, I'm in the latter, and you're — well, you're not."

Lisa started to speak but stopped. A promise is a promise.

Morgan smiled, obviously surprised by her restraint. "I think the poll is off . . . but not by much. Other reports show more folks who think like I do, but it's far from a majority. But none of that matters." He sighed. "I'm making a hash of this. Let me start over."

Morgan continued. "I believe the Mayan prophecies, and I have committed a great deal of time and effort to making sure I'm not wrong. I know your thinking is far from mine, but we still have — I think — a great relationship. I know your faith has kept some distance between us . . ."

Lisa's eyebrows rose.

Morgan waved a hand. "I phrased that wrong. Our different views have kept us from going the next step in our relationship. I've been fine with that. But we're only a few weeks from the day." He stopped and looked at the table.

"Andrew . . ." Lisa reached across the table and touched his hand. "Just say it."

He nodded and then stood, something Lisa didn't expect. "You're right. Come with me." He rounded the table and took her hand.

"Where are we going?"

"This way." He led her around the pool and to the telescope. The device was as tall as Lisa and looked as if it had just been removed from the box.

"How long have you been stargazing?"

"I set it up yesterday. This is why I was awake in the wee hours. I wanted to make sure I knew how to work the thing before you got here."

Lisa blinked several times. The more Morgan talked, the more confused she became.

He removed an electronic device from a clip on the tripod. Lisa could see a digital readout. The display's glow was so weak that she could barely read the numbers. Morgan looked at his watch and then entered the time on a keypad. The telescope began to move. He replaced the device in its holder and then walked to the home's rear door, opened it, and turned off the lights.

"This is kind of spooky." Lisa had trouble

seeing Morgan walking back to her.

"Give your eyes a few moments to adjust." The telescope stopped. "Everything is digital these days. If you have the right coordinates, the computer will direct the business end of the telescope to the right spot in the sky."

"And just what is the right spot?"

Morgan leaned forward and peered through the eyepiece near the top of the device. "Take a look."

Where Morgan had to bend to place his eye in the viewer, Lisa could stand straight. It took a few seconds for her eye to focus properly. "The white spot?"

"Yes."

"It doesn't look like a planet or a star."

Morgan spoke softly. "It's not. You're looking at an asteroid — a mile-long asteroid."

Lisa backed away and looked to the sky. "An asteroid?"

"Yes. It's official name is 2012 GA12, but a lot of people call it the Hammer of God. It's from an Arthur C. Clarke novel."

Lisa's mind began to race. There was something in Morgan's voice: something foreboding. Her mind struggled to shuffle the information in her brain. "You're not telling me . . . I mean, there have been

379

reports from amateur astronomers, but the professionals dismissed them."

"They had to."

Lisa needed to sit down. Her knees felt hollow. Morgan helped her back to the outdoor table and then turned the exterior lights on.

"What do you mean, 'They had to'?" Lisa wished for a handful of antacids.

"The asteroid is due to hit on the twenty-first or a day later."

"Surely someone is doing something."

Morgan shook his head. "What can they do?"

"Blow it up?" Once the words cleared her lips, she realized how silly she sounded.

"Even if some government in the world was set up to do that, it might make things worse. Instead of one large asteroid, the world would be pummeled by several slightly smaller asteroids. Not that that matters. The thing is big, Lisa, real big. Imagine shooting a missile into a mountain. It might do damage, but in the end, the mountain remains in place."

"It isn't right to keep this secret. I need to write a story . . . maybe call some television people —"

"What would that achieve? Panic. Nothing more. What would billions of people do?

380

I can't stop you from telling others, but I don't advise it. Since this has been kept secret, governments must have conspired to keep it under wraps."

"I know how to fix that."

Morgan leaned over the table. "Do you? Really?"

"I'm a reporter. I know how to tell a story."

Lisa saw the hurt on Morgan's face. "How long will it take you to gather information? You don't have the time. Even if you did, they wouldn't let you get very far."

"They? They who?"

"The government would not allow you to cause a panic. Nothing can be done to protect billions of people. All you could do is alert them to their coming demise. Do you want to do that?"

"I don't know."

Morgan again reached across the table and took Lisa's hand. "I've struggled with this. I understand the shock you feel."

"How did you find out?"

"Quetzal. He keeps us posted on the Hammer of God and other . . . things."

Lisa felt cold.

"Let me tell you the rest."

"There's more?"

"Come with me."

"Where?"

"I can't tell you until you agree to join me. Quetzal has made arrangements. I can bring one person with me. I want you to be that person."

Lisa shook her head and pulled her hand away. "Andrew, I don't believe in the Mayan prophecies. I think it's all nonsense. It goes against biblical revelation."

"Does it?"

"Of course."

"I'll be back in a second." Standing, he walked to the house.

Lisa shivered in spite of the outdoor heaters. She gazed skyward again and wondered if she really saw what she had just seen.

Morgan reappeared and took his seat again. He held a book — a book easy to recognize. "This was my son's Bible." He opened the book and turned to the end. He ran his finger over a page and read aloud:

"The second angel sounded, and something like a great mountain burning with fire was thrown into the sea; and a third of the sea became blood, and a third of the creatures which were in the sea and had life, died; and a third of the ships were destroyed.

"The third angel sounded, and a great star fell from heaven, burning like a torch, and it fell on a third of the rivers and on the springs of waters. The name of the star is called Wormwood; and a third of the waters became wormwood, and many men died from the waters, because they were made bitter.

"The fourth angel sounded, and a third of the sun and a third of the moon and a third of the stars were struck, so that a third of them would be darkened and the day would not shine for a third of it, and the night in the same way.

"Then I looked, and I heard an eagle flying in midheaven, saying with a loud voice, 'Woe, woe, woe to those who dwell on the earth, because of the remaining blasts of the trumpet of the three angels who are about to sound!' "

Morgan turned the Bible and set it in front of Lisa. "Revelation 8:8 13." She saw tears in his eyes. "Lisa, I want you to come with me."

Lisa watched Morgan pull from the portico of the Marriott hotel. The conversation had turned awkward, and Lisa finally admitted that she was too shaken to make decisions about anything, let alone one dealing with her sudden departure to places unknown.

He said he understood, asked her to think about it, and then drove her to the hotel.

After walking her into the lobby, he leaned forward and kissed her on the top of the head. It was the most demonstrative he had ever been.

Lisa moved to her room and sat on the bed. The image of the Hammer of God she had seen through the telescope seemed to float inside her eyes. She couldn't get rid of it. Although it was a small image in the eyepiece, it grew in size and detail in her mind.

Shocking as the sight was, hearing Morgan read from verses from the Bible — especially those verses — was more stunning.

"Something like a great mountain . . ." The apostle John's words rang like a bell in her mind. "That certainly could describe an asteroid."

She felt ill again. Rising, she paced the fourth-floor room, taking notice of nothing but the gray-blue carpet. Her skin felt warm. The thermostat read seventy-one, a comfortable temp for her. The heat was coming from inside her body.

She opened the sliding door and let in the night air. Her thoughts rolled around her head like loose marbles. From the balcony she could see the courtyard below. Children played in a large pool, an elderly couple soaked in the spa, traveling businessmen and women unwound on the first-floor patio. The sound of life rose in the air. Night birds coursed through the air.

"Dead. All dead, and they don't know it."

Lisa sat in one of the two patio chairs. Her breathing came in ragged inhalations. A moment later, she leaned forward and began to weep. Five minutes later, tears turned into prayer.

The paper in Garrett's hand shook.

"Take a deep breath." His captor spoke calmly.

He did.

"Again. I don't want to hear any tension in your voice."

"Then throw the gun out the window."

His captor smiled, but Garrett saw no humor in it. "What, this little ol' thing?" He pressed the weapon to Garrett's forehead. "Read it again."

Garrett tried but stumbled a few times.

"Close enough." The man with the gun pulled a small digital recorder from this pocket and set it on the battered table tucked in the corner of the forty-dollar-a-night hotel. Garrett doubted most people spent the entire night. "I can edit it on my computer." He pressed the record button and motioned to another paper.

Garrett got the idea and lifted the paper. "Hey, Uncle Rodney, it's Garrett. I went out of town for the weekend and my car broke down. No need to worry. I have it in the shop, but it's going to take a few days, so I'm going to kick it with some friends. Of course, this means I'll be missing a few days of work. I'm sorry about this, but you know how the piece of junk I call my car is. I'll check in later."

The gunman switched off the recorder.

"You've been most cooperative. We have a few more of these to do."

"Why are you doing this?" Garrett had a feeling he knew the answer.

"I think our last meeting would have taught you to stay out of other people's computers."

"You left me for dead."

The man nodded. "Well, in my defense, you looked dead. I don't usually make those kinds of mistakes." He raised the gun and pressed the muzzle to Garrett's temple. "Now, what did you do with the information?"

"Nothing."

Garrett felt the metal of the weapon dig into his skin. "I want names. Did you tell Lisa Campbell?"

"You already have her. Why ask me?"

The man eased back on the gun enough that Garrett could straighten his neck. "Actually, I don't."

"But the picture . . ."

"Come on, kid. You're a computer jockey. You know you can't trust photos these days."

"You faked it?"

"Not hard to do when you know the right people."

Garrett felt the need to vomit.

CHAPTER 30

When Lisa awoke, she was still dressed and reclined on top of the covers. Next to her was the file she intended to show to Morgan after last night's dinner. That changed when he walked her to his telescope.

She rose, moved to the restroom, and gazed in the mirror. "Yuck. I look like I slept outside." Truth was, she hadn't slept much at all.

She turned on the shower, disrobed, and climbed in. The warm water and gentle noise helped her think. Not that she wanted to think.

The water poured over her, easing the tension in her neck and shoulders but not the stress in her mind. She had spent much of the night in prayer, asking God for clear direction. What should she do? When faced with a tough decision, she "tried on" ideas like someone trying on shoes. If one felt comfortable, she went with it, if it didn't, she tried something else. This morning, nothing was comfortable.

Morgan's offer was kind. Last night, she saw an aspect of him she had always known was there but which he kept at bay. In his eyes, she saw genuine concern. Dare she think it? Love?

For a fleeting moment, she was ready to agree — to say something sappy like, "I'll follow you anywhere." The moment evaporated.

Other thoughts troubled her. The verse from Revelation wasn't new to her. She had read through the Bible several times, having read the New Testament itself even more times. That included the book of Revelation. The book confused her, infused as it was with first-century descriptions and symbolism that were hard to understand. She had been taught, and deeply believed, that just because the book was symbolic didn't mean the future events held in its pages would not come true. Besides, there were many other Bible verses that spoke of the second coming of Christ. Was the Hammer of God a fulfillment of some of those prophecies?

But she was certain that other events would come first. Hadn't Jesus taught the disciples — and through them, the church

— to be alert for the signs?

Maybe this was one of those signs. Maybe this was the beginning of the great tribulation, God's punishment upon the world. The thought disquieted her soul. She firmly believed that believers around the world would be caught up in the air to meet Jesus and be spared the wrath of God.

Maybe that was about to happen. Normally a happy thought for her, she hoped the rapture wouldn't occur while she was in the shower.

Minutes later, she had toweled off. She felt cleaner, but still confused. She dressed, then returned to bed. The night had been restless, and she was operating on just a few hours of sleep. The bed looked good, but she fought off the urge to slip beneath the covers. Instead, she knelt by it, propping her arms on the mattress. The position made her feel like a child saying her evening prayers. That didn't matter.

Alone in the hotel room, she returned to prayer. One hour later, she rose, packed, and headed for the lobby.

The airport waiting area buzzed with activity. Disembodied voices poured from overhead speakers, giving instruction about the number of bags passengers could carry aboard. The air carried the smell of thousands of people, and the muted sounds of hundreds of conversations. Lisa found a corner of a waiting area freshly emptied by a departing flight. She had several hours to kill. Buying a ticket at the last minute deprived her of choices. She took the only flight that had open seating. For a few moments, she thought of renting a car and driving the thousand miles from Oklahoma City to San Antonio, but then she did the math. Sixteen hours of nonstop driving would give her lots of time to think, but she just didn't feel up to it.

Once again, guilt rose in her like Old Faithful. Should she call Morgan, explain why she left so suddenly, and let him know that it was not personal? She just . . . needed to leave.

"We have to stop meeting like this."

Her heart stumbled. She turned her eyes from the window overlooking the tarmac and saw Morgan standing a few feet away. He wore a simple smile.

Garrett had spent the night taped to the chair. His abductor had allowed him to use the bathroom under gunpoint and then made him use a roll of duct tape to bind his own legs and one arm to the chair. His captor secured the free arm. The tape over his mouth remained. Garrett could feel a rash forming beneath the glue.

The man stepped into the hall. Garrett could hear him talking. There was only one voice. He assumed the man was on a cell phone.

On the nearby table rested the notes he had been forced to read into the recorder and the fabricated photo that lured him into the car. Now that he could study it, Garrett could see that it had been cobbled together from several photos. Lisa's head had been digitally added to the body of another woman. He chastised himself for being so gullible. He wondered if stupid people were allowed in heaven. He knew the answer, but his self-loathing kept him from believing it.

The door opened, and Garrett tensed.

"I got good news, and I got bad news, Binky. Which do you want to hear first?" Garrett met his eyes. "Oh, that's right, you can't talk." He carried an overnight bag. "I had to make a quick run to the car." He opened the bag and removed a plastic bottle and large pad of gauze.

He unscrewed the top. "The good news is, you're going to get to sleep." He poured fluid from the bottle and onto the gauze. "The bad news? You don't get to wake up."

Garrett's heart pounded so hard he expected his ribs to crack.

The kidnapper stepped close and forced the gauze over Garrett's nose. Garrett tried to hold his breath but he could do so for only so long. He tried to scream, but the tape and medical gauze muffled the sound. He fought his bonds. He squirmed.

The room went dark.

"Have you ever noticed how much time we spend in airports?" Morgan slipped into the seat next to Lisa. Her face warmed. "We met in an airport."

"Actually, we met in a Roswell theater."

He shook his head. "Only technically. We sat together and exchanged a few words. Our real meeting took place when I offered you a ride home."

"I remember. Very gallant."

He leaned back and extended his long legs. "So . . . you weren't going to say good-bye?"

"I'm sorry . . . I just . . . you see . . ."

"You reporters have a way with words."

"Hey, I'm flustered here."

"I can see that. Let me try. You're confused about my offer. You're frightened because a monster asteroid is going drop on everyone's head. You're ticked off that no one has revealed pending doom. And none of this fits your theology. How am I doing?"

"Annoyingly well. Still, there are things you don't know."

"Such as?"

Lisa pursed her lips and looked away. "I don't know how to piece all this together. Normally, I'm a pretty sharp gal, but I feel adrift. Do you know what I mean?"

"About you being smart? Nope, don't have a clue."

"Funny man. How can you be so casual about this? I was slipping out of town without telling you."

"Lisa, this isn't a romantic comedy. We're both adults. You have a right to leave any-time you like. I have a right to look for you."

"Speaking of which, how did you find me?"

"Long or short story?"

Lisa eyed him. "The shorter the better."

He grinned. "Went to your hotel. You were gone. Gave the guy behind the counter a fifty. He said you took the shuttle to the airport. There are only so many flights to San Antonio."

"Clever boy."

"My mother always thought so. Now tell me, what is it I don't know?"

Lisa pulled her carry-on bag close, opened

it, and removed the folder. "I was going to show this to you last night." She handed him the folder.

Morgan opened it, and Lisa watched him read the summary page and then glance through the documents. He nodded. "Okay, what about it?"

"What do you mean, 'What about it'?"

"It's a list of accusations against Quetzal and Maya2012. Am I supposed to be surprised?"

"Andrew, this should destroy your opinion of Quetzal. He's been lying to you."

"He has?"

Lisa opened the file. "Okay, first, his name isn't Robert Quetzal. It's Robert Sanchez."

"I know."

"You know. He lies about his name, and yet you trust him?"

"Who wrote *Huck Finn*?"

"Mark Twain —"

"No, Samuel Clemens wrote *Huck Finn*. Mark Twain was his pseudonym. Quetzal is a stage name. You remember when you were sitting on my floor last year, eavesdropping on my video conference with him? I was invited to a meeting with him. The first thing he told us was his real name."

"Really? Well, what about the part about him being a Mayan priest? He's not even

Mayan."

"Are you sure?"

"He's Hispanic."

"The Spanish and indigenous Indians intermarried. It's part of Central American history. Unless you've done a DNA test, you have no idea if he has Mayan ancestry."

"Did you look at the spreadsheet in the file?"

"Yes."

"And you're not bothered by it? Maybe you should look at it again."

"Turns out, Ms. Campbell, that I'm pretty good with spreadsheets. I am the CEO of a Fortune 500 company. I'm buried to the neck in spreadsheets. Besides, I've seen it before."

"What? That document shows millions of dollars in offshore accounts. Millions of your dollars."

"Yes, it does. Quetzal sent that same info to me and the others. In fact, I have more detailed accountings than that."

"Andrew, if the world is coming to an end, then why does Quetzal need money in offshore accounts?"

"First, no one is saying the world is ending, but it is about to endure a great upheaval. Everything will change and a new society will arise. That will take some seed money. If the world does come to an end, then nothing else matters. Besides, it's not money he's storing — it's gold. Gold has always been valuable. It's safe to assume that it will be the same in the future. If it's not, then money won't matter at all."

"But he's been buying property all over the world."

Morgan nodded slowly. "I know that too."

"Why would he do that?"

"Because many of those are safe areas. He has created several places to wait out the destruction."

"What kind of place can keep you safe from a falling mountain?"

"Come with me and find out."

Lisa cut her gaze away.

"Lisa, I've been to one of the sites. I've seen it with my own eyes. I've seen and studied his plan. It will work. I can take you to a place where we can live for years if necessary." He took her hand. "Come with me."

"I . . . I don't know. If this is what God wants, then maybe I should just wait for it to happen and pray the asteroid lands directly on my head."

"Don't be silly."

"I'm not. Christians have known for two millennia that God will destroy this world

397

and replace it with new heavens and a new earth."

"If God wants to destroy every living thing on the earth, then it doesn't matter where we hide. I don't share your views, but if I did, I wouldn't want to stand before Him and explain why I didn't take an avenue of safety when He presented it. I can hear it now. You say, 'God, why didn't You save me?' And God replies, 'I tried, but you were too hardheaded to listen.'"

"Hardheaded. You think God would use the word *hardheaded*?"

"If the description fits."

She slapped him on the arm.

He laughed and then leaned close. "I know the confusion you're experiencing. I've been through it. No, I don't have all the answers. Is Quetzal getting rich off me and the others? I'm sure he is. We got rich off others. That's what business is: offering a product or service others are willing to pay for."

"I don't think that's the same thing." Lisa expected a very different reaction.

He took her hand. "Look, Lisa, let's say you're right about many of the things you've said. Let's say the volcano in Mexico and all the other natural disasters over the last couple of years are normal. There's still the

Hammer of God to deal with. It's real. You've seen it with your own eyes."

"But if it were a real threat, our government would have told us . . ." She knew the comment was ridiculous.

"We've been through this. They wouldn't tell us. Why would they? It can't help, but it sure can hurt. Their hands are tied just like yours. I suppose on December 21 the world's governments could tell their people to stay indoors but that's it. Come with me."

"No. I don't . . ."

"Promise me you'll think about it. Better yet, promise me you'll pray about it."

"You don't believe in prayer."

Morgan agreed. "But you do."

"I don't know what to think."

"We have a few days. Go home. Think. Then decide to come with me."

"That's a little slanted."

"I know what keeps us apart. My wife and son's deaths still haunt me, and I will love them and mourn them forever, but I've come to care for you. I want you to be safe. If we had more time, then maybe we could find a way to get past what keeps us apart, but we're down to a few days."

He stood and then pulled her to her feet. His arms pulled her close and then released her. "Don't make me go on without you."

Andrew Morgan walked away, and Lisa felt her heart go with him.

CHAPTER 31

December 20, 2012

The pilot of Morgan's jet announced the moment they crossed over the California border. They began their descent a few minutes before.

Donny sat across from him, leafing through an issue of *Popular Science*. He inhaled deeply and set the magazine to the side. "I guess it's time."

Morgan turned his eyes from the window. "Time for what?"

"This." Donny reached into the inside front pocket of his light Morgan Natural Energy coat, a gift from Morgan last Christmas, and removed a white envelope. "Here."

Morgan took it and noticed his name on the outside. "What's this?"

"It's my resignation."

"What?"

"The letter explains it."

Morgan studied his longtime chauffeur

and bodyguard. "This is a joke, right?"

"Do you see any tears of laughter rolling down my cheeks?"

"The attitude is new."

"Sorry, but I've been dreading this."

Morgan ripped open the envelope and removed the letter. "You technically work for the security firm, not directly for me."

"I understand the technicalities, but we've been together for a long time. I owe you this."

Unfolding the letter, Morgan read aloud. "December 20, 2012. I hereby resign effective immediately. I do so for the following reason . . ." He raised his head. "Are you pulling my leg?"

Donny shook his head.

"I do so for the following reason: My client is an idiot." He lowered the letter. "An idiot? Really? An idiot? That's it? No reasons given? No explanation? Just that I'm an idiot?"

"I'm not great with words."

Morgan folded the letter and put it back in the envelope. "I hope you're better with explanations. Why am I an idiot?"

"Because of this trip. It's ridiculous."

Morgan narrowed his eyes. "You don't know where I'm going. How can you say the trip is ridiculous?"

"It's no secret that you're big into this Mayan end-of-the-world thing. Okay, fine. Until now, I've had no problem with that. It's none of my business. Today's date is not wasted on me. My guess is you're flying off to some place you think of as safe, and you're going alone."

"Oh, so that's it. You're miffed that I'm not bringing —"

"Don't go there, pal. I think the whole thing is a truckload of manure. Even if I believed it, I wouldn't leave my family behind."

"Pal. Now you're calling me 'pal'?" Morgan tossed the envelope across the narrow aisle.

"I resigned, remember?"

Morgan leaned forward and rubbed his face. Sleep had evaded him over the last few days. He'd been surviving on catnaps. "I don't need this now."

"Yes, you do." Donny's words were sharp. His tone had always been respectful, but he was doing nothing to hide his anger. "In a few days, maybe around Christmas, you're going to come to your senses and realize that you've made a big mistake. I don't know where you're heading, but there's no place far enough away to keep you from yourself."

"Look, Donny, you want to resign, then fine, but don't tell me what I should be doing."

"Where's Lisa?"

"Why?"

"Oh, brother." Donny snapped back in his seat so hard Morgan thought he'd break the backrest.

"What does she have to do with this?"

"She loves you, man. You have to know that. You must have sensed it."

"We're just close friends."

Donny swore. "Nonsense. You love her, and she loves you."

"You can't know that. Besides, how do you know she's not waiting for me?"

"I called her before we left."

"What? Who do you think you are?"

"You see, this is why I resigned — so that I can talk freely. I'll tell you who I am. I'm the guy who has been willing to take a bullet for you. If I'm willing to do that, then I must be willing to toss some cold truth in the face of a friend — or client."

Morgan released his safety belt and paced the aisle. "I can't believe you called her."

"It's a free country."

"Free or not, there's no way you can know how deep our relationship is."

This time, Donny popped his lap belt and

faced Morgan, eye to eye. "I make my living by being observant. I watch everything. I've seen how that friendly hug she gives you lingers a second longer than it should. I see her eyes. I hear her voice. She loves you, Morgan. Real love. Deep love. Churn-your-innards love."

"She's never said so."

"Have you told her that you're in love?"

Morgan turned. "That's none of your business."

Donny's tone softened. "I know. I know. It's just . . ."

"Just what?"

"It's just that if it were me, and if I could take the love of my life to safety, I'd do it. I wouldn't leave her behind. That's what you're doing, right? Tell me I've got it all messed up, and I'll believe you. Just look me in the eye when you do."

He couldn't turn — couldn't face Donny. The man would see right through him. He lowered his head and set a hand on one of the seats.

"I can't love someone else, Donny. I've tried dating. I just can't betray my wife."

"Oh, for the love of . . . Turn around. Come on, face me."

Morgan did. Donny tapped the left side of his chin. "Okay, this is where you get to hit me. Right on the jaw. I won't fight back. Feel free to put your weight into it."

"Donny, what are you talking about —"

"Your wife is dead. Your son is dead. They are both in the grave. They are not coming back. No matter how much or how often you beat yourself up, they're still going to be dead."

"Watch it, Donny!"

"I have been watching it. Every day, week after week, month after month, I've kept this bottled up because it's none of my business."

"You got that straight." Morgan's heart beat like a piston. He clinched his fist.

"I know you loved them more than life itself. No man was a better husband or father, but they are *dead*."

With blurring speed, Morgan grabbed the front of Donny's coat. He didn't resist. Morgan pulled back a fist, ready to take Donny up on his offer — until he saw the tears in the man's eyes.

Donny kept eye contact, not blinking. Slowly, he put his hands behind his back, offering no resistance. Morgan released him. "Why are you doing this?"

"Ever since the accident, I've watched you withdraw. Oh sure, you go through the motions. You've traveled; you've run your business — best I can tell — pretty well. But you've lost your way."

"I don't think so."

"I do. Look, I don't even blame you. Your wife and son were the best. They were wonderful people and deserved to be mourned forever, but they would want you to move on." He straightened his coat. "Of course, if you're right about this Mayan calendar thing, then I guess nothing matters, including Lisa."

Morgan felt his organs melting. "I asked her to come along with me, Donny. I tried and tried to convince her, but she is so mule-headed."

"Sounds like someone else I know."

"Cute."

Donny lowered himself into his seat and rubbed his temples. For a moment, Morgan felt sorry for him. It took him a lot of courage to say what he had.

"I don't know what else I could do to get her to come along."

"Do you love her?"

Morgan sat. "I don't know how to answer that."

Donny stared at him for a few moments. "Yes, you do."

"Okay, smart guy. If you believed the world was going to end tomorrow, what would you do?"

"I don't believe the world is ending tomorrow, but just in case, I've made plans."

"Such as?"

"I'm having my family and close friends over, throwing some meat on the grill, and playing Ping-Pong."

"The end of humanity, and you want to meet it with Ping-Pong."

"We're going to watch movies too. Popcorn and movies. It's not going to happen, but if it does, I'll be with the ones I love, doing the things I love."

Morgan had no words.

Moments later, the pilot's voice came over the intercom. They were on final approach to Mojave Airport.

The landing went smoothly. Through the windows during the craft's circle of the field, Morgan could see the modified 747 gleaming in the late morning sunlight. It bore no markings. To Morgan, it looked like a giant silver bird waiting for a reason to take to the air.

As his plane leveled on approach, he saw another 747 in the distance, already winging its way north over the Tehachapi Mountains. His heart quickened. This would be the adventure of all adventures. The thrill died quickly as he recalled the reason he was here. He was fighting for survival, but that meant leaving everyone else behind. If he could, he would change the circumstances, but no amount of money could change the fate the Mayans had seen centuries before. All the combined wealth in the world couldn't push a speeding asteroid from its course, stop volcanoes from erupting, or keep the ground from shaking until buildings fell. And it wasn't as if he hadn't tried to save Lisa. Staying behind was her choice.

Minutes later, the copilot appeared and opened the door, extending the folding stairs.

"Can't say I've ever flown into this airport, Mr. Morgan. I've got a new place to put on my résumé."

Morgan slapped him on the shoulder and smiled but could not force words to come. He doubted he'd ever see the man again.

"I'll get your bags, sir."

The desert air was cool and chilled his face. He descended to the tarmac, took a few steps toward the 747, and then paused and looked back at his business jet. Donny was standing in the door, watching him. Morgan gave a casual salute to the man. Donny did nothing.

The copilot moved down the stairs with a

computer bag and two small suitcases.

"I'll take them from here. Fly safe."

"Yes, sir. We look forward to serving you again soon."

Morgan looked away. "Thanks."

"Mr. Morgan." The voice traveled on the stiff breeze.

Morgan turned and saw Charles Balfour standing by a set of stairs leading to the large aircraft.

Andrew Morgan turned his back on Donny and the small jet and walked to Balfour.

"Right on time, Mr. Morgan." Balfour shook Morgan's hand. "You're the last passenger for this flight."

"Will Quetzal be with us?"

"I'm afraid not. He's picking up a few others and will fly directly to the site."

"So everyone showed up?"

"Yes, and they're all excited to be underway." Balfour motioned to the stairs. "If you don't mind, sir. Just leave your bags here. I'll make sure they get stowed properly." Balfour raised a walkie-talkie to his lips.

Shouldering the computer bag, Morgan moved to the foot of the stairs and placed his right foot on the first tread. He paused. This was a monumental step. Everything was about to change.

He put his weight on the step but couldn't raise his left leg. There was no pain, no sense of weakness, just a lack of will to lift his foot and move up the steps. He looked into the open door. A steward smiled down on him.

Again, Morgan tried to start up the ladder, and again he hesitated. Lisa's image flashed on his mind. Then horrific images of her lying dead under debris or choking on dust-filled air played like a movie in his head.

"Is there a problem, Mr. Morgan?" Balfour had stepped to his side. "It's understandable if you're feeling a little nervous."

"I'm not nervous." He removed his hand from the rail on the side of the stairs and looked at it. He could feel Lisa's skin on his fingertips from when he held her hand the night they picnicked in his backyard.

"Mr. Morgan. We really should be going."

Morgan stepped back and looked at Balfour. "I wish you well."

"I don't understand. Did you forget something?"

"Yeah, I did. I forgot many things, including what is important."

Morgan walked back to his plane.

"Leave something behind?" Donny wore a slight smile.

"Yup. My sanity." Morgan looked in the cockpit. "I've changed my mind, guys. Let's get out of here."

"Um, yes, sir." The pilot exchanged glances with his partner. "Back to Oklahoma City."

"Not yet. I want to make another stop first."

"Hey, boss," Donny said. "Some skinny guy is headed this way. He doesn't look happy."

"Raise the stairs and close the door. I've wasted enough time."

Morgan looked out a left-side window and saw Charles Balfour with a cell phone to his lips.

Lisa had just set her suitcase down when the doorbell rang.

"What now?" She opened the door. "What . . . Aren't you . . . ?"

Morgan smiled, crossed the threshold, took Lisa's head in his hands, and kissed her. The kiss was long, gentle, and thrilling enough to weaken her knees.

Although she couldn't see him while in Morgan's embrace, she recognized Donny's voice. "Now that's what I'm talking about."

Morgan pulled back, and Lisa took a deep breath. For the first time in her life, the

412

reporter was short on words.

"Good, I see you're packed." Morgan pointed at her suitcase.

Lisa raised a hand to her chest as if she could slow the machinegun rate of her heart. "Yes . . . I'm going to my parents. To spend . . . you know . . . tomorrow with them."

Morgan stepped to the side and nodded at the luggage. "Do you mind, Donny?"

"Nah, my pleasure." He stepped into the foyer and grabbed the bags.

"What are you doing?"

Morgan answered. "He's helping me kidnap you. You're coming to my place."

"Your place, but —"

"I'm not going. I'm going to spend the time with you."

"But, my parents. I told them I was coming over."

Morgan shrugged. "No problem. I have a big house. We'll bring them too."

"I don't understand."

Morgan kissed her again. "All you need to know is that I love you."

"But —"

"I hate that word. Are you coming, or do I have to carry you?"

For a moment, she wished he would carry her.

CHAPTER 32

December 21, 2012

Morgan never imagined he'd spend this day of all days like this. Donny's family — his wife, two grade-school-age children, and several nieces and nephews filled the area around the pool with noise and laughter. Lisa's parents sat in the shade of an awning away from the hubbub, drinking fruit juice. Donny, as promised, was playing Ping-Pong with his brother, an army sergeant on leave. Like Donny, he was thickly built and looked like he could bench-press a house.

Morgan, wearing a blue swimsuit and a plain white T-shirt, reclined on a lounge chair. Lisa did the same in a matching chair. He pretended to have a good time, playing with the children, helping with the bar-beque, and giving tours of the house. He even shot hoops with Donny and the older children, but the pending disaster was never far from his mind. The laughter was temporary. But temporary laughter was better than nothing.

"We need to talk, Andrew." Lisa's voice was soft.

"Let me guess — you need to tell me how irresistible I am."

"Lying is a sin."

"Hey."

She chuckled. "Sorry, I couldn't resist." She rolled to her side. "I'm serious. We need to talk."

"I'm listening."

"In private."

Morgan turned his head toward her, removed his shades, and raised an eyebrow. "Are you propositioning me?"

"You know the answer to that. Let's go to your office."

Morgan felt a sudden sense of foreboding. He rose, held out his hand, and helped Lisa up. A few moments later, they were in the upstairs office. Morgan closed the door. They sat in a low-backed sofa beneath a large window that overlooked the gated front yard.

"Okay, Ms. Mysterious, you have my attention."

She chewed her lower lip, and Morgan prepared himself for the rejection he was sure would come. He had swept her off her feet yesterday, but she had had an entire night to think things over. As the day progressed, she seemed more introspective. He assumed it was because of her knowledge of what was due to occur.

"I haven't been honest with you."

"You? Dishonest? I don't buy it."

She touched his arm. "When I was here last year, you read a verse from a Bible you said belonged to your son. That got me to thinking."

"Thinking is permissible."

She saddened. "When I first met you, I did some research. You already know that. I even pressed you for an interview you didn't want to give for an article that never came to be. Turns out, no one in your Quetzal group would talk to me. Anyway, during my investigation, I learned more about you and your family's deaths."

"We talked about that on the trip back from Roswell."

"Well, I let it all slide, but I couldn't let it go."

Morgan felt defensive. "Where are you going with this?"

"I read the article about the funeral, where it was held, and who officiated. From there, it was a small matter to link the ministers to the church your son attended."

"You contacted them?"

She nodded. "I did. I spoke to the youth pastor. He oversees the spiritual lives of the senior high school students. He remembered your son very well. Did you know he was thinking of going into the ministry?"

"No. We talked about him going into engineering of some kind. You're saying he was lying to me?"

"No, of course not. Thinking about going into the ministry is a long way from committing to it. Many ministers train in other fields before going to seminary. No doubt he was thinking of engineering too."

"Why are you telling me this?"

"Do you still have his Bible?"

"Of course."

"May I see it?"

Morgan was slow to move. He felt manipulated. He rose, disappeared from the office, and returned a few moments later with the well-worn study Bible. He handed it to Lisa. He noticed her hand was shaking when she took it. It hurt him to see her so nervous.

"The pastor I spoke to said they did a faith exercise."

"I don't understand."

"He asked them to list five things they wanted God to do in their lives. He had

417

them write it in their Bibles." Lisa began thumbing through the Bible. He watched as she checked front and back leafs. "I don't see it."

"Maybe he chose not to participate."

"The impression I got from the youth pastor makes me think otherwise. Wait. He said that that he based the exercise on Matthew 7:7–8."

"Which is?"

Lisa turned to the Gospel. "Here it is. Jesus is speaking: 'Ask, and it will be given to you; seek, and you will find; knock, and it will be opened to you. For everyone who asks receives, and he who seeks finds, and to him who knocks it will be opened.' " She stopped suddenly, turned the Bible to Morgan, and pointed at the margin.

He took the book and read the notes. The sight of his son's handwriting jolted him.

Five things I pray that God will do:
1. Give me clarity about my future.
2. Help me know more about Him.
3. Make me a good student of His Word.
4. Protect persecuted Christians around the world.
5. Help me lead my parents to Christ.

The last item was underlined twice. The

pit of Morgan's stomach dropped like a stone, and his eyes began to burn.

"It's a very unselfish list." Lisa spoke softly.

"That's the way he was."

"Andrew, this may be the last time we have an opportunity to talk about such things. I don't know what the next hours will bring, but if you're right, if the Hammer of God — I despise that name — is going to kill most life on earth, then we need to be thinking about the next life."

"Lisa —"

"No, no more debate. No more give and take. So far you haven't been willing to listen to me. Maybe you'll listen to your son." She took the Bible back and turned to another passage. "Romans 3:23. It's underlined. I shouldn't be surprised." She scooted next to Morgan. "What's this say?"

Morgan read the words, "All have sinned and fall short of the glory of God."

"Do you need proof that we are all sinners?"

He shook his head. "No, that's pretty obvious."

"Okay, now this. Romans 6:23." She turned a few pages and pointed at another underlined verse.

"The wages of sin is death, but the free

gift of God is eternal life in Christ Jesus our Lord." He looked up. "Lisa, look, I know you mean well —"

"Andrew Morgan, we are going to get through this without interruption."

He smiled. "Yes, ma'am."

"There are scores of these, but I'm going to make you read one more." She moved deeper into the book and found what she was looking for. "This one — Romans 10:9–10 — is underlined too." Again she gave him the Bible and he read the words aloud.

"If you confess with your mouth Jesus as Lord, and believe in your heart that God raised Him from the dead, you will be saved; for with the heart a person believes, resulting in righteousness, and with the mouth he confesses, resulting in salvation." He handed the Bible back.

"Why do you suppose these verses are underlined?"

Morgan shrugged.

"What did your son want God to do?"

"He listed several things —"

"You said you love me. If you love me, then stop playing games. What on that list struck you?"

"He wanted help sharing his faith with his mother and me."

"Do you think he talked these matters over with your wife?"

Morgan squirmed in his seat. "Before they started back, my wife and I talked. She mentioned she and Hunter had had a long talk. I didn't pay much attention . . . I was distracted with work." That admission felt like a punch from a prizefighter.

"How did she sound to you?" There was something soothing in her tone.

"I don't know, maybe a little different. Like I said, I was distracted."

Lisa set a hand on Morgan's knee. "Do you think it's odd that Hunter left his Bible behind?"

"I never thought about it. To me, it was just a phase he was going through, or another way to meet girls. It's probably a coincidence."

"Coincidence?" For the first time that evening, he heard heat in her tone. "Was it coincidence that we both show up late for Quetzal's presentation in Roswell? Was it coincidence that we got the last two seats available in the theater? And my canceled flight and your offer to fly me to San Antonio — was that also coincidence?"

"Look, the way you're stringing these events together may make it sound like everything happened by some plan —"

"I'm not finished. How about everything else that happened? My editor assigning me a story that required I get in touch with you again, and despite your reluctance to see me, you ultimately caved."

"Caved? That's a little harsh."

"Was it coincidence that you used his Bible to show me that verse in Revelation?" She took a deep breath. "Your son's spiritual wish was to share the truth about Jesus with you and your wife. I can't be sure, but he may have done that on the trip that ultimately took their lives. He left his Bible behind, and here we are on the eve of destruction reading it, reading verses he underlined — verses he meant to share with you. God has honored his request."

Something warmed inside Morgan. He looked away. To make eye contact with Lisa now would undo him. What she was saying made sense, and he didn't want it to. After all, it was God who let his wife and son die. He had said so to Lisa.

"I would never do anything to diminish their deaths or your sorrow, but you know as well as I do people die daily . . . some tragically. Besides, you can't blame God unless you acknowledge His existence."

He started to speak, but nothing came. She had him with that last line.

"Andrew, if that asteroid slams into us today, it won't be because the Mayans saw it coming. It will most likely be an occurrence of nature, or . . ."

"Or what?"

"Or the beginning of God's judgment on the world. Either way, you need to be ready." She lifted a hand and laid two fingers beneath his chin and pulled his face close. She gave him a slow, lingering kiss. It was devoid of sexuality. It was not the kind of kiss a woman gave a man to seduce him. It was a simple act of unassuming, nonjudgmental love.

He savored her lips, her smell, the texture of her lips, but most of all, he appreciated her concern.

Anger melted away. Uncounted months of bitterness dissolved. Tears trickled down his cheeks. "Will you pray with me?"

"Yes." Lisa slipped from the sofa to her knees.

For a moment, Morgan felt foolish. This was what children did at bedtime. The moment passed. His heart twisted in his chest, and his mind felt on fire.

Ten minutes later, there was knock on the door. Morgan rose and Lisa returned to the sofa. Donny stood in the wide hall outside the office.

"Sorry to disturb you —" He caught Lisa's eye. "Oh, I hope I'm not interrupting anything."

"We're just talking, Donny. Rein in your imagination."

"Of course. I didn't meant to imply . . . Never mind. Did you know someone has bugged your home?"

Donny put away the electronic sweeping gear. It took him an hour to retrieve the equipment from the security company Morgan Natural Energy retained to provide protection for its executives. It took another two hours for him to sweep the structure and grounds, even with the help of his brother.

"Okay, there were remote cameras in the bushes near the gate, a camera in your living room and office, and there were remote mikes throughout the house, including two in your bedroom. There were also two cameras in the backyard."

"I knew they were keeping an eye on me, but I had no idea it was to this extent." Morgan clinched his fists.

"Who you talking about, boss? The competition or that Mayan guy?"

"Quetzal." Morgan's fury rose. "The competition might bug my office. I can't imagine them bugging my home."

"Not so noble as you first thought." The comment would have offended him if anyone other than Lisa had said it.

"I met with Balfour, and he knew about Lisa. He admitted to keeping an eye on those who were part of the group, but I never thought he'd go this far." Morgan looked at one of the pinhole cameras Donny had retrieved. "Why would they put cameras in my bedroom?" Realization dawned on his face. "Candy . . ."

"Figures," Lisa said. "It would explain why she was so . . . aggressive. Photos of you and her together could be used to blackmail you into cooperation."

"There was no 'me and her together.' Besides, I'm no threat to them. I doubt they did this to everyone who signed on."

"I was the threat. I'm a nosey reporter who was going to write unfavorable articles about them."

"What now, boss?"

"Destroy them."

"How about the cops?" Donny said. "They may want this for evidence."

"Too late. They're long gone and out of reach of the police."

"Hey, everyone, you need to see this." The voice came from the living room. Someone

425

had turned on the television. Morgan saw Lisa's father pointing at the screen. "I hope you don't mind, but I'm a bit of news junkie."

"I don't mind at all . . ." Morgan saw a photo of the Hammer of God. "May I have the remote?" He rewound the DVR, started the news segment over, and turned up the volume.

"These stunning photos were recently released from the European Space Agency. It is being described as the nearest pass by an asteroid in history. It flew within 100,000 miles of the earth. That's about half the distance to the moon. Although not the first to pass within the 240,000-mile span between the earth and the moon, it is the closest on record.

"The photos came from Dr. Michael Alexander of the ESA, but he has not made a public statement. NASA has assured us that the earth is not in danger. In fact, 2012 G12 — as it has been labeled — has already passed through our orbit, and it is speeding its way toward the sun. Unlike many asteroids that have long, elliptical orbits around the sun, 2012 G12 will most likely pass so close to the sun that it will be destroyed. It's ironic that on this day of all days, we would see a potentially destructive asteroid pass so closely — if you call 100,000 miles close."

"Praise God," Lisa whispered.

"Indeed." Morgan put his arm around Lisa. "You're going to remind me of this over and over again, aren't you?"

"That I am. Every day, until you're old and gray."

"You know, the day isn't over yet."

EPILOGUE

December 23, 2012

"You had better figure a way out of this, little man, or you're gonna be the first casualty in this group."

Balfour saw Rickman's face darken another shade of red. He tried to push him away, but he was not a strong man.

"I'm trapped, just like you. I'm in the same predicament."

Sonya stood by Rickman. "You promised us safety and enough food to last months. We've done an inventory, and with two hundred mouths to feed, the food that *is* here won't last more than a week. Everything else is empty boxes and barrels!"

"I ordered the food. I really did. Does it make sense that I would lock myself away with you if I thought we'd run out of food?"

Rickman took another step closer and poked Balfour in the chest hard enough to leave bruises. "Maybe you've got a secret way out or something."

"No, I don't. Something has gone wrong."

"No kidding, genius. Where's Quetzal?"

"I don't know. He was supposed to be here with us."

"He's not," Sonya said.

"Something must have happened."

"I'll tell you what happened. You took our money and then buried us alive in this bunker."

"He must have tricked us. He tricked me too. I'm a believer like you. He's . . ."

"He's what?" Sonya pressed.

"Nothing. I didn't mean anything by that."

"Maybe I should start breaking fingers until we get some answers."

"No, please, don't. I've tried to open the blast doors, but my code doesn't work."

"Neither does our communications system. We can't contact anyone. We have children here, Balfour. I'm not going to sit by and watch them suffer. Not when I can make you suffer."

"I'm telling you the truth. I've been tricked too. Maybe the asteroid hit —"

"We would have felt it, buddy. Something that big would be felt."

"Not if it hit the ocean. Perhaps the magnetic storms from the sun knocked out communication. Maybe there's no one to contact. Maybe —"

A grinding sound stopped the inquisition. The blast door behind them began a slow descent into the floor.

"See," Balfour said. "He's come back. Maybe he's brought the rest of the food, or . . ." He ran out of words. He turned, thankful to the one who — whoever it was — had figured out how to open the metal door. His smile disappeared when the door descended enough for him to see fifty uniformed, heavily armed Russian soldiers.

He did, however, recognize one man. Andrew Morgan stood with his arms crossed, his heavy jacket making him look even more muscular.

Morgan pointed at him. "These people want to talk to you, Balfour. Where's Quetzal?"

"Not here. I don't know where he is, and, trust me, if I did, I'd tell you."

"Your man Jaz — is he here?"

"Just me, Mr. Morgan."

The soldiers moved forward. One took Balfour by the arm and led him away.

"What are you doing here?" Rickman was still abrasive. "I heard you chickened out."

"Saving your skin, it appears. Lucky for you, I changed my mind. I figured you

430

wouldn't want to be stuck in there when there's a perfectly good world out here."

"So nothing happened?" Sonya showed relief.

"Not what you're thinking. The Hammer of God sailed past without so much as a wave."

Sonya broke into tears. The tough facade crumbled. Even Rickman took a few moments to catch his breath. "The others need to hear this."

"They will. You will all be the guests of the Russian government for a few days."

Rickman stiffened. "We didn't do anything wrong."

"I've told them that, but as it turns out, Quetzal didn't buy the use of the facility as he said he did. He just crossed a lot of palms with bribes, an easy thing to do in a country that is nearly broke."

Sonya sniffed. "How did you get here?"

Morgan shrugged. "I'm in oil. Russia is a big producer of the world's oil. Naturally, I know a few people who know people in the Russian government. I'm here to tell them who the bad guys are. I will also be spending a few days here. They have questions for me too."

"It appears I was wrong about you, Morgan." Rickman slapped him on the shoulder.

Morgan slapped him back. "It appears I was right about you."

"Hey, what's that supposed to mean?"

Morgan just laughed.

Robert Quetzal Sanchez sipped a margarita as he watched the sun ease down to the horizon, its light glinting off the ocean and the villa of his new home in Venezuela. He put his feet up on the patio railing. It had only been a few days, but he was feeling at home in his new digs.

He opened the local paper and smiled at the Spanish headline. He translated it. AMERICAN CEOS RESCUED FROM RUSSIAN PRISON. Prison? Reporting in Venezuela was always suspect.

He had been willing to let them all die. Fewer people to worry about seeking revenge. No matter. He had their money and had covered his tracks well. His only concern now was boredom.

He wondered about Jaz and Candy. Part of the deal was they would part as wealthy friends, never to see each other again. They had chosen their own new homes in new countries.

In real life, the bad guys often got away.

Two days after Christmas, Morgan was still

in Russia, helping law enforcement unravel the details of Kamchatka. Although thousands of miles away, he called daily to let Lisa know he was safe and to tell her of his love. He also asked for prayer. Something she never tired of.

She wished he were here now. One day after the world was to end, officials found Garrett Vickers' body in a San Antonio landfill. Through detailed and professional detective work, the police were able to trace his murder back to a hotel in the city's outlying area. Because of the poor state of his remains, it had taken a long time to identify his body. Truffaut had received two other phone messages from Garrett, but he was always on the office line and after hours. He had tried to reach Garrett on his cell phone several times, but it always went to his voicemail.

Rodney Truffaut was devastated, as was Garrett's mother. Lisa stood next to her, ready to catch her should she faint.

The minster stood at a small, well-used lectern. Lisa was certain he was saying good things, comforting things, but she forgot the words as soon as he spoke them.

There was nothing Lisa could have done to prevent the murder. Even so, she felt guilty.

The Mayan doomsday passed, and the world continued on as it had before, but the funeral reminded her that every day, the world ends for someone. She pledged never to take those she loved and respected for granted.

And still the world turns. For her — for everyone — the future remains a mystery.

DISCUSSION QUESTIONS FOR
THE MAYAN APOCALYPSE

1. Before reading this novel, what were your thoughts on what might happen on December 21, 2012?
2. What do you think of Lisa Campbell's actions throughout the novel? Would you have done anything differently if you were in her shoes? Why or why not?
3. Andrew Morgan tells Lisa at one point that he doesn't see any difference between what Christians believe about the rapture and what he believes about the Mayan prophecies concerning December 21, 2012. Do you think there is a difference? If not, why? If so, how might you explain that difference to someone like Morgan?
4. Throughout the novel, Morgan blames God for the loss of his family. Balfour tells him that *God* was just another word his father would "sling around" as if the term were not referring to a real person. But Lisa tells Morgan that he cannot blame

God unless he acknowledges His existence. If you acknowledge the reality of an all-knowing, omnipotent God, how does that affect your view of the future?

5. When researching 2012, Garrett and Lisa both ponder how the earth seems obsessed with its own destruction. Lisa wonders how anyone could anticipate the end of life on the planet. Why do you think some people are so fascinated with this topic?

6. Why do you think God didn't keep Jaz from murdering Necco and Garrett? In the Bible, God also let horrible things happen to Job. Why do you think God allows such tragedies?

7. What might we learn from the fact that Quetzal, Jaz, and Candy all get away by the end of the novel?

8. After reading this novel, why do you think some people are convinced that the world will end on December 21, 2012?

9. Morgan's loss of his family haunts him throughout the novel. Do you know anyone who has lost loved ones recently? If so, how might you encourage them?

10. Share with a friend what impacted you the most about this novel.

ABOUT THE AUTHORS

Mark Hitchcock is the author of more than 17 books related to end-time Bible prophecy, including the bestselling *2012, the Bible, and the End of the World.* He earned a ThM and PhD from Dallas Theological Seminary and is the senior pastor of Faith Bible Church in Edmond, Oklahoma. He has worked as an adjunct professor at DTS and has served as a contributing editor for the Left Behind Prophecy Club for five years.

Alton Gansky is the author of 30 books — 24 of them novels, including the Angel Award winner *Terminal Justice* and Christie Award finalist *A Ship Possessed.* A frequent speaker at writing conferences, he holds BA and MA degrees in biblical studies. Alton and his wife reside in Southern California.

The employees of Thorndike Press hope you have enjoyed this Large Print book. All our Thorndike, Wheeler, and Kennebec Large Print titles are designed for easy reading, and all our books are made to last. Other Thorndike Press Large Print books are available at your library, through selected bookstores, or directly from us.

For information about titles, please call:
(800) 223-1244

or visit our Web site at:
http://gale.cengage.com/thorndike

To share your comments, please write:
Publisher
Thorndike Press
10 Water St., Suite 310
Waterville, ME 04901